WATER AND FIRE

.<>.

VOLUME ONE

THE FIRST ELEMENT

By Samuel R Bell

TABLE OF CONTENTS

Prologue...6

TRAINING

Twelve Years... 19

New Friends... 32

To the Land of the Polar Bear...42

Training...50

The Right Way...64

Flight Into War... 76

OUR DESTINY

The Battle of Wateria...90

Following The Spark...99

Dancing For the Moon...108

An Injury and Some More Questions...128

Implications of a Rosebush...137

The City in the Sky...150

Our Destiny...165

THE MANOR

Prophecies of Before and Now...184

Training, Again...194

The Last Element...208

The One Who Knows...221

The City in the Ground...233

The Catacombs of Nalur Shaa...253

The Thorny Rose...272

A Reunion and an Announcement...288

Epilogue...297

THE BOND

THE MOST POWERFUL MAGICAL FORCE IN THE WORLDS

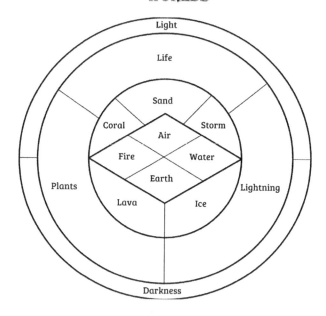

FOR RILEY

PROLOGUE

Deep in the frozen mountains of the Water Kingdom, a woman and her husband sat impatiently. A single lamp lit the room, glowing on the ornate windows on the far side of the room and the huge, circular rug. A blizzard roared about in the night just outside. The man sighed and glanced at his wife. She grimaced, holding her swollen, pregnant stomach. He placed one hand on her shoulder, and another against her chest.

"He'll be here soon, I promise," the man whispered into his wife's ear. He wore a simple band of gold around his head, one that had been passed down from a long line of kings before him.

Suddenly, out of thin air, sand began to appear and swirl in hypnotic tornadoes in front of the couple. They watched as the tendrils of sand twisted, grew, and flowed into the vague shape of a person. The sand tightened into the form of a man, then bleached into flesh and simple clothes. The man stood before them, fully formed. He had arrived.

"Mark," the woman breathed, her face breaking out into a wide smile. She shifted her weight over to face him. "You're—

He interrupted her.

"It's them," he said, walking forward. He was still breathing hard from the exertion of bringing himself to the room. The woman's eyes bulged, her hand going to her stomach. "This conflict is too great for a Setter to handle."

"Mark, if this conflict is coming as soon as you say it is, why can't you fight it? You're a Setter in the height of your power, these are the kinds of conflicts you're supposed to stop," Aidan said.

"I'm aware of the role I play in this world, and I know that as the current Setter I cannot stop this conflict," Mark said. "My magic will leave my body, and it will become the magic of the new Balancers."

"Lose your magic?" the woman asked. "But—

"And... it's going to happen tonight," he said, wiping the sweat off his forehead.

"Mark, are you sure? I don't know if we're really ready for this," the husband said, his eyes wide. "Our family isn't ready, and neither is our kingdom. The Mesipar Sea War was only eight years ago and we've barely had time to—

"Aidan," the woman said, placing a hand on his arm. "We're going to be fine. If what Mark says is true, then these three are supposed to bring peace, not chaos."

"I just... I'm just anxious, that's all," Aidan said, patting his wife's hand.

"Now," Mark said, stepping forward. "I have to leave. There's one last thing I have to do."

"I see," the woman said, looking down. "So..."

"Yes," Mark said, nodding. "I've made my peace with it."

"Then go," Aidan said, looking outside at the blizzard. A gust of wind howled across it, snow slicing into the glass. Aidan sighed, as his eyes began to fog up with tears.

"I will," Mark said, stepping back. "Just remember. You must make sure that nothing happens to them until they are at their full power, or when the time comes for them to be called into action. Balance must be preserved."

He turned away from them, taking in a ragged sigh.

"It must be preserved at any cost."

"*Ramalcha*," the man whispered, closing his eyes. His skin turned back into sand; his body momentarily formless. A moment later, he snapped back into being, the sand turning back into flesh.

He now stood at the edge of a thin knife of stone, the sea to one side and a basin that dipped far below the water level to the other. He looked down into the basin, featureless except for an imposing manor in the center, warm light coming from its vaulted windows and grand doorways.

The cliff almost went to a dead drop, so he took a deep breath and held a hand out over the void before him. Calling up the magic within himself, a slab of stone suddenly burst out of the cliff face. He stepped down onto the precipice, and created another step, working his way slowly down the cliff. Finally, his feet touched the sandy ground of the basin. He turned towards the manor.

A dark figure was waiting for him, his voluminous robe silhouetted by the light from the manor. The figure held a dancing flame in his hand. The fire played around but never quite touched the man's open palm.

"Hello, old friend," the man said, the fire illuminating a crooked grin peeking out from between the folds of his hood. The man made a fist with his palm, the flame blooming into a large blaze. Pulling his arm back, the fire coalesced into a tight ball.

"Conner, we don't have to fight," Mark said, holding his hands out. "I'm only here to try to convince you not to go down this path. You should never have trusted Palos."

"Palos only wanted what was best for this world," the other man, Conner said. The fire in his palm pulsed angrily. "You're too narrow-minded to understand that this is the only solution."

"Please Conner, we can end this now," Mark said, stepping forward. "You don't have to go to war with the water people."

"I gave them a chance to give me what I wanted, but they didn't take it," Conner said. Assuming an attack position, he angled one leg back in preparation to lunge forward.

"I see," Mark said, closing his eyes. He took a deep breath, calling up the deep magic within him. It bloomed from within him and tingled on the surface of his skin. "You have proven yourself to stubborn to change. I hoped it wouldn't come to this."

"And yet it has," Conner hissed, launching the fire at Mark.

Mark raised his arms, the earth below him melting and crashing up into a wall of boiling lava. He thrust his hands out, the lava scattering across the basin. Conner leaped back, his fireball sputtering out as he escaped the lava. Mark pulled his hands back in, and kicked out with one leg, a spear of ice materializing out of thin air alongside it. The spear was melted by a shield of fire Conner quickly conjured up before it could impale him.

Mark swept his hands out, the sandy ground of the basin boiling up in a wave that threw the other man off of his feet. Mark rushed forward and drew his hands together. The sand snaked around Conner, encasing him completely. Mark touched the sand, causing it to bleach and harden into sandstone. Conner struggled against his prison, thrashing his head about.

"Conner, tonight I will die, and my power will be passed on to the Balancers," Mark said calmly, looking forlornly at his former ally. "If you declare war on the water people, it will cause an imbalance in the Inner World that will destroy it. It would be a conflict only the Balancers could stop."

"The Balancers aren't even born yet," Conner spat. "By the time they would come to full power, I'll have eliminated the water people. The Balancers will be mine, and I can use them to *save* us."

The man glanced at the sky, where a full moon had nearly reached its zenith. It was almost time.

"If you're so concerned about what I'm going to do, why don't you just kill me now?" Conner taunted. Mark shook his head.

"Because if you are truly trying to bring the Untamable Mights back," Mark explained, "then killing you would only put them in far more evil hands."

"What are you talking about?" Conner asked, raising an eyebrow. Mark looked up to the moon. He felt something suddenly change within him. It was the magic. The thrumming power within him was starting to leak out of his body, spiriting itself away.

"I..." Mark stammered, his hands starting to tremble.

"Mark... what's happening? Mark?" Conner asked, his eyebrows turned up in concern.

"Conner," Mark said, turning away. Most of the magic had siphoned out of him now, the emptiness crushing his chest and weakening his legs. His vision was so blurry that he could barely see the moon above. His brown hair suddenly began to bleach to silver. "In time you'll realize your mistakes. You'll realize the gravity of your decisions."

"Mark..." Conner trailed off, noticed Mark start to break down. Mark fell to one knee, all of the color draining from his hair and face. He looked up at the moon. He felt the last of the magic flow down his arms, into his hands, and out of his palms. The last few tingles trickled away, flying off into the night.

"Balancers... please protect this world."

Conner watched in horror as Mark's body fell to the ground, lifeless. It laid in the moonlight, frail and contorted.

"Your Majesty!" a guard shouted, three others running out of the manor to Conner. They surrounded him, three of them starting to break down the sandstone shell around him. The first knelt before him.

"Are you alright your Majesty?" the first guard asked, kneeling before Conner. Conner looked at Mark's body.

"Yes, everything is fine," he said. "However, as soon as you release me from this sandstone, I need to send a message."

"Of course, your Majesty," the guard said. One of the other guards broke off a piece holding Conner's arm. He stretched it out, clenching his fist. He inspected it, opened his palm and created a small flame.

"Send word to the Water Kingdom, that I, Emperor Conner of the fire people, am declaring war," he said, crushing the flame with his fist.

.<>.

Across the world, the woman held her three newborns in her arms, happy to have a moment alone after all the chaos of the past few hours. She had given birth to two boys and a girl, who she now had in her private bedchambers. She sat on a huge mattress, blue silks and blankets pooled around her. Behind her, in the huge circular window, the blizzard had begun to die down.

The first, a boy, she had named Kiefer. The second was a girl, with bright blue eyes who she had named Jamison. The third and youngest she had named Samson the Fourth, after her father. She hugged all three of them tight, tears in her eyes. They were perfect, and she loved them.

But she couldn't stay.

She put each of the babies in a crib and began to arrange a few things. First, she grabbed a small but ornate box she had set aside before the birth. Running over to the door to make sure it was locked, she drew a sapphire necklace and a tiny silver telescope out of a tiny compartment in her closet. She placed them in the box, along with a sealed letter she'd written right after her husband had left about an hour ago. She closed the box and put it aside, sighing.

She stood up and looked out the window, feeling sick. She'd just given birth to three children, three children with powers not seen in thousands of years. And as much as she loved them, there were more urgent matters to attend to, more pressing things she needed to take care of. Turning from the window, she went to her closet and opened the same drawer that had held the telescope and the necklace. She pulled out a worn letter, her eyes hovering over the corner where someone years ago had signed *Urgently, Julian.* She pocketed the letter and began to gather other supplies. She readied a bag full of clothes and tools she would need, her children completely unaware of the gravity of what she was doing.

The door suddenly opened, Aidan standing in the doorway. He saw her half-packed bag, supplies were strewn around the room.

"Marin," he said, breathing. "Wh... What is this?"

"Aidan, I," Marin stammered, stepping back. "I thought I said I wanted two hours alone."

"I came here to tell you that the fire people just declared *war* on us," Aidan said, stepping towards his wife. "Are you... are you running away?"

"No, I—

"Is this because they might be the Balancers?" Aidan asked, pointing to the newborns. Marin shook her head and held out a hand. "Marin, prophecies are not always followed. They might not even be—

"Aidan, no, that's not it," she said. "It's... a vision. My mother saw something and I can't stay here."

"Your mother?" Aidan hissed. "I thought we agreed we couldn't trust her."

"We never agreed on that," Marin said, walking to her closet and grabbing the last of her things. Aidan grabbed her shoulder as she walked back towards her bag. She wrestled her shoulder out of his grip.

"Marin, why are you leaving? You just gave birth, your children need their mother," Aidan begged. Marin sighed, placing the last of the things in her bag and closing it.

"I know they need me, but they need me alive, which is why I have to go," she said, pulling her arms through the straps of her bag. "Don't worry, I have people who can take care of me where I'm going."

"But where is that? Marin, please don't tell me you're running away because you're scared of what the *possibility* of the Balancers means for our family," Aidan said, placing a gentle hand on her cheek. She held it, a tear in her eye.

"Aidan, please, I can't tell you why I have to leave or you will be in danger as well," she said. "I will send you letters, and any type of correspondence I can."

"You can't do this," Aidan weakly said, his voice shaking. He knew that nothing he said would convince her. He knew his wife better than anyone; she had made this decision long ago.

"Who have you told?" Aidan asked.

"My parents and I've already said goodbye to our other children," she said, choking a bit.

"How... how long will you be gone?" Aidan asked. His wife, her hand on top of his, pulled it down.

"A year at the most," she said. "And I will send letters, so if they stop coming after a year..."

"A... a year?" Aidan stammered. "Are you sure this is—

"Aidan, I'm sure," she said, her voice strong. "I'm leaving three newborns behind, I *have* to be sure."

"Please be careful," Aidan said, pulling his wife in close. His wife melted into his embrace. She wanted to stay like that forever, but she couldn't. Even so, that moment would stay with her for the years to come.

"Okay," she said, pulling away. She turned to her three children. "Bye, Kiefer."

She placed a hand on his cheek, the baby squirming around and whimpering a bit. She placed a hand on Jamie's heart, the baby squeezing her eyes shut. "Goodbye Jamison."

She then moved onto Samson. She placed her hand gently on his head. Marin leaned in, knowing that of the three of them he had the hardest road ahead. The simple fact of her lineage had cursed him with the same gift that had nearly ruined her life once before. She prayed in vain it wouldn't ruin his life as well.

"Goodbye Samson," she whispered. She then turned to the window and took in a deep breath.

"*Obroullard preneva,*" she said. Her body and her bag suddenly turned into mist. The cloud dissipated, leaving nothing but a thin band of sunrise slicing in from the window.

Aidan turned to his three new children.

His wife had just left on a quest he knew nothing about. His friend Mark was dead. His country was at war again. And he now had to raise three more children, children who had far more responsibility than any other in the entire Inner World. He looked at his children, the light of the rising sun illuminating them.

The sun rose on a new era for the Inner World.

The sun rose for the return of the Balancers.

WATER AND FIRE

.<>.

PART ONE

.<>.

TRAINING

TWELVE YEARS

The shimmering globe of water floated before my outstretched hand. Droplets sprinkled off of it, melting the crisp snow beneath as I pushed my hand forward. The water bubbled backward in synchrony with my bare, shivering hand. I concentrated with my entire being to just hold the water suspended in the cold winter air.

"SAMZ!" Kiefer yelled from behind me on the wooded path we were hiking. My concentration broke and the water was released from my control and splashed onto the snow. I turned back and saw his bundled-up form jogging after me, his cheeks flushed red in the chilly winter air. His sandy hair flopped around his head and mischievous face as he ran after me.

"Kiefer, really? That was the most I've ever been able to control," I asked, slowing down for him. He caught up and supported himself with his hands on his knees. His blue jacket and pants had streaks of snow and ice on them from slipping on ice and attempted snowball attacks.

"Well I'm sorry I didn't see that you were using your powers," he said sarcastically, catching up to me.

"It's fine," I said, pulling my mitten back over my icy hand.

"We should keep going though, Jamie might be a bit angry with me," he said sheepishly, looking back up the path. My head dipped back in exasperation.

"Kiefer, what did you—

"KIEFER!" someone else shouted from down the path. Wearing a deep purple outfit nearly identical to mine and Kiefer's, came Jamie. Her long, brown hair was temporarily tied up in a bun and sequestered inside of a bulky, blue, knitted hat our grandmother had made for her. She had an uptight, disapproving look on her face. She stomped down the path towards Kiefer and me.

"She, uh," Kiefer mumbled, glancing back at Jamie. "Might be a bit mad. Stay calm."

"I'm mad because you hit me in the *eye* with a *snowball* and you used your *magic* to make it faster," she said, catching up to us. She frowned and lunged forward to push Kiefer before I shoved my body in between them.

"Guys, don't fight," I asked, stepping back. "Dad's not in a good mood today and we shouldn't make it worse."

"To be fair though, Dad is *never* in a good mood," Kiefer countered, crossing his arms.

"He's never in a good mood for a valid reason," Jamie said, stepping towards Kiefer. "It makes me sad too sometimes."

"Why? We never met her," Kiefer said, for the thousandth time.

"She's still our mother and people we care about knew her!" Jamie said back for the thousandth time.

"And fighting about it won't change anything and will only make Dad angrier," I said for the thousandth time.

We'd had this fight so many times it was starting to get tiring. "Anyway, we really should be getting back to the castle or Dad is going to—

"Dad's going to do this, Dad's going to do that," Kiefer mocked, throwing his hands around. He put them on his hips. "What you mean is *Maddie* is going to be mad if we're not back."

"It doesn't matter," I said, continuing down the path. "If we're not back soon, someone will be mad and we'll all have to deal with it."

Kiefer and Jamie trudged after me, both of them probably rolling their eyes. Above, the light gray overcast began to sprinkle snow down upon our path, the winds whistling through the trees around us promising an oncoming blizzard that night.

"Do you think Dad's going to talk about it tonight?" Kiefer asked suddenly. Jamie and I looked at him.

"Kiefer, knowing Dad he'll just want to talk about our birthday tomorrow," Jamie asked.

"But he just gave up the search for mom a month ago, a search that started eleven years ago tonight," Kiefer countered. "I kind of feel like the anniversary of his search for Mom, now that it's over, is bigger than just another one of our birthdays."

"I don't know, but worrying about it won't change anything," I reminded them. "Let's just get home first, and then get through dinner. Whatever it's going to be about."

Kiefer and Jamie shrugged, continuing to follow me down the path. Around us, the snow began to fall harder, and the wind began to sing.

.<>.

"Um, Dad?" Maddie asked that night at dinner. We were eating in the family dining room, a high-ceilinged wooden room that was much smaller than the one we used for hosting. Our castle was built into the side of a mountain, this dining room carved into it near the base. Maddie, sitting next to Dad, folded her hands across her thin frame after running one through her wild mess of brown curls. "Can we talk?"

"Of course," Dad said, at the head of the table. Tonight, it was lined with three pots of beef stew and three plates of rolls to feed our huge family: my dad, me and my nine other siblings.

"Well, I was just wondering if..." Maddie trailed off, biting her lip. She was the eldest, twenty-three years old, the spokesperson for the children of our family and two years away from becoming a ruler. She also was our main caretaker when Dad was away. She was a lot of things. My dad sighed, rubbing the bridge of his nose.

"I know what you want to know," he said, taking in a deep breath. "And no, I haven't made a decision."

I glanced at Jamie and Kiefer. Kiefer had been right, and it had only taken a few minutes for them to get to the topic.

"I don't think you should make an announcement," said Erin, the second oldest. She was the bookworm of the family, holding an encyclopedic knowledge of nearly everything in our library. She straightened her glasses.

"Well, shouldn't he?" asked Ezra, my oldest brother as he leaned back in his chair. He lazily held a spoonful of soup out in his hand, letting some of the broth drip on the tablecloth. He was definitely doing it on purpose to annoy Erin. "I think the people deserve to know."

"Ezra—

"Well, whether he tells them or not I was talking to some of my friends from Elmonee and they said that they already think that you're not looking for her anymore, and before you ask, no I didn't say anything to them, but still, they already think you've stopped so do you really have to make an announcement at all?" Emily babbled. Her twin brother Anthony leaned forward to offer his opinion.

"Okay, but just because your friends think so doesn't mean everyone else does," he said, shaking his head. Next to me, my brother Miles rolled his eyes.

"Yeah, I'm with Anthony on this one," he said, shrugging. "Making the announcement would get rid of any conspiracy theories."

I thought it was kind of ironic that he brought that up. He was usually the one most likely to be fooled by a conspiracy theory. Not that I would actually comment that out loud.

"Miles please—

"But he doesn't have to, right?" asked Luke, the youngest brother before Jamie, Kiefer and I. Miles patted him condescendingly on the head, even though he was only a year older than him.

"I trust whatever Dad thinks," Jamie said. Kiefer and I, at the end of the table, looked at each other. Dad sighed.

"Kiefer? Samz? Either of you want to contribute?" he asked, exhausted. Kiefer and I shrugged. This debate had been a dinner topic ever since Dad had told us that he wasn't going to look for Mom anymore. He hadn't told the people of the Water Kingdom yet, who all knew about his trips, that the search was officially over.

I was a little sad that he was stopping his expeditions. Besides the fact that he was giving up on Mom, the expeditions had been such a large part of my life since I was a child. He'd brought us on many of his trips, all over the world. At home I didn't know many people outside of my family, but I'd met so many more people on his trips. I even had a friend from the Earth Territories I still sent letters to every now and then. Now, that part of my life was over.

While we constantly debated the reasons for Dad telling or not telling, we never talked about the reason he came to the decision in the first place. It had been the war. The war with the fire people had become increasingly tense since the Battle of the Lost Man's Pass a few months ago, and Dad's brother and sister, the other Emperors, needed him back in the Water Kingdom instead of traveling the world. When he decided to stop looking for Mom, he said he would continue after the end of the war, even if there was no end in sight.

"Let's... table this discussion for now," Dad said, leaning forward in his chair. "There's something much more important we need to discuss."

"What is it?" Maddie asked, jumping forward. There was something more important than *Mom*, he had to talk to us about? Kiefer perked up, probably thinking the more important thing was our birthday. Dad pushed his empty plate aside and cleared his throat.

"Look, it's no secret that these past years I've neglected to teach you all water magic as well as I should have," Dad said, hanging his head a bit. I thought back to the measly orb of water I'd managed to levitate earlier. It was pathetic compared to the great acts of magic that water mages like my Dad could do. "I've talked to your Aunt Sophie, and we've agreed to finally give all of you the training you need."

The table erupted into mixed reactions. Ezra and Miles looked mildly disinterested while Emily had grabbed Anthony by the shoulders and started to shake him wildly, already babbling about all of the cool spells and forms she wanted to learn. Jamie crossed her arms as if she felt she already knew enough water magic, while Kiefer just grinned.

"When do we start?" Maddie finally asked, her voice cutting through the chaos. Everyone quieted down.

"In a few weeks, Sophie and I will be taking all of you north to the Land of the Polar Bear, where we trained at your age, and where all of your royal ancestors have trained since the founding of the Water Kingdom," Dad explained. "Any questions?"

"I guess, why now?" Ezra asked, leaning towards Dad. "The war is getting worse, why are you *and* Aunt Sophie both going to teach us water magic? I thought Uncle Drew needed both of you."

"The war had recently escalated, yes," Dad said, nodding. "However, based on the current movements of the fire people, we should be getting a brief window of calm around the time we plan to train you."

"But still, why now? Why didn't you teach us..." Ezra trailed off. "Um, never mind."

"No, no, you deserve an answer," Dad said, nodding. "These past few years have been hard. On our trips to look for your mother, I never had time, and in between I was almost always planning the next expedition. I know that it's not fair to you, but that's the way it played out and I want to rectify that."

There was a brief silence at the table as we listened to Dad. He paused for a moment, before pushing his chair back and standing up.

"I'm sorry, I'll give you more details later on the training, but I have a meeting with some delegates from the Storm Empire tomorrow and I need to check in with the Pataoban interpreters. Maddie, make sure everything is ready for the triplet's birthday tomorrow," he said, breezing out of the dining room. He slammed the huge mahogany door shut, echoing through the vaulted wood ceiling.

"C'mon," Maddie said, standing up. "Let's clean up."

As Maddie directed the cleanup of dinner, Miles briefly pulled me aside to the huge window at the end of the dining hall. It looked out over the dark, glacier-laden mountains and the whistling snowstorm.

"Samz, I don't like this," he said, looking out over the mountains. In his faint reflection in the glass, he noticed one of his meticulously combed hairs was sticking out and swiped it back into place. "Dad has had time to train us in the past few years, but he hasn't."

"Well he's been searching for Mom so..." I trailed off.

"But there were times in between trips he could have, or during them," Miles said.

"Okay, but we were busy," I said. Miles shook his head.

"Sure, but there was still *time*," he insisted.

"What are you getting at?" I asked.

"Okay, fine. The war is getting worse, and we barely know how to control our element," he said, running another hand through his brown hair to make sure it was all perfect. "I think he's training us because he knows we might have to fight soon."

"Us?" I hissed, glancing over at Maddie. She had staunchly supported the idea that we were never going to go into battle because, according to her, Dad would 'never do that to us.' Or rather, she would never let us. *Not like there's much of a difference,* my mind grumbled.

Miles turned away from the window, leaned on the wall and crossed his arms.

"It makes sense, doesn't it? Maddie comes of age soon, the war is getting worse, and Dad just gave up the search for Mom," he said. "We're in danger, and he wants to teach us how to protect ourselves."

"Or maybe he's realizing that we're the only royalty in the Water Kingdom who aren't good at water magic, and he wants to fix that," I offered. Miles shook his head.

"Dad could care less about our image," he said. "And even if he did just a little bit, he wouldn't do all of this just to change that."

"Really?"

"Whatever," Miles said, pushing himself off the wall and standing up. "I just wanted to tell someone what I was thinking."

"Okay..." I said, watching him leave the dining hall.

.<>.

Before bed, I stood in front of the tapestry of the Bond hung just before the staircase that led to my tower. I stared at the blue diamond near the center that symbolized water. The circular tapestry had been handed down from generation to generation of water people royalty.

"Samz, it's time for bed," Maddie said, stepping up behind me. She put a hand on my shoulder and looked up at the tapestry.

"What are you looking at?" she asked softly. Sown into the very edge of the tapestry was a ring split in two. The top half of the ring was white and represented the element of light, while the bottom was black and represented the element of darkness. In the center of the tapestry, one diamond split into four smaller ones. The top one symbolized air, the bottom was earth, the right and left were water and fire respectively. A circle split into five parts surrounded the core diamond, representing the elements of sand, ice, lava, storms, and coral.

In between the center circle and the outer ring, there was another ring, but this one was different. It was split into thirds, the top purple, and the bottom two yellow and green. They symbolized life, lightning, and plants. While all the other shapes and colors stood for all the types of elemental magic and the eleven nations of people that controlled them, no one had the magic of those three elements.

"Maddie, why do people even put plants, lightning, and life on the tapestries of the Bond if no one controls them?" I asked. Maddie shrugged.

"Well, there *were* people that controlled them, depending on which legends you believe in," she said, kneeling down next to me. "Some people believe that there used to be people who controlled them but they died out a long time ago. Others think those people thought they were better than us and left to go live in the Upper World. There's one legend that says that the animals could control the magic of life, there's another that says it all came from one city full of people who had power over the stars."

"I don't think I understand..." I said, looking back at the tapestry. Maddie sighed.

"Well, whether anyone ever controlled them or not, they are a part of the Bond, and their magic does exist in our world," she explained. "And it's very important to our world too."

"How?" I asked. Maddie pointed to the tapestry.

"Imagine trying to build a world with all of the elements, *except* for the third ring," she said. "It's fine, but there are no plants living there, no animals living there, and no magnetism to hold it all together."

"Okay, I guess that makes sense," I said, looking down from the tapestry. It didn't, but I shouldn't have been bothering Maddie this late. Maddie sighed and patted me on the back.

"You should get to bed," she said, standing up. "It's your birthday tomorrow!"

"Right," I said, turning away from the tapestry and going up the staircase. I went into my room and pulled myself into bed, thinking of the mother I never met, the magic I was about to learn and the magic I still didn't understand.

Of course I had opinions about what I thought Dad should do about Mom. I just... never really told him. Growing up with nine older brothers and sisters, I'd been born in the background. I felt safe there. Dad was always stressed about Mom and the war, Maddie was always worried about the problems all of my other siblings had, so I never really felt like my problems merited their attention. So, it had always been my instinct to keep to myself. If I had a problem, I would deal with it on my own. If Dad was deciding whether or not to tell the kingdom he had given up the search for Mom, I wouldn't give my input.

Maybe if Mom hadn't left, for whatever reasons that had caused her to leave, maybe I would have been more outgoing. Dad would only have to focus on the war, and he could have taught us water magic when we were younger. Maddie could have just been a normal kid, not having to raise all of her siblings.

But she was gone, and I had never met her. Twelve years had passed, and we were moving on.

It took me a while, but I eventually fell asleep.

At least until Ezra threw a wolf at me.

NEW FRIENDS

The way the events that night played out made it *seem* in my groggy state after being forced awake that Ezra had thrown a wolf at me, even though it wasn't like that at all. However, that was the explanation my brain instantly invented when I woke up to a wolf cub being launched at my chest and Ezra standing behind it with an outstretched arm.

"EZRA!?" I yelled before the wolf cub nailed me in the chest, his tiny puppy claws digging into my chest. His momentum, however, carried his hind legs past my chest, over his body, and into my head. I tried to roll over but didn't have time before he'd landed on my face, my mouth full of long wolf fur.

"*Coffin!*" Ezra hissed, rushing forward as the wolf and I untangled from each other. Once I did, he sat on my bed, his head looking too large for his body and his eyes a shocking bright green. He was panting, his little pink tongue sticking out of his mouth. His coat was dark gray, with a lighter gray stripe running from his snout to his forehead, and a black racing stripe running from the back of his neck to his tail. He sat still for one moment before his adorable face broke into another snarl and he lunged for me again.

This time Ezra grabbed him around the waist and held him up as he struggled to escape.

And then the wolf talked.

"Let... me... *goes!*" he squeaked.

And then the wolf turned into light.

"Crap, crap, crap, crap," Ezra breathed as the light snaked out of his hands, boiled, then compressed and flashed into a new form. Left where the light had been was a small robin with piercing green eyes.

"Did he just..." I breathed, realizing what exactly that flapping bird in front of me was. The bird then flapped forward, opening its beak to bite me. Just before it could, Ezra wrapped what looked like a collar around its neck. The bird's eyes went wide as it turned back into light, flashed, and was a wolf again.

"That morphing collar should help when you're training him," Ezra said, holding the growling cub back. "So... happy birthday! This is your present!'

"Is that...?"

"A morphing wolf? Yes," Ezra said, grinning. I took a deep, shaky breath in.

Morphing wolves were incredibly rare and incredibly powerful magical animals, considered by some to be *the* most powerful. Hence the name, they're born as wolves, and stay as wolves in their natural state, but have the ability to shapeshift into any animal. They had the intelligence, lifespan, and speech ability of a human. Some even had the power to transform *other* beings into new forms.

"He's... feisty," I noted, the tiny wolf trying to squirm his way out of the morphing collar.

"Yes he sure is," Ezra said, through his teeth. "I met him and his two siblings in the mountains the other day, struggling to survive."

"We weres *not*," the wolf insisted, trying to pull backward out of the collar.

"Well, I offered them a chance to live with us, and they allowed Coffin to stay with us," he said.

"Coffin?" I asked. The wolf whipped his head at me, staring me down.

"That's *me*. I ams Coffin, and I *don't* needs your *help*," he growled, pawing at my sheets and drawing them in.

"Yes you do, and this is Samson, your new Master," Ezra said. "And you're going to behave for him."

"Nooo," he whined, sinking down into the bed.

"Ezra, are you sure? I mean, he doesn't want to be here at all," I said, reaching out a hand towards the cub. He noticed it and tried to bite it before I swept it away. He shoved his face into my bed.

"Samz, I'm sure," he said, smiling. "His siblings Squeto and Getel are still trying to find their old pack. Until they do, they said Coffin could live with you."

"Coffin," Ezra said, lightly touching Coffin's back. He perked up, glaring at Ezra. "Will you stay with Samz if he gives you something to eat?"

"Um," the wolf thought for a second, staring off into space with his huge green eyes. "Fine."

"Okay," Ezra said, reaching into his pocket and pulling out a few strips of smoked bacon. He handed them to me, Coffin sniffing the air as he did. I took the cold bacon in my hand.

"Now Coffin," Ezra said. "When I let you go, you have to *gently* go up to your new Master and let him feed you the bacon. If you do it calmly, I'll give you more bacon. If you attack him, that is the only bacon you'll get for the rest of the week."

"Whats?" Coffin whined, his hind legs slumping. "Why can't I just haves *all* of the bacon *now?*"

"Because you have to be nice to Samz first," Ezra said, pointing to me. "Ready?"

Coffin stood up. Ezra took his hand off of the collar.

Coffin lunged forward, his tiny teeth flashing as he tore the bacon out of my hand. I panicked, falling back as Coffin gulped down all of the meat in seconds. He stepped onto my chest and ate the few crumbs he's dropped.

"Coffin!" Ezra shouted. Coffin sheepishly looked back at Ezra. Frowning, he walked over to the window and took out the rest of the bacon he had in his pocket. He unlatched the window and opened it, letting the freezing outside air and a few flakes slice into my room. Nonchalantly, he stuck his hand with the bacon out the window and dropped it. My room was situated high up on the mountain, the bacon tumbling down to the ground several stories below.

"NO!" Coffin yelped, leaping off of my chest and onto the ground. Ezra shut the window and crossed his arms. Coffin pawed at Ezra's feet, whimpering.

"I wanteds that bacon," he whined. I suddenly felt bad for him and climbed out of my bed.

"It's okay," I said, patting him on the back. "I'll go get you some more from the kitchen."

"Really?" both Ezra and Coffin asked, although Ezra was disappointed and Coffin was excited. I whispered into Ezra's ear.

"*Look, if I give him bacon I'll seem like the nice guy and he won't hate me,*" I whispered. Ezra shrugged.

"*Alright, this might work, I guess,*" he said. I led Coffin across my room and opened the door. To my right was a line of nine other doors that led to my sibling's rooms.

"C'mon Coffin," I said. He waddled along next to me, his head barely reaching my knee. I passed Jamie's room, and then Kiefer's when I heard something. I paused, hearing a vase clatter to the ground and break. I grabbed the door handle of Kiefer's room, yanked it open, and was immediately bathed in blue light.

In Kiefer's window, sat a giant, blue, swan-necked bird whose glow lit up the whole room. Kiefer stood cowering by an alcove on the side of his room, where he'd just accidentally knocked over a vase. The bird had opened the circular window, letting in the cold winter air from outside.

"Kiefer," I hissed, walking over to him. Kiefer glanced back at me, his eyes wide and trembling. "What is—

"RARARAR!" Coffin growled, leaping through the doorway and onto the bed. He stood his ground on top of Kiefer's sheets, baring his teeth at the huge bird. The bird arced its neck around, boredly regarding Coffin. Ezra poked his head into the room, his eyes bulging when he saw what was inside.

"Kiefer," he breathed, stepping forward. "That's an aquanix."

"Wait, what?" Kiefer asked, raising an eyebrow. "I thought they were just in fairy tales."

"They're so rare they might as well be," Ezra said, stepping towards the aquanix with an outstretched hand. "Hey, you can come in, maybe even close that—

The bird snapped its beak at Ezra, stretching its neck right over Coffin. Ezra stumbled back, guarding his hand.

"Geez," he said, glancing at Kiefer. "I... Kiefer, you go up to it."

"Yeah, nope," Kiefer said, shaking his head. "Not gonna do that."

"Yes, you're gonna do that," Ezra said, his voice suddenly stern. "I might be wrong, but I think this aquanix has chosen you."

"Chosen me? What?" Kiefer hissed, crossing his arms. "Why?"

"I don't know, I heard that's what they used to do. When they still existed," Ezra said.

"Still existed? But then why is there one right there?" Kiefer asked.

"Just approach it, see what it does," Ezra said, grabbing Coffin before stepping back to the edge of the room. "Go."

"Okay..." Kiefer said, stepping forward slowly. "Hey... bird."

"Oh boy," I muttered under my breath, shaking my head.

"I see you like... sitting in windows," Kiefer said, kneeling on his bed. The bird turned its neck, inspecting Kiefer. A gust of freezing wind blew through the room, snowflakes billowing around its blue feathers. "And letting really cold air in."

The aquanix suddenly lowered its head and pressed the top of it to Kiefer's chest. The light began to flow from its feathers, down its neck, and into the point of contact between them. Kiefer shivered as the light disappeared, the aquanix no longer glowing. There was a silence for a few moments as the bird entered the room, stepping off the edge of the window. The wind slammed it shut. Kiefer began to stroke the neck of the aquanix.

"So...?" Ezra asked. "Did you get anything?"

"I did," Kiefer said, as the bird began to coo. "It's a she, and her name is Shinux."

At that moment Dad appeared in the doorway, his hair disheveled and his night robe wrinkled. He saw Kiefer and Shinux, his eyes going wide.

"An aquanix?" he breathed, stepping forward. "This is..."

"What?" Kiefer asked, looking over his shoulder. Dad stepped back.

Shinux squawked, turned, and threw the window open with her beak. Kiefer reached for her as she dove out into the night.

"Dad!" Kiefer hissed. "You scared her off!"

"It's okay Kiefer," Dad said, stepping towards him. "When an aquanix chooses someone, they only return to help them in times of their greatest need. When you need her, she will return."

"Greatest need?" Kiefer asked. "But when am I ever going to need an aquanix?"

Dad sighed, walking over to the window.

"I'm not sure," he said, shutting the window. He stood for a moment, silent. Kiefer and I glanced at each other, uncomfortable. Even Coffin was silent. Dad suddenly turned around.

"Well... we're having a bit of a change in plans," he said. "We leave tomorrow for your training. Ezra, go tell your siblings. Kiefer and Samson, start packing."

"Wait, Dad!" Ezra said, dropping Coffin and chasing him as he marched down the hall. Coffin scampered over to me and started to bite the end of my robe.

"Kiefer, do you know what that was all about?" I asked, pointing a thumb over my shoulder. Kiefer shook his head.

"I'm not sure, but I don't like it," Kiefer said, pulling his feet up onto his bed.

"Well... Happy Birthday to us," I said, shrugging.

"Happy Birthday," Kiefer said, turning back to Shinux. I left his room, Coffin scampering around my feet.

"Who ares those people? What wases that *bird*? Where *is* this place?" Coffin babbled as I went back into my room. I slumped down on my bed, Coffin jumping up next to me.

"Mr. Human? Or, no, whats was the thing..." Coffin muttered, closing his eyes and thinking. "Oh! Rights. *Master*."

"Master?" I asked, poking my head up.

"That's what my brother said I hads to call you," he said, rolling onto his back and stretching out his paws.

"Okay," I said, my mind still mulling over what Dad had said. He'd seen Shinux, and then immediately decided to start our training? What did Ezra mean about aquqanixes not existing? And Dad saying Shinux would return in Kiefer's greatest time of need? After what Miles had said about Dad training us to prepare us for battle, it didn't sit well with me. What did Shinux appearing have to do with the war?

I suddenly felt a burning itch on my left hand and held it up to scratch it. My palm up to the light, I noticed a circle of green had appeared near the base of my middle finger. It was the source of the itch, so I went to scratch it off. I had never painted, or done anything that would have gotten dye on it. However, itching did nothing to get rid of it.

I stood up and went over to the pitcher of water next to my bed. Concentrating, I held my right hand over the top of the pitcher. A small blob of water floated up to meet it. I rubbed it into my palm, but the water did nothing to get the circle of the dye out of my hand. Annoyed, I dried it off with my bedsheets, hoping it would rub some of it out. It didn't.

"Master? What are you doing?" Coffin asked sleepily from where he's settled into my blankets. I looked at the circle as if I could make it disappear with the sheer force of will. Nothing happened. Sighing, I stood up. I could get some real soap the next morning, and really get it out, wherever it had come from. If it wasn't dye, it was probably some weird bruise, even though it wasn't sore. But for now, I had to pack.

TO THE LAND OF THE POLAR BEAR

That morning, after breakfast and a short time for my siblings to give presents Jamie, Kiefer and I, Dad ordered us to meet him with our bags right outside the huge doors at the entrance to our castle. It seemed like a fairly simple task. Simple when you don't have to factor in a morphing wolf cub.

"It's too cold," he complained, as I opened the main door a crack. I'd already spent nearly half an hour convincing him to leave my tower. "I *hates* the cold."

"Coffin, you have fur, you'll be fine," I said, grabbing his collar as I pushed the door with my back. It towered high above me, the dark oak wood riddled with traditional carvings. Bright morning light reflecting off the fresh snow burned into the entryway as I tried to squeeze Coffin out of it. As I grabbed him by the collar, he pulled his neck back and locked his hind legs into position.

"Ughhhh," he whined, throwing his head back. "I... justs... *got here*. Last... night..."

"And now," I said, the door sliding outward a few more inches as I pulled him along, "you're going to come with us to the—

He suddenly let go, all of the force I'd been using to try to pull him out of the castle sending both of us sprawling out into the snow. *What a great start to my birthday,* I thought to myself as I grabbed for Coffin trying to dash back inside.

"It... is *colds* on my *paws*," he whined as I scooped him up. He snuggled into my coat, growling. "Betters."

"How's it going with Coffin?" Jamie asked, walking calmly out the door. "By the way, you have snow in your hair."

"Oh really," I mumbled sarcastically, shaking it out of my hair. In front of me, the main doors stood impassively, the rest of our mountain rising behind it. Compared to most mountains, it was fairly small, and its front face was nearly a vertical cliff. Windows, balconies, and towers poked out of the mostly uncarved rock, all the way up to the pointed peak where Dad had a private observatory. Taller, snow-streaked mountains rose behind it and on either side of it. I stood on the snow-packed cobblestone road that stretched to my right, left, and straight ahead, where it disappeared into a pass between the two mountains across from ours. The town of Elmonee lay at the end of the road that went between the two mountains.

Four carriages with horses waited outside, servants loading our bags onto them. A moment after I placed mine down in the snow a servant swooped by to pick it up. Dad stood in the center of the carriages, directing all of the movements. Suddenly, a column of gray water vapor appeared in front of him, churning up from nothing. The mist collapsed into the form of a woman bundled in a tight coat and carrying a small, spartan pack. Her dark blond hair spilled around her shoulders and framed her stern face. She wore a small golden amulet, a water droplet carved into its face.

It was Sophie, Empress of the Water Kingdom, and my aunt. She instantly turned to Dad.

"Well Aidan, it's good to see you," she said. "On such short notice."

"I know, I'll explain on the way," Dad explained, leading her to one of the carriages.

"Who's that?" Coffin asked, peeking up at me.

"That is my aunt," I said. "She's going to teach the girls water magic."

I stepped up to the carriage closest to me. It was almost full, one spot left next to Ezra. I climbed in, Coffin jumping out of my arms and immediately curling up under one of the seats. I closed the door and looked up at the castle. I had no idea how long I was going to be away from it, but in a way, I missed it already.

.<>.

"What are you reading?" Emily asked, leaning over to look at Erin's book. Erin shuffled her feet over.

"A book," she said dismissively. Emily rolled her eyes.

"What's the book *about*," she asked.

"It's about Gaila, a Setter from about a hundred years ago," Erin said tersely, pulling the book closer to her.

"What did she do again?" Anthony asked, staring out at the frozen countryside. Erin sighed.

"She was a lava person with earth and storm magic as her Setter elements," Erin explained, her voice devoid of inflection. "She united the warring halves of the lava people tribes into the country we know them as today."

"Right, I think I remember learning about her but all the Setters get all mixed up in my head cause they all controlled different combinations of three elements and they all stopped certain wars or did other big things and it all kind of starts flowing together after a while," Emily said. I looked out of the window, trying to tune out the conversation. The Setters, certain people born with powers over extra elements every now and then, were interesting, but talking about them always led to the same argument. Erin shrugged.

"Gaila was an important Setter, and she was the last one before Mark," Erin said.

"Mark, who was the last one before our *current* one, wherever they are," Ezra corrected. Erin groaned. This argument among my siblings, and most of the rest of the world, was getting old.

"We don't *have* a current Setter," Erin said. "They're not always born right as the one before them dies, they only are born in times of need. After Mark died, no Setter was born."

"And a war between the water people and the fire people isn't important enough for one to be born?" Ezra said, throwing his hands out. "They're out there, they're probably just too young to realize they can control two extra elements."

"Actually, most Setters realized their powers from a very young age," Erin said. "If there was a Setter who was supposed to stop the war, we would know about them by now. But we don't, so obviously whatever magic gives birth to Setters doesn't think this war needs one to stop it."

"Maybe the Setter is a fire person, and the fire people just don't want us to know," Anthony suggested.

"Why would the Setter be a fire person? I thought they were supposed to be born in places where they could be the most effective at solving the world's problems," Emily said.

"It's not always apparent at first why certain Setters are born where they are," Erin said. "Some Setters don't have to use their powers to solve stuff until they're adults. Others are literally born in warzones. But the point is that we do not have a Setter to solve this war for us. We have to fix it ourselves."

"I honestly don't get why this war is still going on," Ezra said, switching from one touchy subject to another. Ten minutes in the carriage and we were already arguing about things we shouldn't have been talking about. *Maybe I should bring up the debate about the Upper World, just so we hit every controversial topic* the snarky part of my brain whispered.

"Sure, we beat the sand people in the Mesipar Sea War twenty years ago and were pretty harsh to them," Ezra said. "But like... why did it take eight years for the fire people to respond to the sanctions we put on them? Why do they even care so much about the sand people?"

"That's how the war *started*," Erin said. "But because they struck us, we had to strike back, and then it became personal between the two nations. Now it's all about prisoners of war, revenge for casualties, even disputes over island colonies in the Lesser Ocean. Dad's been pretty tight-lipped about what would end the war."

"Well, we're obviously not trying to conquer each other, because it's been twelve years and—

"Invasions take time," Ezra said, interrupting Anthony. "I think we're just trying to soften them up before we invade, eventually."

"Okay, but why would we want their land? It's across the Lesser Ocean *and* the Eastern Sea, which really isn't convenient for anyone because to get to either continent it takes a long time by boat, even water people boats and it's too far to Vaporite," Emily said.

"You *could* Vaporite there," Anthony said.

"No, you couldn't," Emily said, lightly punching her twin's shoulder.

"*I* could," he said, pushing her back, into Erin.

"*You* couldn't," Emily said, pushing Anthony against the side of the carriage.

"I *could*," he said, pushing her into Erin again.

"I—

"*Enough!*" Erin shouted, pushing Emily and Anthony away from her. "Just let me read in *peace*."

Emily and Anthony squabbled with each other, while Erin tried to read and Ezra stared out the window. I looked down at Coffin, snuggled into my jacket.

Even though there had been hundreds of Setters born in the last two thousand years, there really wasn't much known about them. They were born into random nations, with power over as many as three elements other than that of their own people. Sometimes they'd be born right as the previous one died, or sometimes there would be decades, even centuries until the next one was born. There were remnants of groups that had guided and trained past Setters in their other elements, that were still looking for a current Setter. In twelve years since Mark's death, they'd found no one. The world often waited for Setters to solve their problems for them, but for now, it looked like we were on our own.

.<>.

Hours later, we arrived. Stepping out of the carriages, a huge compound spread out before us. White mountains surrounded the valley on all sides, glaciers flowing down towards the center where the bright, wooden compound stood. Several buildings branched off of the central lodge, which had a high, steepled roof that shed snow easily. Warm, golden light glowed from the windows and a high watchtower behind the main lodge.

Dad and Aunt Sophie led us into the compound, the doors guarded by men in thick, fur-lined armor. We settled down in a hall of rooms, Kiefer and I choosing a small room together. Coffin was still asleep, so I quietly transferred him into his bed.

Later that night, after a dinner where Dad and Aunt Sophie had lectured us about the importance of the Land of the Polar Bear and the compound held in our family, Kiefer and I retired to our room.

"Good night Kiefer," I said, blowing out the candle.

"Good night Samz," he said, pulling a blanket over his head. As I tried to sleep, I banished thoughts of Setters and Mom and arguments about the war. I decided I needed to focus on the positives.

Tomorrow, I'm going to finally learn water magic.

TRAINING

"The legends say that of all the elements, water was the first to come into existence," Dad said. He pulled water from a bowl next to him into the air and began to dance it around his fingers. We were inside, in one of the large training rooms. We sat around him in a semicircle as the water swirled and spiraled around his arms.

"Every water person in our kingdom has been born with the power of our element," Dad explained, the water briefly looping around his head like a crown. "Water is a part of us, as we are a part of water, understand?"

A few of us glanced at each other, not understanding.

"Listen," Dad said, pulling his hands together. The water coalesced into a sphere above his head. "As we are a part of water magic, it even affects our biology."

"Like how we can hold our breath for longer than others," Miles offered. Dad beamed.

"Exactly. Water magic makes it easier for our lungs to hold our breath underwater. It even develops certain muscles more to make us adept swimmers," Dad explained.

"It also takes twice as long to dry off if we're wet," Ezra muttered.

"Right," Dad said, nodding to him. "Water naturally clings to us, just as dirt clings to earth people or smoke clings to fire people. We are all a part of the elements we control."

Dad continued, releasing the water and resuming its dance.

"The best way to learn water magic is to observe how water moves in the natural world," he said slowly, his voice soft and lilting. "How the waves of the ocean crest, how rivers flow from waterfalls, how it bubbles up from natural springs."

He spread his arms out, and the water he'd been controlling split into six spheres, floating in a line above his hands.

"Now, one by one I will give each of you some water," Dad said. "I want you to hold it above your hands, using only your magic to keep it aloft. Keep in mind the way water behaves naturally. Now, who wants to go first?"

"I'll go," Ezra said, lazily raising his hand. At his age, he's pretty much taught water magic to himself and didn't really need much training. Dad dropped a finger, and one of the spheres floated down to Ezra's outstretched hand. It settled into the air above his fingers. Anthony went next, then Luke and Miles.

"I'll try," I said, holding my hand out. Dad passed the water from his control into mine. I held my hands out, my fingers shaking as they splayed. The water shakily gathered itself into a sphere again around my straining hands and arms. It vibrated above my hand as Kiefer got his water.

"Now," Dad said, looking down the line of us. "When you control water, don't spread your fingers out. Keep them close together. If you tried to swim with open fingers you'd go nowhere. If you tried to cup water in your hands like that it would all splash to the ground."

I closed my fingers and immediately relaxed. The tension released from my arms and shoulders. The water stopped vibrating and began to calmly churn itself. Next to me, Dad pulled the water from the floor and gave it back to Kiefer.

"Now, take one of your hands, and try to extend the water," he said, taking the last of the water from the bowl and demonstrating. I pulled one of my cupped hands away from the other. One part of the water poked out of the sphere and followed my hand. It began to vibrate as it had before, a few droplets spilling out onto my crossed legs. I took a deep breath and fought the urge to spread my fingers as I pulled the water into a line.

"Now, compress it back into a sphere," Dad ordered, demonstrating up front. I slowly brought my hands back together, the water shakily forming a sphere.

"Good," Dad said, smiling. "Now, I will take your water back."

He stretched his hands out, and the water was ripped from my hand. It splashed over to Dad, who siphoned it back into the bowl.

"Now," Dad said. "I'm going to give each of you a bowl of water to practice with for the rest of the day. Practice shaping it, communicating with it."

"What if we already know water magic?" Ezra asked, raising a hand. Dad coughed.

"*Everyone* will get a bowl, regardless of how much water magic they think they know," he said. "Ezra, stay here as they leave, I want to talk to you."

Ezra rolled his eyes as we filed out of the training room, taking a bowl from the table. I glanced back just as I walked into the hallways, as Dad looking disapprovingly at Ezra.

.<>.

Sitting on my bed, I tried passing the water from one hand to another. The water sloshed back and forth in the air, raining droplets onto my bed. I groaned, dropped the water back into the bowl and fell back on my bed. Coffin dozed at the foot of my bed.

"You know, it's okay if a couple droplets fall," Kiefer said from his bed, his bowl of water in the corner of our room. "In a real fight, it's not gonna matter if you blast someone and a couple droplets of water get on the ground."

"I know, but this is just a tiny bit of water, not a whole blast like they use in the war," I said, holding my hand above the water. I began to move it in a circular pattern, the water swirling lazily. "I should be able to control it easily."

"Samz, it's fine. We're gonna learn, this is only the first day of training," Kiefer said. "I can't wait to get better though, I get where you're coming from."

"Yeah," I said, pulling up a blob of water. It rested on the underside of my palm.

"What do you think Dad was going to talk to Ezra about?" Kiefer asked. I shrugged.

"I don't know. Responsibility. Respect. Not being cocky," I said.

"So... telling Ezra not to be Ezra?" Kiefer chuckled. I laughed.

"I guess..." I said, dropping the water back into the bowl.

"Speaking of Ezra, when do you think we're gonna start learning spells?" Kiefer asked, rolling over on his bed. I rolled my eyes. Kiefer had a tendency to jump between several conversation topics in the span of a few minutes. It annoyed others, but as his closest brother, I'd gotten used to it and didn't mind.

"I don't know, probably not for a while," I said. "Spells are kinda dangerous if you ask me. With spells, you just say a word and concentrate and then... stuff happens. And you don't really have to do anything."

"Isn't that the point? To make magic easier?" Kiefer asked.

"Well yeah, but I think Dad just wants us to learn regular magic before learning serious spells," I said.

"Ezra told me there used to be a water spell that could make someone choke on their own spit," Kiefer said. "He doesn't know the incantation, though."

"That's probably a good thing, for Ezra and for everyone else," I said, putting my water aside. I'd had enough of it for one day. I laid back on my bed as Kiefer rolled over. We both stared at the dark wooden ceiling.

"Do you think Dad's worried?" I asked.

"About what?" Kiefer asked. "The war?"

"Well yeah but... specifically us," I said. "Why else would he choose to train us now?"

"Because he's not looking for mom anymore? I thought that was the point? Plus an aquanix visited me."

"I mean... well..."

"What? What?"

"I mean, Miles was talking to me. He says Dad thinks we might be involved in some sort of fighting soon, and he wants to teach us water magic so we'd be protected."

"Well sure. Of course he wants us to be protected," Kiefer said.

"But when have we ever actually seen fighting?" I asked. "I mean, when you think about it... have you ever actually seen a fire person?"

He thought for a moment.

"No," he said, already chuckling to himself. "But I would imagine they'd be pretty hot!"

"Kiefer," I groaned, trying not to laugh at his terrible joke. Unlike Jamie, who actually disliked his jokes, I just pretended to. Kiefer was funny, even when it wasn't the right time to be.

"I'm sorry, I'm sorry, I have been waiting for months to use that since I thought of that—

"You've been thinking up that god awful pun for *months?*" I asked.

"*No*, the thinking was like, two seconds, but waiting for the *opportunity* was a different story," he said, calming down. "But to answer your question seriously, no. I have never actually seen a fire person."

"Exactly," I said, the giddy feeling of his joke subsiding. "We've never had a need to know water magic until now. He could have taught us before, but he didn't."

"You could be right," he said, shrugging. "Or you could be turning into another Miles, and the good Lord knows we don't need another one of those!"

"Kiefer!" I said, failing this time to hold in any laughs or chuckles. We both cracked up for a few moments, at Miles' expense.

"So... why are you spending so much time worrying about being perfect with your water?" Kiefer asked, sitting up. "I mean, water magic isn't about how perfectly you can execute it, it's all about power."

"Power?" I said. Kiefer grabbed his bowl from the corner and placed it next to mine.

"Sure," he said, holding his hand out above his bowl. The water flowed up from the bowl and gathered around his hand. Several droplets sprinkled down onto the bed. "In a real fight, it doesn't matter how perfectly you hit someone, it just matters how *hard!*"

On the last word, he punched his hand forward, the water jetting across the room and splashing onto the wall opposite us.

"See, there's a bunch of water on the ground, but does it matter?" Kiefer asked, motioning to the splashes on his bed and the floor that traced the path his water had taken. "I hit my target, so does it really matter that some of the water spilled onto the ground?"

"I guess not," I said, pulling the water from my bowl up around my hand, just as Kiefer had done. I pulled my hand back and glanced at Kiefer. "I guess I'll try it."

I punched my hand forward, and most of the water made it across the room, lightly splashing against the wall. It was much lower than Kiefer's blast had been.

"Ah, you'll get the hang of it," Kiefer said, standing up. "I should... probably get us some more water."

.<>.

"Ugh, is that seriously what Kiefer told you?" Jamie said the next day after lunch. On our second day, Dad had started to teach us fighting stances. Jamie and I were practicing with some burlap dummies in one of the training rooms. We both had barrels of water next to us and were practicing some of the stances Aunt Sophie and Dad had taught us.

"Yeah. Water magic is all about power, not precision," I said, whipping a small jet of water at the dummy. It splattered against its chest, the dummy barely moving.

"I mean, power is important for water magic," Jamie said. "But precision is a *lot* more helpful."

"How... so?" I asked, punching another weak blast at the dummy. Most of the water spilled out onto the ground before it could reach it. I dropped my stance and turned to Jamie.

"If you are precise and careful with where you hit," Jamie said, pulling two globs of water out of the barrel and into each of her hands, "you can be a lot more effective in your fighting without wasting water."

She turned to the dummy, and sent one small but sharp jet at the hip and another at the head. The dummy, unbalanced, began to tip over on the post it was tied to. She hadn't even used that much water. She folded her hands, and released her fighting stance.

"Huh," I said, pulling two spheres of water out of the barrel as she had. I tried the same attack she had, but the blast at the hip hit too high and the blast to the head was too weak. The dummy moved a little but not much.

"That was good," Jamie said, smiling. I rolled my eyes. "I'm *serious*. I wasn't great when I started either."

"Sure," I said, grabbing the discarded lid of the barrel and putting it back on top.

"Samz, don't be mad, you'll catch up, I promise," she said, as I closed the door of the training room. I wasn't as good as Kiefer or Jamie, both of whom had already excelled in water magic. They both already had ideas on how it was supposed to be used. And I didn't.

.<>.

A few minutes later I bumped, literally, into Coffin. I'd been turning a corner when he'd run into my legs. We both stumbled for a few moments, gathering ourselves.

"Master!" he yelped, running around my legs. "What are you doings?!"

"Trying to learn water magic," I said, crossing my arms.

"Why?"

"Because I'm a water person, so I have to," I said, shrugging.

"Why?"

"Why do I have to or why am I a water person?" I asked, looking down at him. He thought for a moment.

"Yeses."

"Never mind," I said, looking back down the hall.

"You seems... angry," Coffin said, waddling next to me.

"I'm not angry, just a little frustrated," I said. "Everyone seems to have water magic already figured out, and I don't."

"Well... I don'ts understand it either," Coffin said, cocking his head. "Don't feel bads."

"Right..." I said, thinking for a moment. "Coffin, what does your morphing magic mean to you?"

"Huh?" he asked.

"I mean, what do you think is the most important aspect of your magic?"

"... huh?"

"Ugh," I said, rolling my eyes. "Just... why do you think you have morphing power?"

"Oh!" Coffin said, beaming for a moment. "Uh... because... because... I can."

"That's... it?" I asked. "Just... because you can?"

"Yeps," he said, licking his nose. "I morph because I cans. Except when *someone* putses and *evil* collar on me."

We came to an intersection in the halls of the compound, just as Maddie was coming in from the right.

"Samz! How's it going with training?" she asked, changing directions to talk to me. I shrugged.

"Fine—

"He's *angry*," Coffin interrupted, softly growling. Maddie looked at me.

"I know that magic can be frustrating to learn at first," she said, nodding. "If you want to practice with me, I'd be happy to—

"He doesn't *understands* it, and he's *angry*," Coffin piped up, headbutting my leg.

"*Coffin*," I hissed. I turned back to Maddie. "What Coffin meant to say was that I was a little annoyed that everyone else seems to have figured out what water magic is to them, and it makes it so much easier for them to learn, but I can't. Everyone's saying different things and I don't know who's right about it."

"Right," Maddie said, sighing. "I struggled with that as well when I was young. I was Dad's oldest child, and everyone wanted to be the first to make me into a great water mage. I don't know if they thought they'd get special treatment when I became a queen or whatever but it was confusing for me too."

"Really?" I asked. Maddie, of all of us, barely needed any training. She had been amazing with water magic since a young age, how had she ever had time to be confused about it? Maddie leaned in.

"But it was our grandmother, Mom's mom, who told me the big secret about water magic," she said, placing a hand on my shoulder.

"What is it?" I asked. I'd never met my maternal grandmother, she and the grandfather I'd been named after had been traveling the world for as long as I could remember.

"Water magic... is whatever you want it to be," Maddie said, leaning back. I frowned.

"What? How is that helpful?" I asked, crossing my arms. Maddie smiled.

"Water is... kind of a weird element," Maddie said. "Other elements have simple ways of learning that work for everyone, but water doesn't. Each person learns water magic differently."

"So you're telling me that Dad teaching all of us as a group is wrong?" I asked.

"No, not really," Maddie said. "There's a reason why water people pass magic down through families. Water magic is unique to each person, so it's traditionally taught by older family members who know their younger relatives best."

"I'm... kind of lost," I admitted.

"Look, at some point, you'll figure out what water magic means to you, some aspect of it you can fixate on. Once that happens, you'll be able to forge a personal connection with our element," Maddie explained, putting a hand on my chest as if she were pressing the secrets of water into my heart.

"Dad and Aunt Sophie are teaching us because they know us best, they're our family. They can help us connect to our element," she explained. "After you make that connection, magic becomes so much easier."

"So… since Kiefer and Jamie already have figured out what water magic means to them, they'll learn faster?" I asked. Maddie shrugged.

"Maybe. Maybe not. You've only been learning for a couple days," she said, standing up. "Look, if you ever want to talk, or practice, I'd love to help you."

"Okay," I said. "Can I ask one question right now?"

"Sure," she said, folding her hands.

"What does water magic mean to you, specifically?" I asked. She thought for a moment and then shook her head.

"I'll tell you eventually," she said, patting my head. "But for now, you need to find the meaning of water magic your own way."

"What?" I asked as she began to walk away. "Just tell me! Can you give me some ideas at least?"

"Not yet," she said. "Not yet."

THE RIGHT WAY

It happened the second we went out of sight of the compound, even though I'd warned both Jamie and Kiefer against it. Usually, Jamie assumed the job of stopping Kiefer and me from doing stupid things, but on this rare occasion it was my job and I was not good enough at it to stop them. At this point in our exploration of the Land of the Polar Bear, even Coffin had decided it was too cold. I'd taken off his morphing collar to allow him to shapeshift into a bird and fly back to the compound. Jamie and Kiefer both wanted to explore the bottom of a snowy ridge that steeply dropped down into a frozen stream, and practice magic with natural water.

"This is amazing!" Jamie said as she stood by the bank of the stream, and wall of snow marred by our footprints rising behind her. Removing her mittens and casting them aside, she drew her hands up. Water flowed from a hole in the ice up into a whip. She swept her hands in an arc, the water splashing into the ridge behind us. "See Samz? Isn't this worth it?"

"No," I said, shivering. Snow had fallen down into my loosely laced boots and made my feet soggy. I'd been able to pull some of the melted water out of my socks, but I didn't have great enough control over it to completely dry them yet. We'd been in the Land of the Polar Bear for two weeks, a little over halfway through our stay.

"Ah, ignore him," Kiefer said, stomping on the ice. A hole of water opened up beneath his boot. He threw his mittens aside and began to practice some new forms we'd learned that morning. In two weeks, we'd progressed from controlling small blobs to conjuring whole whips of water. If we concentrated enough most of us could produce a fairly powerful jet of water, Kiefer especially.

"I'm just saying, Dad, Maddie, and Aunt Sophie wouldn't like us being out this far, where we can't even see the compound," I said, throwing a mittened hand up at the ridge.

"We'll be fine, and if they come looking for us, we have a good reason," Jamie said. I rolled my eyes. This morning all of us had gotten a lecture about how practicing magic with naturally-occurring water was incredibly important for learning mages. They'd told us to go seek out natural water to practice with during the afternoon.

"Jamie's right," Kiefer said, blasting a ball of water across the river. "This is the best source of natural water in the whole valley. They'll be proud."

"There are definitely better places that are *closer* to the compound," I said. "Like that pond, that was kind of frozen but also kind of slushy. Or... or the..."

"Exactly," Jamie said, her arms slowly windmilling from one side to the other. The whip of water hypnotically looped and spiraled in front of her. "This is the best place and frankly, the water here is noticeably easier to control."

"Yeah," Kiefer said, punching a ball of water across the ice again. "Just try it."

I sighed, my shoulders sinking in defeat. I needed more practice; Jamie and Kiefer were already far ahead of me in their ease with water magic. It couldn't hurt, and we wouldn't even be there that long. I took off my mittens and pocketed them, my hands open to the freezing air.

"Let's just be quick, we don't need a lecture from Dad or Maddie," I said, punching a hole through the ice with my foot. I took a deep breath and shifted my weight down towards my feet. I stretched my hands out and felt the shimmering power of the ice-cold water from the river. I rose up and pulled a long whip of water out of the hole. Kiefer was right, the water did feel easier to control, like it was more willing to listen to my hands and thoughts.

I bent the whip to one side and pulled it out of the hole, and slowly began to loop it into an infinity sign.

"See?" Kiefer said, pulling more water out of his hole to blast it across the river again. "Isn't it so much better than that old barrel water?"

"It is," I said, throwing the whip up, the water formless for a moment. It began to crash down, so I held my hands out, most of the water stopping in midair. I refined it back into a whip. "It really is."

Maybe that would be what water magic meant to me: water being used in its natural state. But as I began to think about it, that idea would never work. Water people didn't always have natural water available. In battle, most carried them in leather pouches, or in the most dire situations, summoned new water into existence using only their magic. I wouldn't always be next to a river, or lake or ocean. I sighed and continued to shape the water and practice different fighting stances.

"See, this was a good idea," Jamie said, breaking off the end of the whip to send it splashing across the river. "I—

Fire exploded around one of the pine trees across from us, the flames instantly tearing through its needles and jumping to the other trees. We all dropped our water in shock as two men in thick black coats rushed out from either side of the tree, holding their bare fists out. My heart began to beat so violently in my chest I was afraid it was going to leap right out of it.

"Who are those—

One of the men punched his fist forward. As he did, flames began to form around his knuckles, blooming into a fireball as his arm reached full extension. The fireball exploded from his fist, burned over the river to Kiefer. Kiefer ducked, the fireball burying itself in the snow behind him.

We were being attacked by fire people.

My chest pinched in terror as they kicked forward in sync, two fireballs arcing towards us. Jamie, Kiefer and I threw up our hands, the water from the river rushing up in a wall in front of us and saving us at the last second. The smoldering water splashed down just as one of the men, his mouth obscured by a black cloth, shouted a muffled spell. A double helix of white fire burned out of his fists, the loops of flames growing larger and wider as they crossed the river, big enough to get all three of us. We screamed, throwing our hands up and pulling the river into a wall of water again. This time it wouldn't be strong enough. I could feel the heat prickling on my skin through our useless shield. I squeezed my eyes shut.

The river exploded.

The two men were thrown back into the forest by one surge of water, another splashing up and vaporizing the double helix of flames. We dropped our water and looked behind us.

Dad and Aunt Sophie rode the snow down the ridge, water melting into a slide at their feet. They skittered down to the bank of the river and crossed in front of us. In sync, they thrust their hands up and forward, the whole river blasting into the fire people and again and sending them up into the tops of the pine trees. Dad and Sophie threw their hands down, the water dragging the two fire people down through the branches and into the snow. The two fire people suddenly disappeared into smoke.

Dad and Aunt Sophie relaxed, dropping their arms. Dad turned back to us, his face an unreadable mask.

"Come," he said, his voice echoing up the snowy ridge. "Let's get back to the compound."

.<>.

Dad sat us down in his office, not having said a word since we left the ridge. Aunt Sophie had split from the group once we reached the compound, so she could take a patrol of guards out to see if there were any more fire people in the woods. He sat us down on the chairs across from his desk and took the large seat opposite us. A blazing fire burned in the hearth behind him.

"What were you three thinking?" Dad asked, his voice low and dangerous. He looked up at us. "What were you *thinking*?"

"You were the one who told us to go find natural water to use," Jamie said. "The stream was the best place. It's not like we were *planning* on getting attacked."

"You were out of sight of the compound where the guards couldn't see you," Dad said, shaking his head. "Do you know *how* your Aunt and I came to your aid so quickly?"

"Um..." Kiefer said, looking back and forth between Jamie and I. Dad sighed, and looked at me.

"Your wolf told us," Dad said. "He flew back here and told me that you'd gone down to the ridge. Sophie and I never expected to find you being attacked by fire people."

"Exactly! So why are you so mad at us if it wasn't our fault we got attacked?" Kiefer asked, crossing his arms. Dad slammed a fist on the table.

"It is your fault that you went somewhere you shouldn't have," he hissed. "You could have been *killed*. Do you understand that? You could be dead right now if it hadn't been for that wolf telling us where you were."

None of us said anything. Dad stood up.

"Look, I am glad that you are safe, but I am angry that you got yourselves into a situation that could have been fatal," he said quietly. "Go to your rooms."

.<>.

"No, they're not ready," Aunt Sophie said. I'd been walking to the kitchen in the middle of the night to find something to eat; dinner had been too awkward for me to eat much. I'd been passing by the door to Dad's office just as I hear Aunt Sophie.

"Sophie you saw them," Dad said. "They were helpless. They need to start learning spells."

"Aidan, if they can barely handle regular magic, how could they ever be ready for spells?" Aunt Sophie shot back. I leaned against the door, pressing my ear to the cold wood.

"It's not about how ready they are," Dad said. "It's about was best for them. We need to accelerate their training so if something like that happens again, they'll be able to defend themselves."

"Teach them spells this early and they might get hurt without a fire person ever coming near them!"

"They're my children Sophie. I want them to be safe."

"They're the future rulers of *our* kingdom, not just yours. I want them to learn magic the *right* way," Sophie insisted.

"What would be our other options? Confine them to the limits of the compound? Even then there's a chance a fire person could get in."

"We could get more security."

"No," Dad said. "We've already asked too much of Uncle Drew by having both of us step away from the war. We can't ask for more trained men."

"You're right," Aunt Sophie said, sighing. "What if I went back, in exchange for more guards?"

"No, that's not a good idea," Dad said. "We'd be more vulnerable if only one of us were here. You leaving would not be quiet. If our enemies found out they would surely attack us again."

There was silence for a few moments.

"Look..." Aunt Sophie said. "I know how... complicated spells are for you. For Drew and me as well. I don't want to repeat our mistakes."

"Me either," Dad said. I heard him shift in his chair. "What if we only teach them a few spells. Say, one defensive spell, one offensive spell."

There was more silence.

"Fine," Sophie said, her voice shaking. "I will go prepare the water staffs."

Realizing she was about to leave, I peeled away from the door and scampered around the next corner. I was out of sight just as she opened the heavy door.

.<>.

"Now, you must all understand that using a water staff is just to get you started on learning spells," Dad explained, passing one to each of us. They were simple wooden staffs, carved with flowing patterns surrounding a circular blue gem embedding into the middle of it. The staff felt light but sturdy in my hands as Dad passed one to me, giving one to each of us as we stood in a line. Placing the end on the ground, the staff just reached up to my shoulder.

"Spells require much concentration when you are first learning them, and the water staffs will ease the effort usually required to learn one," Dad explained, handing the last staff to Anthony. "They also allow you to produce water from nothing. In a few months, you should no longer need your staffs. Please be careful with them, they are incredibly rare."

"Dad? What if we already know how to use spells?" Ezra asked, boredly raising his hand. "Can I go practice somewhere else?"

"In... in a minute Ezra," Dad said, faltering as he often did with Ezra. "For now just... work with the rest of your brothers."

"Fine," he said, rolling his eyes.

"Now, usually spells are not taught until one has a good grasp on regular magic," Dad explained, walking to the center of the training room to face us. "You are all still beginners, and this *is* a bit early, so I am only going to be teaching you two spells."

"What if we already know a lot?" Ezra asked, raising his hand again.

"Then take this as a refresher," Dad said, holding his hands together. "Now, the first spell is a very simple but very important defensive spell used by all water people."

He pointed to Ezra.

"Ezra, send a blast of water at me from that barrel in the corner, since you are so eager to participate today," Dad said. Ezra shrugged and pulled his hand back into a fist. The water in the barrel quivered. He thrust his fist towards Dad, the water splashing out and spinning in a foamy jet towards Dad.

"*Seela!*" Dad shouted, crouching down into a defensive posture with his legs and arms wide. As his hands swept from his chest outward, an expanding bubble of blue light solidified into a glassy circle of deep blue water. The water was strange; it wasn't transparent and seemed to be more solid than regular water. Ezra's blast bounced right off of the shield. Dad stood up, drawing his hands together. The strange water shield evaporated into mist.

"Dad?" Miles asked. "I just... couldn't you have just redirected that? It was water."

"It was, for the sake of the demonstration," Dad said. "But it won't always be water, and you won't always be able to redirect it. The Seela spell augments the water to be stronger and thicker than regular water. However, the changes it undergoes makes it too unstable to change back to normal water. If the shield is broken or you deactivate it, you won't be able to get that water back."

"Wait," Luke said. "I thought you said you could only produce water from nothing with a water staff. You just made water from nothing."

"The Seela spell automatically pulls water out of the air to form the shield," Dad explained. "However, with a staff you can produce more water and make a stronger shield."

Dad instructed us to hold our staffs out, one hand near the gem and the other stabilizing the back.

"Let's practice that first spell," Dad said. "Focusing your energy on the gem will help your magic."

Ezra lazily made a Seela, Luke following him right next to me. I gripped the staff, and focused on the blue gem.

"*Seela!*" I yelled. The water staff thrummed with power, a blue shield of water instantly blooming out of the tip of my staff. It just... happened. There was hardly any effort on my part. Pretty much all I'd had to do was say a word and concentrate a bit. I lowered my staff, dissolving the spell, feeling impressed and nervous at the same time.

Over the course of the day, we learned one other spell. This one, the incantation being "Carwavo" produced a cone of water from the end of the water staff. The water just came into being at the end of the staff, no barrels or water pouches required. Once we'd learned that spell, Dad had us practice using the Carwavo spell against the Seela spell.

It was completely different from regular magic. It required no forms to memorize, hardly any physical movement, and very little effort. Most days of training I'd go to lunch all sweaty, but I'd barely broken a sweat that whole morning. Spells made magic *so* much easier. Even so, there was something in the back of my head, that memory of what I'd heard Dad and Sophie talk about. It was easy, *too* easy, and I knew that there were worse spells than Carwavo. But for now, it felt nice to finally be able to do water magic just as well as Kiefer and everyone else.

Suddenly, the door to the training room slammed open, Aunt Sophie rushing through with a string of guards at her wake. I dropped the Seela I was maintaining against Kiefer's blast as Dad ran up to her.

"Aidan, we just received an urgent message from Drew," she said. "The fire people are moving in on the Capital."

"The Capital? What are they—

"The letter said that their forces are a lot stronger than we anticipated and we don't know where all of the troops came from—

"How long ago was that letter?" Dad asked.

"Not long," Sophie said. "But we need to leave. Now."

FLIGHT INTO WAR

"I can't say I'm surprised," Kiefer said as he haphazardly threw his clothes into his bag.

A few days ago, scouts had discovered a massive invasion force in the Lesser Ocean, one that had seemingly appeared out of nowhere. While Drew was scrambling to figure out where all of the fire people had appeared from, he'd called Dad and Aunt Sophie to join him in the Capital, the nearest major city near the invasion force. Dad had given us two hours to pack. We were leaving by sundown.

"Kiefer," I said, at least trying to fold my clothes a little bit. "This is serious."

"Samz, the second Dad told us that we were finally going to get training, I thought it was too good to be true," he said. "I was right. Our training got cut in half, which is better than I expected but still not great."

"At least we got to learn *something*," I said, latching my filled bag closed. "It's a lot more than we knew before coming here."

"It's still not much," Kiefer said. "Just yesterday we were attacked and we were basically helpless."

"At least now we know some spells," I said, putting my bag aside and neatening my bed.

"Two. We know two spells," Kiefer said, closing his bag. "Honestly at this point, I'm thinking of looking for a private trainer."

"What?" I hissed. He was seriously thinking of moving forward with water magic without me? I was already behind, didn't he know that? "You can't do that."

"I can," Kiefer said. "I've thought about it, and I can. So I will. It's the only way I'm ever going to learn water magic at this point."

"Kiefer, it's not traditional for a prince to learn from someone outside of his family," I said, shaking my head. While most water people learned magic from their own families, some hired private trainers to learn. It was a relatively new trend, one looked down upon by older water people. "People would talk. It just wouldn't be a good situation. You can't."

"I can though," Kiefer said. "It's not *your* decision, it's *my* magic. I can do what I want with it."

"But Kiefer you..." I struggled for a moment. I couldn't let him move on without me. I wondered for a moment if I would ever consider getting someone else to train me, but banished the thought. It wasn't right for just one of us to get a trainer. "... Dad's going to be furious."

"Well, it's his fault we don't know any useful water magic, so I don't really care how he feels about it," he said. "Or how Maddie feels about it."

"Dad might continue our training later," I said. "Couldn't you wait?"

Kiefer paused, looking back.

"No," Kiefer whined, releasing his shoulders. "I've been waiting for years for someone else to teach me magic, and at this point, I've been waiting for too long. It's *my* turn to decide what to do with my magic."

"But—

"And you can too," Kiefer said, picking up his bag. He walked to the door.

"Fine," I said. "If I can choose, then I choose to learn from Dad. Cause that's how it's supposed to be."

"Okay," Kiefer said. "When we get to the Capital, I'm going to start looking for someone to teach me."

He turned and slammed the door. I flinched, grabbing my hand. I suddenly noticed that the green pigmentation was still there. I held my palm out and almost jumped.

The pigmentation had been *growing*. The dot of green now had part of a curving line etched into the skin. I closed my fist, deciding to ignore it for now.

.<>.

"Jamie, we need to talk about Kiefer," I said as we both dragged our bags down the hallways of the compound.

"What is it?" she asked.

"Well, since our training got cut short, he wants to get a private trainer once we get to the Capital so he can keep learning water magic," I said.

"Oh," Jamie said, looking down the hall. She shrugged. "Okay. Good for him."

"Okay?" I asked, pausing for a moment. "You're not mad at him?"

"No," she said. "I don't blame him. That's actually a good idea. I might do it too."

"What?" I hissed. "I thought you of all people would understand what a terrible idea that is."

"Is it though?" Jamie asked. "We're water people royalty. We should be the best in the kingdom when it comes to water magic, and we're not. If we wait around for Dad to teach us, we'll never be."

"Really? You don't think it's a little..."

"A little what?"

"A little... unfair. I guess," I said. "The point of being taught water magic by relatives is so that the ideas and values behind it are consistent with the values of our kingdom. If he goes and trains with some private trainer they won't be."

"So? We're fighting a war," Jamie said. "We need to fight, and Dad needs to help Uncle Drew and Aunt Sophie. He can't help if he's overseeing armies, so we have to learn water magic from someone else."

"But does it have to be a private trainer?" I asked. "Couldn't it be... I don't know... Maddie, maybe?"

"You have to learn from someone who's a master, and Maddie is not a master," Jamie said.

"By technicality," I said. "She's as good as or better than a master. She just hasn't completed her great act or been granted the title."

In the Water Kingdom, to teach others, one had to be a master. To become a master, Maddie would have to train, which she had, then complete a 'great act' of water magic. If enough masters deemed her to be worthy, she'd be an official water master.

The problem was that opportunities for her to complete a great act were few. Most achieved their great act in battle, which Maddie had never been in. There were other ways, but almost all of them required intensive, years-long training, which Maddie also hadn't had.

"Yeah Maddie hasn't done either of those things, so she's not a master, and you can't learn from someone who isn't a master," Jamie said.

"Oh, so *now* tradition and rules matter?" I asked. Jamie rolled her eyes.

"It's not just that. You're siblings. You'd argue. Learning from your sister probably isn't the best idea," she said.

"Neither is getting a private trainer," I shot back.

"Look, none of our choices are great," she said, arriving at the massive front doors. "But sitting around and choosing nothing is the worst thing we could do."

She pushed the door open, cold snowflakes and wind blasting into the compound. Heavy, wet snow splattered to the ground from the swirling gray clouds above. A big storm was coming.

.<>.

We stood in a circle in the driving snow. It piled around our bags, our shoulders, and along my neck under the curve of my hood. Coffin sat in my pocket, morphed into a mouse. We stood in a circle holding hands, bags and water staffs strapped to our bodies.

"This should be very quick, but for our large group we need all the help we can get," Dad shouted, over the wind. "Who here knows the Vaporition Spell?"

Maddie, Ezra, and Erin briefly broke the circle to raise their hands.

"Good, we're going to need you to help us teleport to the Capital," Dad said. "We're going right to the courtyard in the middle of Uncle Drew's Palace. Do you all know where I'm talking about?"

They nodded.

"Good," he said. "Now, on the count of three."

I squeezed Jamie and Kiefer's hands.

"One."

Coffin squeaked.

"Two."

A tree in the forest cracked in half, snow showering down as it fell under the weight of the heavy snow.

"Three! *Obroullard preneva!*" they shouted.

I'd only Vaporited with someone once before, and it was not an experience I liked to repeat. In the space of a single moment, my entire body dissolved into mist. It started at the five who had shouted the spell, their bodies and bags instantly unwinding into mist. The mist continued to devour the people closest to them, until the spell reached my left hand. First my arm unwound into mist, then my torso and left leg. When the transformation reached my eyes, the view of the Land of the Polar Bear was smeared to shifting gray. For a moment my body was formless, my thoughts heavy, muddled and broken.

In a second, we lurched back into reality, the mist snapping back into my physical body, and the gray of my vision condensing into the central courtyard of Uncle Drew's palace.

"Good job," Dad said, his voice sounding far off as my brain reorganized itself. Everyone said that Vaporiting got easier once you have learned to do it yourself; being a passenger makes you a lot sicker.

Coffin, my passenger, hopped out of my pocket and unmorphed on the ground. He leaned over to a stumbling Miles and barfed on his shoes. Just as he did, a man wearing blue armor, a cape, and a simple crown walked up to Dad and Aunt Sophie. He had long brown hair, a prominent nose, and a permanent scowl.

It was Uncle Drew, the High Emperor of the Water Kingdom.

"Aidan, Sophie, good to see you," he said, briskly walking up to them. "Now, let's get going. The fire people could be here any second."

.<>.

From our room, we could see the coast-facing part of the capital of the Water Kingdom. The city of Wateria was nestled into the base of two mountains, two ridges reaching out and hugging the sides of the city. Two rivers flowed into the city from beyond the mountains, filling its thousands of fountains and canals. The palace had originally been built in the style of ancient water people design: all spires and domes and arches. Over time, the palace and the city had adapted to more modern architecture. Now, circular towers, rounded stain glass windows, and steep triangular roofs spread out from the palace, getting increasingly shorter as it reached the city limits. Most of the buildings were painted in blues and sea-greens and grays. Opposite the mountains, a massive harbor faced the passive Lesser Ocean. Thousands of miles away, across the ocean I looked at, was the home of the fire people.

"This is a nice view," Miles said, putting his bag down next to his bed. Our room had two beds, the other one that usually would have been claimed by Kiefer. "But I have to ask—

"Look, I just don't really want to share a room with Kiefer right now," I said, sitting down on my bed. Coffin jumped into my lap, his claws digging into my pants. "I know it's what we always do, but we're... kind of in a fight."

"About what?" Miles asked, sitting down on his.

"He... he wants to get a private trainer, to teach him water magic since Dad can't," I said, crossing my arms. "I tried to talk to Jamie about it but she *agreed* with Kiefer. Since when have they ever agreed on anything?"

"Well, Kiefer and Jamie are different but the one thing they have in common is that they're driven," Miles said, shrugging. "I can see why they'd both want to do that."

"Please don't tell me you think it's a good idea," I said, Coffin biting the fabric of my blanket.

"Don't worry, I think it's a terrible idea," Miles assured me. I breathed a sigh of relief.

"I know, right?"

"Yeah," Miles said. "I want to learn water magic too, but I want to learn it the right way. They're just going to find someone who's just going to dump a bunch of spells down their throat and never teach them any *actual* magic."

"Yeah. Spells are kind of—

"Lazy, and overrated," Miles said. "I do *not* like using spells. They offer no room for creativity in your magic. Trust me, I know what these trainers are like. They give you a bunch of spells, send you off, and get their next client."

"I don't know. If Kiefer and Jamie are serious about getting someone to train them, they'll do their research," I

84

said. "Or at least, Jamie will and Kiefer will trust her judgment."

"I could talk to them," Miles offered. "I don't know if they would listen to me but I could try."

"No, you don't have to do that," I said, waving him off. "They're set in their ways."

"Ugh, that's so annoying," Miles said, falling back on his bed. "They're gonna learn magic so wrong."

"Well, then that'll be their fault, I'm kind of over complaining about it," I said, standing up as I pushed a sleeping Coffin over onto my bed. Miles sat up.

"Maybe we should go on a walk," he said, standing up. "Go see the city."

"Sure," I said. "Anything to get my mind off the whole upcoming battle thing and Kiefer and Jamie."

Coffin snored from the bed.

"Is he going to be fine, or is he going to puke all over my stuff again?" Miles asked. I shrugged.

"There's literally no way of telling," I said, crossing my arms. "He's... chaos. Given form."

"Great," Miles said. "I guess we'll just roll the dice."

.<>.

Outside in the city, a brisk sea breeze blew up the sloped street, the fresh smell of salt mingling with the other scents of the city. Small, two-story buildings rose on either side of us, small markets and restaurants spilling out onto the cobbles. People clad in ocean-colored tunics and robes milled about, not being very discreet about looking at Miles and me.

"It's kind of nice to not have to share a room with Luke," Miles said. "He's fine sharing a room with it's just nice to have a change."

"Same," I said, as we walked towards the harbor. "I've been sharing a room with Kiefer for a bit too long as well."

"So I guess I was right about the whole... getting attacked thing," Miles said. "Remember? When I talked to you the night Dad told us?"

"I... guess you were," I said. "Even with two weeks of training, we were kind of useless."

"That's because you've only been doing it for two weeks," Miles said. "Even I'm still not great at it. And I've been practicing by myself for a while."

"I know," I said. "I did a little bit, but not much more than holding water. Shooting it and shaping it is a lot harder."

"I know," he said. "We'll figure it out. Without cheating and getting a trainer. And without excessive spells."

"Exactly," I said, sighing. "I just don't want to be behind them."

"You won't be," Miles said, shaking his head. "If they learn a bunch of spells, they'll only give off the *illusion* of being better. All they'll know is a bunch of fancy words and how to focus. *You'll* know water for what it is."

"Right," I said. "Both of us. We just need... some practice."

"Right," Miles said. "Just some real prac—

BOOM

A giant fireball interrupted Miles by crashing right into a building next to us, the burning payload smashing through the roof. People rushed from the building, screaming and splashing water on themselves from a nearby canal.

We looked around, as another flaming projectile crashed into a building a few streets away.

"Oh my God," Miles said, his face turning pale. "The fire people are here."

"Well," I said, my stomach flipping. "You said you wanted some practice."

On the horizon, the black hulls of ships began to come into view. Fire tore up the two ridges hugging the border of Wateria, fire people surging over it.

The fire people, for the first time in the war, attacked the capital of the Water Kingdom.

END OF PART ONE OF

VOLUME ONE

OF THE WATER AND FIRE SERIES

.<>.

PART TWO

.<>.

OUR DESTINY

THE BATTLE OF WATERIA

"Uh, Miles?" I asked as foghorns began to sound throughout the city. "Should we get back to the palace, or—

"I..." Miles stammered. Fire people, looking like a tide of black coming over the ridges flowed into the city. Around us, blue armored water people rushed to the outskirts of the city to stop the fire people from burning through it. Others used the water from the canals and fountains to put out fires started by the bombs. "I... don't..."

He was frozen, his eyes wide and his face white. His fists were clenched, nearly in an attack position. His chest fluttered with quick breaths. His eyes darted around, his lip trembling with each blast from the firebombs. He was helpless.

Strangely, seeing him frozen in terror made a profound feeling of calm wash over me. My shoulders relaxed and all of the tension released from my hands. He was in trouble and I had to help him. I might not have been able to save everyone in the city but I could save him.

"Miles," I said, placing a hand on his shoulder. He flinched, his head whipping back towards me.

"S-Samz?" he said, his face briefly silhouetted as a firebomb streaked behind his head and exploded a few blocks over, shaking the ground. Screams pierced the sky. I took a deep breath.

"Let's get back to Uncle Drew's palace," I said, keeping my voice low but still loud enough to be heard. I just had to save him, and that would be enough. "We'll be safe there."

"Okay, okay," he said, shaking as he turned around to face me. I grabbed his arm.

"Let's go," I said, turning up the street where Uncle Drew's palace stood impassively in front of the two mountains. The firebombs had punched black holes into the cityscape as it sloped back up to the palace. I grabbed Miles and started to jog up the street, following a thin tide of people also headed towards the palace.

"I'm sorry," Miles said, pulling his arm out my grasp. "I don't know what's happening to me—

"It's fine," I said, plowing on. I paused for a moment, looking back at Miles. Color was starting to flow back into his face, and he wasn't shaking as much. That was good. I turned back, but before I could go, something flaming dropped out of the sky.

It was a fire person, flames jetting from their hands, slowing their descent as they touched down onto the street. People scattered from the one fire person as they stood up, the black visor of their helmet shuttered. The insignia of the fire people, a fist surrounded by flames, was punched in red in the center of their breastplate.

Miles froze up again behind me, all the confidence he gathered shattered the moment the fire person blasted down. The other water people screamed, running into the buildings on the side of the street, Miles and I the only ones not moving.

The fire person turned to us.

They held a bare palm out, fire igniting from thin air. They slashed their hand in an arc, the fire extending into a whip. I stepped back, pushing Miles slowly as he froze up. My heart started to pound, until I remembered the promise I'd made to myself. The fire person turned in a circle, the fire whip burning into a crackling hoop. I had to protect Miles. I could save him. Coming from in between the two buildings behind us, a canal flowed into a tunnel under the street we were on. The fire person began to expand their hoop, the heat burning against my face. I had to protect Miles.

I thrust my hands forward, and the water from the canal, more than I had ever controlled before, exploded around Miles and I. It flowed into a thick, swirling wall around us, the fire person snapping their head towards us as their hoop of fire burned nearer. I assumed a fighting stance, widening my feet, pulling my elbows in, and dropping my torso. The swirling wall of water around me dropped along with my body, flowing lower and wider across the cobblestones. Moving my foot forward across the ground in an arc I threw my hands out, the water jetting into two different streams. I clapped my hands together and brought my other foot forward, the two jets of water blasting through the hoop of fire and hitting the fire person from two directions.

"Samz..." Miles breathed. "That was—

The hoop of fire faltered, the fire person only briefly stopped by my attack, which I still couldn't believe I'd actually done. Part of the visor had been broken off, half of her face revealed. Glaring at me, she resumed control of the smoldering hoop, the fire flashing brighter than before and burning right at us.

"Miles, help me," I said, throwing my hands up over my head. Miles followed me, helping me pull the water over our heads and into a thick wall in front of us. The fire made contact with the buildings on the street, Miles and I nearly pushed back into the canal.

"Miles, if we get in the canal we can get off of this street," I said, only a few feet left before the fire pushed us into the canal. Our wall of water was thick but the fire was slowly burning through it.

"Alright," Miles said, looking back at the canal. He seemed to have calmed down. "Let's do it. On three."

"We don't have time for three, jump *now!*" I said, jumping back into the water. I splashed down into the cool canal, the firebombs and the screams muffled by the water. Miles splashed next to me just as I was about to surface.

"Let's go!" I said as Miles bobbed to the surface. The canal flowed parallel to Drew's Palace, mostly in between houses. I could feel the magical invigoration of being nearly submerged in my element vibrate in my muscles.

We pushed ourselves down the canal until we reached a bank where we could climb back up onto the street. I got out first, reaching down to help pull Miles up. Miles awkwardly crawled onto the stones, dripping with water.

"Okay," I said, standing up. The canal had brought us farther downhill, Uncle Drew's castle farther away. The street was mostly clear. The firebombs had slowed, most of the fire people stopped on the outskirts of the city and taking time to regroup. The air was still thick with smoke and screams. "So, we're a little farther down than we were before, but at least this street is clear."

"Right," Miles said, trying to control the water to flow out of his clothes. "Let's go."

We started running up the hill towards the palace, already tired from our swim in the canal. Our feet pounded against the vibrating cobblestones, as another volley of firebombs slammed into the city. The smoke began to block out the sun, causing bands of darkness to appear across the hill in front of us. My throat burned from breathing hard in the smoky air.

Suddenly, a chorus of screams erupted from the east side of the city. Miles and I whipped our heads to see a fiery explosion tear a hole in the cordon the water army had formed around the edge of the city. We watched as the fire people poured down the ridge and into the city, spilling into the streets.

"Oh no, no, no," Miles said, freezing up again. His eyes became distant and glassy as he watched geysers of flames burn ever closer as the fire people advanced.

"Miles, not now," I said, dragging him along. His legs stiffly marched behind me as he kept his eyes glued on the advancing destruction. One building three streets over suddenly exploded; the fire people were a lot closer than we thought. They'd be on us any second.

Miles and I reached a bridge spanning one of the canals, but before we could cross it, Ezra and Kiefer darted out from one of the streets parallel to the palace that ran along the canal, blasting fire people as they ran in our direction.

"Kiefer!" I shouted, running down the few steps I'd taken over the bridge to meet him at the foot. Five fire people followed them, blasting the buildings on the side of the street as they did. Right now, it didn't seem like the fire people had a strategy other than to burn any building in sight. They weren't organized or even really moving towards the palace.

"Samz, c'mon, you and Miles have got to help Ezra and I fight off these fire people," Kiefer said as I met him.

"What? We're supposed to be getting back to the palace," I said, shaking my head. Kiefer raised an eyebrow and Ezra came up behind him.

"We can't leave our people behind," he said. The fire people had nearly caught up to us. Neither of them seemed scared. In fact, they both seemed almost... angry.

"Miles, look alive, they're here," Ezra said, assuming a fighting stance as the fire people spilled out to the intersection.

Ezra whipped a blast of water out of the canal behind him into the face of one of the fire people, sending them careening down the street. Kiefer sent a tight blast at one of their shoulders as two fire people launched writhing whips of fire at us. Ezra pulled his fists in tight and expertly stepped in a circle, a wave of water sweeping the fire away before it could reach us. Kiefer, Ezra and I stood shoulder to shoulder, and pushed the wave outward, knocking three of the fire people off of their feet.

The last remaining fire person pulled their fists in, muttered a spell, and threw their arms out. A tight, blindingly white jet of fire exploded from their chest, arced over our heads, and slithered towards Miles.

I'd almost forgotten about him! I was supposed to be protecting him! My heart racing as the jet of flames neared Miles, I threw up and thin wall of water and shouted, "Seela!"

The Seela spell formed a moment before the jet of fire hit it. A shower of golden sparks flew off of the fire as it drilled against my spell. Red cracks began to form in the wavering shield, my power fading. Miles suddenly unglued his feet from the street and started to run back. He dove into the canal just as the jet of fire shattered my Seela and burned a dark hole into the street behind us.

"I'm coming Miles!" Ezra shouted, running between Kiefer and I to grab him. Kiefer and I turned around.

Miles was in the canal, Ezra struggling to get him out. All five of the fire people had regrouped. For the first time during the whole battle, I felt a cold fist of fear close around my chest. I couldn't move as the fire people ignited their fists. I couldn't breathe as they drew their arms back, the fire hissing and spitting. I couldn't do anything. But Kiefer, soaked in water, his jaw set, punched a fist forward.

But water didn't come out of it.

Lightning did.

Blue electricity pulsed around his knuckles, crackling up his arm as it extended. The water at his feet tingled as the lightning exploded out of his hand in an expanding wave of destruction. The cords of energy struck the metal armor of the fire people, their bodies convulsing as the electricity conducted on their armor.

Thunder boomed across the city as they fell, their armor smoking. Kiefer, wasting no time to puzzle over what happened, grabbed my arm and started to pull me over the bridge. His hand was burning hot, something in his palm briefly glowing against my skin. The glow quickly died as we reached Ezra and Miles, sopping wet on the other side of the bridge.

"Kiefer, what was—

"We need to go," Kiefer said. "Let's get back to the palace."

"But—

"He's right," Ezra said, pulling a shivering Miles to his feet. "We need to go."

I glanced back over my shoulder at the twitching fire people. I wanted to know how that had happened, but I couldn't stay to investigate. We had to get back to the palace. We shambled our way up the street, the water army starting to take control of the battle. Fires were dying all around the city as civilians and soldiers put them out. We saw a few fire people being dragged away in chains as prisoners of war. We also saw water people, civilians and shoulders, being carried towards the palace as medics tried to tend to their burn wounds.

The guards at the palace ushered us in and whisked us through a series of halls and tunnels until we reached a room in the underbelly of the palace. The rest of our family was there, huddled around small couches and dimly lit candles.

After we hugged everyone, and settled down as the sounds of battle died, I didn't say anything. Kiefer had created lightning. I was the only one who'd seen it. He was a water person. There were no lightning people.

So how had he made the lightning?

FOLLOWING THE SPARK

My behavior after the Battle of Wateria was apparently so concerning that Erin felt the need to confront me about it after a week. Jamie and Kiefer both had found a private trainer, a man named Master Sevett I'd met briefly when I went with them on their first day. Luke had also decided to get a private trainer, although I hadn't met his. Ezra had started the process of joining the water army. Miles went to a small, calm town outside of the city to see a therapist. Maddie was waiting to hear from a group of masters if she'd earned her title (she'd been nominated after taking out ten fire people at once during the battle). Emily and Anthony spent most of their time helping Dad. Apparently, spending almost whole days in the library as I was doing wasn't what most people did after a traumatic battle.

After the battle, I couldn't get over the fact that Kiefer had controlled lightning. I'd barely had time to speak to Ezra or Miles about it, even though they'd only heard it. Besides the fire people who'd been blasted, I was the only person who had seen. Kiefer avoided me most days. The only way I could figure out how he could have possibly made lightning was research. So, I went to the vast library nestled into one of the mountains to try to find any instance of a water person making lightning.

I was poring over a book of battles from three hundred years ago in a brief war we'd fought with the ice people. The summaries included notable acts, which lightning would have been if it had been used. I wasn't really sure why I was so concerned about it, there were more pressing things I should have been worrying about. My magic, the fact that we'd just been attacked, or even all the weird ways my siblings were dealing with the battle. It wasn't just something to distract me from those things, it was *vital* for me to figure out.

I turned the page, still reading about a battle that had taken place right near the ice people's capital of Tarchenglass when someone stepped up to my table. It was Erin, her glasses reflecting the candlelight. I was deep in the archives, literally inside the mountain. Stacks rose up to the far off ceiling above me. My table was in the middle of an intersection, strewn with books and notes and lists the librarians had given me.

"The librarian told me you would be here," Erin said. I was surprised. Conversations like these usually happened between Maddie and I, not Erin. Erin realized this too and quickly added, "I know, you're expecting Maddie but she's busy with the masters trying to find out if she earned her title. She wanted me to talk to you."

"About...?" I asked, placing my pencil down.

"Look, I get more than anyone that the library is a calm place to... gather your thoughts..." she said, biting her lip. "Um..."

"Okay," I said, looking back at my book. Erin sighed, rubbing her eyes under her glasses. She sat down on the chair across from me.

"We were just a little... concerned," she said, sitting up a bit.

"About...?" I asked, looking around at my piles of books.

"I'm just... what are you even researching?" she asked, leaning forward. She suddenly turned from being concerned to being energetically curious. "If you want, I can help you."

"Um..." I said, unsure of what to say. I hadn't told anyone that Kiefer had made lightning yet, and I wasn't really planning on it. At the same time, I was pretty terrible at research, and Erin was amazing. She could help me make some actual progress. It couldn't hurt.

"Samz...?"

"Can you promise not to tell anyone?" I asked, leaning across the table towards her.

"Of course," she said, nodding. I looked around. This part of the library was mostly deserted, only a few librarians organizing books.

"During the battle... Kiefer... did something he shouldn't have," I said. Erin's eyes widened. "No, no, not like that. Like... shouldn't have been *able* to do."

"Oh" she said, sighing. "You had me there for a second."

"He... I know this sounds crazy but I saw it happen," I said, wondering for a moment if it had even happened at all. Had I hallucinated it? No, he'd definitely done it. We couldn't have gotten away from those fire people any other way. "He made lightning, and electrocuted a bunch of fire people."

"Well, there are some records of people from the Upper World experimenting with electricity, so he could have used one of those devices," she offered.

"No, he didn't have any device on him. The lightning came from his hand, like it was an element he controlled," I explained. "Lightning people don't exist, so I was trying to see if there was a way that water people could do it."

Erin thought for a moment, tapping her finger on the table.

"Well, lightning is usually produced by clouds, which are made of water, but then again only storm people can control clouds and even then they have no influence over where the lightning of their storms strike," she said, explanations and possibilities ticking and whirring inside of her head as she rattled off her answer. "Could he have been able to harness static electricity by, I don't know, rubbing the cloth of his robe together? No, that would have taken time and I'm sorry but I don't believe it's something Kiefer would think of doing and even if he did, it wouldn't be able to produce anything powerful enough to take out five fire people. Could he have amplified it through water?"

"No, there was no water involved," I said. "Well, there was a puddle at his feet, but otherwise he just punched his fist. Lightning came out of it."

"That's not..." Erin said, shaking her head. "That shouldn't... be possible. If a water person ever made lightning, even long ago, I think we'd know about it."

"So, looking over these books on old wars isn't going to help?" I asked, feeling the weight of disappointment in my chest. I really had wasted the past week.

"Probably not," she said, shaking her head. "If a water person had made lightning in battle you wouldn't have to go all the way to the archives to see if it happened."

"So... where *should* I look?" I asked.

"Well, I wouldn't look at the history of the water people just yet," she said. "First, I'd look into lightning magic."

"But that's not a real thing," I said. Erin shook her head.

"Lightning magic is real, it just can't be harnessed by humans," Erin said. "Or at the very least if it ever was, it hasn't been for a long time. Long enough to be something generally thought of as mythical. But there *are* books where it's mentioned, and it's not very many so you shouldn't have a very large pool of books to look at."

"Where would I find them?" I asked. Erin stood up.

"Wait here, I'll be back in ten minutes," she said. After what felt like an hour, she came rushing back with a small stack of books. She placed the stack on the table and started to spread them out.

"*Origins of the Inner World,* you'll be able to find some good information on not just lightning but all of the elements. It's a good read if you're interested in basic magical theory, I love it," she said, placing the largest book in front of me. "*Legend of the Eastern Sea,* takes a look at the real-world influences on a legend involving lightning, among other things. There's bound to be something about it in *History of the Catacomb War*, it also is probably mentioned in *Prominent Setters and their Achievements*. The Setters had powers over multiple elements, and combining some of them might have allowed them to at least create lightning."

There was one book, the smallest of the five left in her stack, she picked up, pausing before she placed it in front of me.

"*The Lives of the Balancers*, although that one doesn't have great credibility," she said.

"How so?" I asked.

"I mean... just look at the author's name," she said, crossing her arms.

"*Written by Andromeda of the City of Cosmos, Prophetess of King Embernam, Amateur Biographer (among other professions)*," I read. I read it a second time.

"See? First off, it's a book about a legend, but it's talked about as if it were fact. The events of this book are mentioned as legend in *History of the Catacomb War*," Erin said. "And the City of Cosmos, which the author claims to be from, is also a myth. There's no such thing as a prophetess. On top of that, this book is a copy of the original, written nearly two thousand years ago. But one of the main characters does use lightning magic, so it will at least give you some ideas."

"Oh," I said, taking the frail book and placing it on top of the stack. "I'll still read it. I'll take any sort of information at this point."

"No problem. I can try to find more but most other books would only mention it in passing," she said, stepping back. "If you give me more time I can do some research in some of the water magic books, and see if there's anything there. If a water person could create electricity, it would be a very complex form of water magic. I suppose it *is* a possibility Kiefer could have somehow tapped into it. If such a form even exists."

"Thank you," I said, smiling as I opened *Origins of the Inner World*. I was surprised that she'd been so helpful, with something that I thought she'd write off as a hallucination. Well, most people would. Erin was way too curious.

"Okay," she said, starting to turn, but pausing. She looked back. "You should read those outside of the archives. Somewhere with light."

She tapped her glasses. "You don't want to end up like this."

"Alright," I said, picking up the books. She helped me pick up the others strewn about the table.

"I think these librarians are getting tired of me anyway," I said as she led me out of the archives.

"When I come of age and get to run this place, I'll let you come whenever you want," she promised.

.<>.

A week later, when I was starting *History of the Catacomb War*, Miles came back from therapy. I was reading on my bed, Coffin gnawing on the metal post when he opened the door.

"Miles!" I said, putting the book down and jumping up. "I didn't know you were back."

We hugged. Miles released me and put his bag down, which Coffin immediately attacked and started to bite.

"Yeah, well, I'm here," he said, sitting down on his bed.

"How was therapy?" I asked. Miles had gone to a doctor in one of the quiet towns outside of the capital and had lived there for two weeks after the battle. He seemed a lot calmer now, more balanced.

"It was actually really helpful," he said, sitting forward. "I don't plan on going into another battle any time soon, but if I did, I'd be better."

"That's good," I said. Even though him freezing up at the battle had helped me find a connection to water magic, I didn't want Miles to be scared of fighting anymore. Well, at least not so scared he froze up and couldn't move.

"I actually... I wanted to talk to you about an idea," Miles said. Coffin ripped through one of the straps on Miles' bag so I walked over and picked him up.

"Yeah?" I asked as Coffin thrashed in my hands. I settled him down in my lap, where he started to scratch at the fabric around my knee.

"Well, one of the reasons I froze up during the battle was because I didn't feel confident in my water magic," he

106

said. "So, my therapist said that the easiest way to stay calm in battle is to learn more water magic."

"Right," I said, sheepish. I'd completely neglected to learn water magic in the past two weeks. It didn't take much observation of Kiefer and Jamie sparring in the courtyard below to know that I was behind.

"I know that neither of us wants to get a private trainer, so do you want to try to get better at water magic with me?" Miles asked. I paused for a moment. Learning water magic would take up the time I needed to research. *Origins of the Inner World* only taught me about the mechanics of lightning and its assumed values. *Legend of the Eastern Sea* had talked mostly about the legend of a secret archipelago where different mythical creatures controlled all of the elements, only a brief conclusion at the end debunking the existence of such a place. So far, *History of the Catacomb War* hadn't revealed anything. It had taken me so long to get so little information, the last thing I needed was another thing to take up time. However, Miles and I both needed to get better at water magic. At the time, it mattered more.

"Of course," I said. "Let's learn water magic."

DANCING FOR THE MOON

"I think you're supposed to pull your elbow back more for that move," I said, trying to match up the diagram in the book to Miles' body. We were in a small training room near the base of the palace. A semicircular window took up most of one wall, illuminating a deep, circular pool at one end, with various dummies and spigots attached to the wall. We'd been working there for a week and a half, Erin providing us with books on water magic and occasionally joining in on our sessions.

"I don't think my elbow can go any farther back," Miles complained, dropping the stance. "Let's try a different one."

"Fine," I said, flipping the page. It had been frustrating for us, trying to just learn from books and tips we could get from our older siblings. We never went to Luke, Jamie, or Kiefer.

"I'm boreds!" Coffin bubbled from the pool. He was in the form of a small, gray dolphin. He stuck his snout over the edge of the pool and spat water at me. I held my hand up, the water pausing in midair. I flicked my hand forward, the water splashing back at him. Coffin dove right before the water hit him, splashing the wall with his tail. He'd been behaving better recently, so I gave him a few hours every day with no morphing collar.

"Maybe we should just call it a day," Miles said, sitting down at the edge of one of the low barrels. "We did a lot yesterday, and we have to go get ready for Maddie's ceremony soon, *and* we have the Moon Dance after that."

"I know," I said, crossing my legs. "Maybe just one more form?"

"I guess," Miles said, standing up. Suddenly, the door opened, Dad poking his head in.

"Dad!" I said, jumping up. He stepped through the door, both of us hugging him. The past three days he'd been out on a scouting mission, and even before that, we'd hardly seen him. We let go.

"It's good to see you two," he said, looking around the room. "How's the training going?"

Coffin chose that moment to jump out of the pool and unmorph, his fur soaked.

"They're *bad* at it," Coffin said, shaking his fur out. I rolled my eyes.

"He's kidding," I said, Coffin grumbling something like "*Am nots*". "It's slow, but we're getting better."

"I'm glad," Dad said. "Don't worry, in a few months we'll be able to start regular training again."

"Yeah," Miles said, not making eye contact. Dad sighed.

"I know you both are frustrated but believe me when I say that we are doing everything we can to find time for me to train you," he said. "Nothing makes me prouder than watching you two take initiative and find your own way to learn water magic."

"Thanks," I said, Miles glumly kicking debris from a dummy our blasts of water had destroyed.

"Samson, can I talk to you for a minute? Just a short walk around the palace?" he asked. I glanced back at Miles.

"We can start again tomorrow. Could you also take Coffin back to the room?" I asked. Miles nodded silently, turning away from Dad and I.

"I'll see you before Maddie's ceremony," Dad said as we walked out of the training room.

.<>.

"Is Miles alright?" Dad asked. "Do you think he needs more therapy?"

"No," I said, shaking my head. "He just really needs to learn water magic, and he's frustrated that you can't teach us."

"I know," he said, as we walked out of one of the doors and into a garden planted on a terrace. The nearly repaired city spread out below. The garden was sparse at this time of year, only a few green bushes alive. Winters were warmer in Wateria than at home, but even so, many of the flowers hadn't bloomed yet. Dad sat me down on a bench in front of one of the fountains. It showed a golden man in a large crown, dripping in jewelry command a carved hurricane. Water flowed from holes and folds in the carved clouds of the storm. It was a gift the Storm Empire had given us twenty years ago when their current ruler, the one depicted in the fountain, came into power.

"I wanted to talk to you about Jamie and Kiefer," he said. "They won't listen to me about their private trainer."

"What about Luke?" I asked.

"I've nearly convinced him to stop, but I can't get to Jamie or Kiefer," he said. "I've tried to tell them why it's wrong, they won't listen. I've even promised that they'll get to learn from Maddie once she gets her title tonight but they don't want to learn from her. I don't know what to do."

I didn't either. Of all people, I'd been the one to try to convince them against it the most. Did Dad not know how much I tried? How they ignored me now?

"I'm... I'm out. I've told them everything I can and they won't listen," I said. "It's really starting to hurt my relationship with them. They don't talk to me anymore, if they can help it."

"What?" Dad hissed, his head whipping towards me. "They're not talking to you?"

"No, but please don't talk to them about it, it's really not that big of a deal, I'm fine," I said. If Dad got angry at them for not talking to me that would only make them even more annoyed with me.

"It *is* a big deal. You three are triplets, you can't ignore each other like that," Dad said. "I had no idea it had gotten that bad."

"They just think I'm jealous that I'm not as good as water magic as they are. That's all they'll hear if I try to talk to them," I explained. "So... I can't really help with that."

"I'm sorry," Dad said, looking to the fountain. "I've been so focused on the war I haven't even noticed what's been happening in my family. I don't even have the energy to stop Jamie and Kiefer from taking private lessons."

"Dad, it's not your fault and we all know that," I said. "We all want to win this war. I mean, Ezra is even trying to get into the army."

"I know," Dad said, sighing. "I'm nervous about him too."

"Why?"

"The last time I saw him, before I left, he's been so... angry," Dad said. "The battle didn't scare him, it just fueled his hatred for fire people. It makes me uneasy."

"Oh," I said. During the battle he'd been pretty brutal towards the fire people, but it hadn't scared me at the time. It kind of did now.

"I'm sorry, I shouldn't be telling you all of this," Dad said, looking off.

"No, it's fine that you told me," I said. "It's actually good. If you need help with family stuff, I'll do what I can."

Dad looked at me, smiling warmly. "I'm so proud of you. You know that?"

"Dad," I said as he hugged me. I felt warm, happy, and for the first time in a few weeks, I felt safe. Dad released me, looking down at my head.

For a second, he noticed something over my shoulder, his eyes flashing with concern for just a second before returning to normal. He awkwardly smiled again, and stood up. I glanced over my shoulder, seeing nothing as I stood up.

"Well, thanks for letting me talk to you," Dad said. "I'll see you in a few hours at Maddie's ceremony."

"See you," I said as he briskly walked away. The second he went out of sight, I looked back over my shoulder where Dad had looked. We'd sat next to a withered rosebush, which was right over where my shoulder had been. Most of the branches were black with shriveled brown leaves, except for one.

Wait.

When Dad and I had entered the garden, almost all of the plants, including the rosebush, had been dead. But now, there was a single red rose in full bloom in the center of the rosebush, right behind where I'd been sitting. It had *not* been there when we arrived. Shivering, I left the garden, leaving the rose behind.

.<>.

A few hours later, I sat in a stiff pew, trying not to itch the old fabric of my ceremonial robes. Everyone in the hall wore the same type of robe, hoods drawn, some with white sashes signifying them as masters. Seven masters stood in the front of the room in a semicircle around an

113

ornately carved porcelain bowl of water, Maddie in her robe kneeling before the bowl. The hall was a small church like room near the top of the palace, filled with five rows of pews facing the raised floor with the masters. A tapestry behind the masters depicted the history of the water people, while the other three walls were cut open with arched windows that overlooked Wateria.

The shortest master, the one in the center standing right in front of the bowl, stepped forward.

"After consideration by the selected council, we have decided to grant Princess Madison Alma the title of water master for her actions in the Battle of Wateria," she said, her voice echoing through the room. "Master Huith will read to the present witnesses the process we took to grant Madison Alma the title."

The man to her right stepped forward, holding a few sheets of paper. For a few minutes, he droned on about their deliberations, description of her great act, interviews with masters who had worked with her, and interview with Maddie, and all the other things that qualified her for the title of master. It went on for a while, Kiefer started to get fidgety next to me.

Master Huith finally finished, folding the paper and putting it into the pocket of his robe. The first woman stepped forward again, holding her hands out. Each of the other masters held a hand out, water flowing from the bowl and into the air above their hands. The first master took her water, which floated above her head.

"Rise, Madison Alma, and take the water from each of the masters," she said. Maddie stood up, and held her arms out. Starting from the edges, each master gave their water to Maddie, until she had a large sphere floating in front of her, above the bowl.

"Now pass the water back to each of the masters." Maddie did so. The woman turned around and took a white sash from a rack behind her. She walked around the bowl and placed it over Maddie.

"Congratulations, Master of Water, Madison Alma," the woman said, stepping back. Maddie turned around, smiling as we clapped for her. As our family rushed forward to congratulate her, I turned to Kiefer.

"Kiefer," I said, but he walked right by not, pretending not to hear me. I sighed and decided to ignore it for now. At least I was making an effort. For now, I just had to focus on Maddie.

.<>.

Twice a year, the water people come together in a celebration called the Moon Dance. The Moon Dance was a time for water people to come together and celebrate our heritage.

I'm not really sure how the Moon Dance started; there are a lot of different stories and legends. Some people say that since the moon is the master of the ocean, and the ocean is the greatest source of natural water, we should celebrate it. Some people say that water people started celebrating the moon because the fire people started celebrating the sun, some say it was the other way around.

Never mind how the Moon Dance came about, it was held on two nights of the year when the full moon was at its largest. We would dance traditional water people dances, masters would sometimes put on shows, and there was always really good food. It didn't matter how you were feeling, you were expected to go. I didn't want Dad to think something was wrong with me, even if there was, so I went.

I arrived alone, Miles having gone early, probably to flirt with the Waterian girls. Normally, Kiefer and I would watch Miles embarrass himself. I entered through a door near the band, the vaulted ceilings of the ballroom rising high above me. People done up in elaborate suits and dresses danced traditional dances in the center of the circular marble floor. Everyone wore different shades of blue, silver, and even dark greens. Opposite the band, chefs prepared huge pots of traditional water people foods. I walked towards the edge of the dancefloor, where people mingled in between the columns that held up the domed ceiling. In between each column, a small balcony looked out to the city, where smaller celebrations took place in other halls and citizen's homes.

"Prince Samson," a voice said, appearing behind me. I turned around, his frame taking up most of the area behind me. It was Master Sevett, Jamie and Kiefer's private trainer. He had a wide face and a sharp nose. He quickly bowed, revealing a large bald spot amongst his brown hair.

"Master Sevett," I said, bowing to him.

"I was actually hoping to run into you," he said, giving me a toothy grin. My skin crawled. It was a weird statement; as a prince, I would obviously be at the Moon Dance.

"What did you... want?" I asked, grabbing my hands behind my back.

"Nothing, it's just that I've heard so much about you from your siblings. I wanted to know more than that brief conversation we had," he said, folding his hands. "You didn't think I wouldn't notice that just one of the three of you wouldn't be taking lessons from me, did you?"

"Um... no?" I asked, unsure of how to respond.

"Now, why is that?" he asked, tilting his head down towards me. I knew I couldn't tell him that I wasn't because I thought he was dishonoring water magic by cheap tactics designed only to make him richer. That would be rude. I also couldn't tell him I was still focusing on researching how Kiefer could have possibly created that lightning bolt. Or, I could tell Sevett about my research to make him think I was weird and not worth bothering.

"I just..." I said, my eyes darting to try to catch someone else I knew to drag them into this conversation. I wondered if I should have brought Coffin to annoy people like this into leaving me alone.

"Do you doubt my abilities as a teacher?" he asked, cocking his head a bit.

Yes, absolutely.

"No, not at all," I said, shaking my head. "I'm just not... looking for a teacher right now."

"Is that so?" he asked. He wagged a finger at me, "That's funny because I could have sworn I saw you and your brother Miles training by one of the canals the other day. I would have given you some pointers on your form had you wanted me to."

"I... no... thanks," I said, my mind scrambling for a princely answer. What was I supposed to say that would keep me from accidentally being his student *and* be proper and respectful?

"Sorry?" he asked, tilting he head down to me again. He was *literally* talking down to me. The worst part was that I couldn't lash out at him for being condescending.

"Miles and I are just... practicing," I said, shrugging. "We're all set."

"Are you sure? As royalty you would be one of my priority students and receive the very *best* education in water magic one can find in Wateria," he said, leaning in and speaking out of the side of his mouth, almost conspiratorial. Suddenly, another lanky man dressed up in Moon Dance attire paused as he walked by. He turned around and threw an arm around Master Sevett.

"Oh Sevett you really need to stop filling the little prince's head with that crap," he said playfully, Sevett's turned head grimacing as the other man released him. His voice was thick with a Therbin accent, Therbin being the secondary language of the Water Kingdom. He was balding, with wispy red hair and thick glasses. The man bowed to me. I reluctantly bowed back to him.

"Master Ithcois," the man said. "At your service, your Highness."

"Nice to meet you, Master Ithcois," I said, nearly stumbling over the Therbin name. It had been a while since

I'd studied it. He leaned in, putting his hands together. He reeked of sleazy businessman.

"Your Highness, I can assure you that if you work with me, you'll become a master much quicker than with old Sevett here," he said, pushing a shoulder forward to edge out Master Sevett.

"I'm really not interested in becoming a master right now," I said, my heart beating a little faster. Having one master try to pressure me into learning from him was enough, I didn't need two.

"That's what they all say until they start their lessons with me," Ithcois said, holding a finger up. "I've trained some of the greatest generals in the Water Kingdom army."

That's a lie. They're all trained by official army masters. Not greedy scumbags looking to get rich quick.

"That's... great—

"Oh please," Sevett said, stepping back into the conversation. "Ithcois will just feed you a bunch of spells and send you packing."

You do the same exact thing because you're both fake masters.

"As I said, I'm not really—

"Oh please, you're a prince," Ithcois said. "Of course you want to be a master. Who doesn't?"

I do, more than anything, but I want to do it the right way! Which is as far away as I can get from you two!

"It's just not really a priority for me right now, I—

"Nonsense, learning water magic is the greatest thing a prince can do, and learning it should be done right," Sevett said, both of them walking towards me as I backed up.

"It's just—

"It would be done right if you did it with me," Ithcois said, pointing a thumb to his chest.

"Don't listen to him," Sevett chuckled, waving him off. Suddenly a woman came in on the other side of Ithcois, crossing her arms.

"Your Highness, I'm so sorry these two are bothering you," she said. She looked at me. "None of their students amount to anything. I, Master Aluse, am part of a school with other masters that can—

"Don't listen to Ms. Aluse, she only works with other masters because she's not strong enough to work alone," Sevett said. Aluse turned red with anger.

"Excuse me, the collaboration with other masters results in an education that offers multiple viewpoints on the values of water magic," Aluse fumed. "It's the only way our young mages can learn in the modern era."

"Your Highness don't listen to that nonsense, learning from multiple teachers will only confuse you. Train with me and you'll—

"Ignore him, he's—

"Oh please, both of you are—

"*Enough!*" a voice shouted from behind me. The three masters' eyes went wide as they froze sheepishly. Maddie stepped out from behind me, her arms crossed. Her fresh master's sash glowed in the warm light of the party. She looked down on them, her eyes brimming with cold rage.

"P-Princess Maddie I—

"Sevett, Ithcois, Aluse, my brother will not be learning from any of you, and that is his choice," she said, her voice cold and commanding. "As a prince, it is your duty to respect his decision. If I see any of you talking to my brother at any point in this evening, or hear you've tried to coerce him into learning from you at any other point in the future I will see to it that your titles are revoked. Am I clear?"

The three of them muttered 'yes,' their shoulders hunched. None of them could make eye contact with her.

"Good. Now please, enjoy the Moon Dance," she said, pointing to the door. The three masters scurried off, their robes and suits flapping behind them. Maddie sighed, pulling me out to one of the balconies.

"Maddie, thank you so much," I said, hugging her. "I'm sorry I talked to them."

"It's not your fault," she said, squeezing me. "I went through the same thing when I was younger. I had to learn to tell them to leave me alone. You *never* have to be patient with them."

"Right," I said. "But I don't want to be rude to them."

"Samz, you can be angry at other people," she said, touching my shoulder. "But as a prince... how could I say this... it can't be *hot* anger, understand?"

"Kind... of?"

"If you need to express your anger at someone, it has to be cold anger," she said.

"What... do you mean?" I asked.

"It's like..." Maddie thought for a moment. "You can feel angry but you have to be... not exactly *quiet*... but keep your voice low and firm."

"Right," I said.

"Don't yell or raise your voice. People will actually be less intimidated if you're loud," Maddie explained. "Also, if they're really condescending, never be afraid to remind them of your position."

"I don't really... like doing that," I said, grabbing my arm and looking off at the softly glowing city.

"I know," Maddie said. "I didn't like doing it at first either."

"It doesn't feel fair," I said.

"It's not always gonna be fair," Maddie explained. "You're a prince."

"I... know..." I said, feeling talked down to again. I had to get out of the conversation. "I'm gonna... go back into the ballroom. Thanks for talking to me."

"Samz, please if anyone bothers you again—

"I know," I said, ducking away from her and turning towards the ballroom. Maddie sighed as I re-entered the Moon Dance, the band briefly pausing in their playing.

There was nothing for me here. Everyone in my family was bothering me. All of the guests just wanted to manipulate me. I wasn't even hungry for any of the food. At that moment, as I stood there, the crowd briefly parted. Jamie and Kiefer stood in the gap, laughing with some of the masters. Kiefer briefly glanced at me, his mask of amusement briefly turning to contempt.

The moment passed, something invisible punching me in the gut. The crowd filled in. The band started playing again. I left alone.

.<>.

"Master!" Coffin yelped as I walked back into my room. He scrambled off my bed, tangling my sheets into a knot as he launched himself into my knees. I stumbled as he organized himself at my feet, staring up at me.

"What?" I asked, not really in the mood for anything other than sleep.

"Master there wases a guy who came in here and he was *creepish*," he said, weaving around my legs. "But he gaves me a whole fish if I promised not to bite him, but when he was handings it to me I kind of did bites him and dere maybe was a bit of blood, but it wasn'ts my fault because I mean, it wases a fish and how could I *nots* get excited? Rights?"

"... what?" I asked. I was pretty sure this was another one of his stories, but it was way too normal. There was actually a chance that this had truly happened.

"Yeah, and he got mad so I growled at him cause I coulds take him down, but he just... threw a paper at me, cause he was weak," Coffin said. "He grabbed one of the books. And then I peed on him and he walked out the door."

"Coffin, I thought we talked about peeing on people," I groaned, flopping down on my bed. When I landed I felt something poke into my back. Puzzled, I turned over and opened the tangled sheets of my bed. There, on my bed, was a small envelope with a tiny bite mark in the corner.

"Whoa..." I said, grabbing the envelope. "You weren't making that up."

"I never make *anythings* up," Coffin said resolutely, holding his chin high. I tore the envelope open, a folded letter inside.

"Why would someone..." I said, opening the letter. Dark ink scratched spindly words into the paper. *Dear Samson IV.*

"What does it say?" Coffin asked, cocking his head.

"It says," I said, holding the letter up.

"Dear Samson IV,

I apologize for borrowing the book. It's the only copy and I heard you had it after I visited your library. I'm trying to learn more about the Setters, but the libraries back home are pretty bare, if you can imagine. I've been trying to get in touch with you for weeks but Wateria hasn't been very welcoming to foreigners as of late. If you're reading this letter it means we missed each other. Still want to try to see you soon. I'll get the book back to you as soon as I'm done with it.

Jack

PS I'm doing this project because of some information I heard a few months ago, and I might as well let you know as well:

Mark was the last of all the Setters."

"Who's Mark?" Coffin asked. "Did he write the letter?"

"No, Mark was the latest Setter. He had extra powers so he could solve the world's problems," I said. "The person who wrote the letter was Jack."

"Is *he* a Setter?" Coffin asked. "Also what is a Setter?"

"Jack isn't a Setter," I said, shaking my head. "He was a friend I made a few years ago when dad was searching the Earth Territories for mom. I just... haven't heard from him in a long time."

In Dad's expeditions, we'd gone to the Earth Territories to search for Mom. Three of those times, he'd left us in a small town outside the capital, Ar Shaa. We'd visited a school for earth people, and I'd met Jack there. He was a few years older than me, but we'd become friends pretty quickly. We sent letters when we could, but Jack's family was poor and couldn't really afford it. It had been almost two years since I had sent him a letter. And now, out of nowhere, he had been in my room, taking a *book*.

"Was he the guy I peeds on?" Coffin asked. "And gave me a whole fish?"

"I guess he was," I said, rereading the letter. "It's just weird that no one else saw him. How would he have slipped past the guards? *Why* would he have slipped past the guards?"

"Well, he did takes the book, so he's a thief," Coffin said, jumping up onto the bed. I glanced over at my bedside table.

"Well, I hadn't really read much of the Setters book," I said, reaching for the stack. "But—

Prominent Setters and Their Achievements was still on the top of the stack.

"Why wouldn't he take that one? I thought he said he was researching the Setters," I wondered aloud, flipping through the stack. There was one missing. "He took *The Lives of the Balancers...* to learn about the Setters. What?"

"Who are the Balancers?" Coffin asked, cocking his head.

"Erin said they were a myth," I said. "And the book was kind of rare. But it's still... weird. Why would he give you a fish?"

"Cause he loves me," Coffin said, sniffing my pocket. "You don't have any food."

"Sorry," I said, my throat hollow. It was nice to hear from Jack. It had been years since we'd talked, even more since we'd seen each other. But something was off.

Everything was off. Something was wrong.

AN INJURY AND SOME MORE QUESTIONS

Dad, Uncle Drew and Aunt Sophie stood in front of me. I was pretty sure it was a dream. I couldn't feel or see my body, and everything looked like I was watching it from behind a pane of blue glass. They sat around a small table in front of a fire, in some small room in the palace.

"You just must not have seen the flower when you came into the garden," Uncle Drew said. "I thought you said that Mark was wrong about them."

"That's what I've thought for eleven years, especially after Marin stopped sending letters," Dad said. "I don't know, maybe I'm just on edge."

"We all are," Aunt Sophie said. "Is there anything we can do to help you? We need you to be level-minded if we're going to plan a retaliation against the fire people."

"Find the current Setter," Dad said, chuckling. "At least then we'd know for sure that Mark was wrong."

"Really Aidan, if you wanted me to, I could give my funds to some of the Setter search teams," Uncle Drew said, placing a hand on his shoulder. "I need you to be at peace."

"No, no, it's fine," Dad said, shaking Uncle Drew's hand off. "I was joking about finding the current Setter, mostly."

"I know," Sophie said. "I understand. This war would be a lot easier with a multi-elemental mage on our side."

Suddenly the image began to blur away into royal blue. Their voices distorted until there was silence. Then the blue sank into black.

.<>.

Later that day, I found myself slouched on the edge of a terrace overlooking one of the sparring courtyards, propping my chin up with my fist. Dark bags hung under my eyes, sleep trying to pull down anytime I started to feel comfortable. The brisk morning air was kind of keeping me awake.

After the strange dream I'd had of Dad, Aunt Sophie, and Uncle Drew talking about the current Setter (who apparently didn't exist, according to Jack), I hadn't been able to sleep.

It was a dream, it wasn't real. It took the weirdest events of the day, the rose appearing, Jack taking the book, and turned it into a weird dream. It had been strangely realistic though, and the memory of it didn't fade as the day went on like a normal dream. I decided it was just stress. The night before had been so weird, and my brain had just been too scrambled to show me a normal dream.

The loss of sleep however, meant the only way I could stay awake was watching Kiefer and Jamie practice their water magic. Well, practice their spells. That was pretty much all they were using.

"Brisera!" Kiefer shouted, punching his fist forward. A white jet of water exploded out of the pool behind him,

which Jamie easily sidestepped. As his jet blasted against the wall behind her, Jamie drew two jets out of her pool.

"*Roshur ulak!*" Jamie yelled, flinging the jets forward into a double helix. Kiefer cast a Seela just before the jets hit him, the water exploding outwards. He sent a spell back. They exchanged spells again. More water. Another few exchanges. They'd barely moved their positions. More exchanges. My eyelids started to droop. A sharp slap of water made me jump, only for a moment. More spells. Barely moving. The wind died down for a bit. The sun felt warm and soft on the back of my neck. More spells. More water. I closed my eyes. My neck dropped onto my forearms. More spells. More spells.

"*Onstrac... hela...*" Kiefer stammered, fear shaking his voice. Jamie yelped, my eyes flying open. Kiefer, his eyes wild and arms flailing, was up to his waist in a shaky column of water that was holding him high above the sparring court. My breath got stuck in my throat as the incomplete spell fell apart, the column blasting across the courtyard. Kiefer screamed as he fell several feet to the stone ground.

I could hear his leg crack from atop the terrace.

"Kiefer!" Jamie screamed, her robes sopping wet as she ran towards him. My heart started to pound, a few guards either rushing towards Kiefer or running off to alert one of the medics. I leaped up, and ran down a flight of stairs next to me that led down into the yard. I knelt down in the puddle around Kiefer. The bloody skin on his calf was sickeningly torn back. His ankle was at an incredibly wrong angle that I couldn't look at.

"Ow, ow, ow, ow, ow," Kiefer said, tears filling his eyes as he grimaced. He shivered, his breath coming out in short, quick bursts. He tilted his head forward, saw his ankle, and hissed a curse he'd probably learned from Ezra.

"Kiefer, it's okay, the medics are coming, it's going to be okay," I said, trying not to look at his injury. "Right Jamie? It's going to be all..."

Jamie wasn't talking. Her eyes were fixated on Kiefer's injury. She held her hands up, over Kiefer's calf. Kiefer arched his neck back in pain. Only I saw what happened next.

Her palms suddenly began to glow *purple*.

Wisps of violet energy extended from her fingers to caress the torn skin of Kiefer's calf. As it did, the skin began to *knit itself back together*. The cuts closed, the energy nudging the edges together and sealing them when they touched. A second later, the light went out of her hands.

For a brief moment, a sign on her hand glowed. It was a purple circle, with three lines radiating out of it. The glow died, leaving a dark purple pigmentation on her palm.

Time snapped back into its normal flow, the guards reaching Kiefer, Jamie and I pushed to the back of their crowd. I caught snippets of conversation, some of them about a possible concussion, others wondering where the blood came from if he had no cuts. I looked over to try to find Jamie, but she'd already left.

I walked away, finding a small alcove to myself. People were still rushing towards Kiefer. I opened my palm, looking at my hand.

The green pigmentation had grown again. One dot and two curves of a line had formed.

.<>.

"Erin, I need your help again," I said as I threw open the door to her room. Only Ezra was in there, grabbing a book from her bedside table. "What are... you doing here? I thought you had training with the army."

"I have a few days off. I'm just borrowing a book," he said, shrugging. *Seems like a lot of people are borrowing books without asking these days,* I thought for a second.

"Oh, I just had a research question for her," I said, turning away.

"What is it?" Ezra asked. "I could help you."

Ezra? Yeah, sure, I thought, turning back. "It's just about... something that happened during a training accident Kiefer got into. Nothing big."

"Ugh, let me guess," Ezra said. "He tried a spell, couldn't concentrate, and it blew up."

"Yeah, that's basically what happened. His trainer just keeps giving him a bunch of spells, regardless of whether he's actually ready or not," I said, shrugging.

"That's not how you're supposed to learn water magic. Or at least it's not how they're teaching us in the army," Ezra said, shrugging.

"How do they teach it for the army?" I asked. The way Miles and I were trying so far wasn't working out, it couldn't hurt to hear more ideas.

"Well, the basic principle, or whatever, I guess, is you look at what you're fighting, and do the opposite of it," Ezra said. "Which makes fighting fire people really easy."

I suddenly remembered what Dad had said about Ezra. Ever since the battle he'd been feeling more anger towards fire people. I realized I didn't really want to get caught up in it.

"Oh, that's... interesting," I said, turning to go find Erin. "Tha—

"Like, for example, fire is the element of destruction, so water magic should be about restoration," he said. That made something in me uneasy. People often talked about elements being of certain virtues or abstract ideas. Most people agreed on a few general ones for each element, but others were debated. I'd heard some people call fire the element of destruction, but hearing Ezra say it with such venom made it feel... wrong almost. I had to say something. I shouldn't have. But I did.

"Is it really... the element of destruction?" I said, still turned towards the door. I bit my cheek, which I regretted, at that moment, more than I regretted provoking Ezra.

"Of course it's the element of destruction," he said, his voice low and hoarse. "Did you not fight in the Capital Battle? Do you not see all of the homes that are still burned down? All the people with scars?"

"I'm sorry, I shouldn't have said that," I said, rushing out of the door. Ezra stomped after me, placing a hand on my shoulder. I jumped, ripping my shoulder out of his grip. He faced me, his dark hair obscuring one of his eyes.

"Samz, you're just a kid. You don't understand what the fire people are like. You don't understand what their element is like," he said, shaking his head. "I get that you haven't seen much, but you need to be careful saying things like that."

"I'm... sorry," I said. More because I was scared. There was real darkness in his eyes. A sort of desperation. I didn't want to be around him.

"Fire *is* the element of destruction," Ezra said, stepping back. "That's why we have to win this war. To stop them from burning everything to the ground."

He turned, Erin's book clasped in his hand, and sauntered down the hallway. He turned a corner, out of sight. I still hadn't breathed a sigh of relief. I still felt tense, scared, and jumpy. So many... weird things were happening. I didn't know what to do.

I started walking. As I walked, the thoughts started to flow, the fear melting and turning into a flood. Kiefer somehow had used lightning. I walked. We'd been attacked. I walked. I'd had a strangely realistic dream. Jack had stolen a book from me. I walked. Jamie had healed Kiefer's cuts. I couldn't learn water magic. I had a growing pigmentation on my palm, and Jamie had a complete one. Ezra was being scary. I couldn't sleep. I couldn't trust anyone. I walked. I stopped.

I was in the garden, where the rose had appeared. I stood in front of it, the rose still bright despite the cool wind. I sat down on the bench and placed my cold fingers on the stem of the rose. Why had it appeared? Had it appeared? Had we just not noticed it?

Maybe, I thought, taking in a deep breath, *maybe, for now, it's okay not to know. For now, it might be better to focus on things you do know and can control.* I took a few more breaths, my heart rate dropping to normal. *My life isn't in danger. Strange things are happening but they can't hurt me. I am safe.* I sighed, turning away from the dead rosebush and folding my hands.

Worrying about what was happening was bad for me. If there was no way to figure out the reason for all the strange events, then tearing myself up about it would get me nowhere. I felt my mind center itself, the fearful thoughts flowing away, leaving me with calm.

Something pulsed in the palm of my hand. I pulled my hand up, turning my palm over. My heart flipped.

The pigmentation was glowing, the curving line burning farther down my palm. It suddenly stopped, the light going out of my hand. I closed my palm, breathing a sigh of relief. If it was stopping, it was good.

Except, now the entire rosebush had bloomed.

I jumped back, trying not to scream. The entire bush had been revived. That I definitely would have noticed on my way in. Somehow, someway, the bush had pulled itself out of its winter hibernation and bloomed all of its roses. Maybe when I'd been gathering myself someone had come along and replanted it. *Really? Why would anyone ever replant*

135

a random rosebush while a prince is recovering from a breakdown?
part of my brain mumbled.

I stood up, just as someone else entered the garden.

Dad.

He saw the rosebush, and me standing in front of it.
His jaw dropped. *No.* He turned, and he ran into the palace.

IMPLICATIONS OF A ROSEBUSH

The second I'd made peace with myself Dad had ruined it. He didn't have to *run* away from me. He could have walked, and only made me worry about how I'd somehow offended him. But no, he'd run, now making me worry about what I'd done to make him be scared of me.

It was also the rosebush's fault. It did *not* have to bloom when I was next to it. It could have bloomed any time of the day, and Dad would have just thought it was weird. Now, Dad must have thought that I was some sort of evil rose witch, or something. I wasn't sure. But he'd ran. It must have been bad. Bad that a rosebush had bloomed next to me? Apparently.

I had to talk to someone. I had to get it all out. Everything that was happening. But, anyone I talked to would think I was crazy. No one would believe any of the things I was... actually there was.

I unfroze, looked at the rosebush one last time, and ran into the palace.

.<>.

"A story?" Coffin asked, cocking his head. "But you don'ts... tell stories."

"Coffin, you're always telling me crazy stories," I pleaded. He sat at the foot of my bed, Miles out for lunch with Anthony. Coffin harrumphed and stuck his nose into my bed.

"They're not *stories* it's my *for real life*," Coffin groaned, rolling his eyes.

"Okay, what if I told you... about my real life?" I asked. Coffin jumped up, his tongue hanging out of his mouth in excitement.

"Yes!" he yipped, tipping his head back. "Tells me! Tells me! Tells me!"

"Okay," I said, patting him before he bounced off of the bed. "It actually started the night I met you."

I told him the whole story, all starting when I first discovered the pigmentation, the first weird thing. Coffin listened the whole time in rapture, occasionally trying to guess what bizarre thing would happen next. After a while, the story extended by Coffin's own stories and a brief walk outside so he could go to the bathroom, I finally told him about the rosebush.

"Just when I thought I could deal with all the weird stuff, the rosebush—

"The one your dad wases scared of?" Coffin asked.

"Yeah, the one that had just one rose on it yesterday," I said. "Well, the green thing on my hand started to grow, and all the roses on the bush bloomed."

"Was it pretty?" Coffin asked. I shrugged.

"Not really the point, but I guess it was," I said. "Anyway, Dad saw it, and he ran away."

"I sees," Coffin said, narrowing his eyes. "It all makes sense."

"What... does?" I asked. Coffin usually spouted nonsense, but I was open to anything at that point.

"Your dad..." he said, leaning in. I leaned towards him. He held his snout up to my ear. "He hateses roses."

"... maybe," I said, pulling back. "Or maybe he just doesn't like what the rosebush means. Whatever it is the rosebush... means."

"Roseses mean stuff? I thought they were just flowers," Coffin said, nibbling on his paw.

"Not in this situation," I said, patting his head. "Flowers aren't supposed to bloom out of nowhere. Dad might think something's wrong with me because that happened."

"Did you make the roseses do it?" Coffin asked.

"No, I would know if I made a whole rosebush bloom on purpose," I said, chuckling. Coffin grunted.

"What if it was an accident? I morphs accidentally a lot," Coffin said, suddenly turning into light as I pet him. The light condensed and cooled into a turtle, Coffin biting the sheets in his new form.

"Accident? How could I accidentally bloom a rosebush?" I asked. Coffin unmorphed.

"I don't knows," he said, biting the sheets with his wolf teeth now. "You do water, right?"

"Last time I checked," I mumbled, lying back on my bed.

"Plants... have water," Coffin said, his teeth starting to rip the fabric. I sat up.

"Right," I said, my chest releasing pressure. "It could have been me, because plants have water in them, and I have water magic."

"Okay," Coffin said, turning his head to try to rip the blanket. "Solveds. You're welcome."

"Phew," I said, leaning back on the bed. The roses had just bloomed, because I was emotional, and it caused them to come to life because of water magic. Maybe it was a rare skill, and Dad had just run off to tell someone. Maybe a trainer who could teach me about it.

"So, when are you gonna washes the paint off your hand?" Coffin asked, walking across the bed to lick my hand. I snatched my hand away, opening my palm. The sign was still there. It hadn't grown since the rosebush incident. I still had no idea what it was, or why Jamie had one, or why it was growing, or what it meant or—

I closed my hand into a fist.

"I think I'll keep the paint for now," I said, putting my hand down. The symbol on my palm didn't mean anything. And even if it did, I didn't care. "I think it looks pretty."

.<>.

"Are you okay?" Miles asked suddenly. We were down on one of the rocky beaches on the outskirts of the Waterian harbor. We passed a large stream of water back and forth in a lazy loop, warming up for training. "You don't look too good."

"I'm fine, I just haven't been sleeping well," I said, passing the water back to Miles. A few days had passed since the rosebush incident, and I hadn't seen Dad much since he ran. He barely went to meals, Maddie telling us he and the other rulers were almost ready to launch their counterattack and he was busy. Jamie and Kiefer had interacted with me even less since Kiefer's accident. "Seeing Kiefer get hurt during his training was rough."

"Don't take this the wrong way, but I think, in a sense, it was kind of good for him to get hurt, especially doing a spell," Miles said, shifting his weight and arms forward to pass the water to me. I leaned back on my heels, catching the water as it flowed in front of me.

"Yeah," I said, pushing the water back to Miles. "I guess."

Miles caught the water, and let it splash to the rocks.

"... Miles?" I asked. "What's... going on?"

"Samz, you've been the most against Kiefer going to a private trainer," he said, crossing his arms. "He's finally gotten a reality check, and you have nothing to say about it. There is something wrong with you."

141

Something burned in the back of my head. I'd been trying so hard for the past few days to bury all of my stress, and he had no right to ask me about it. I couldn't tell him about the rosebush, or the dream. I could tell him about Ezra, but he wouldn't believe that that was the only thing stressing me out. *Actually, I could tell him about Jack's letter,* I realized.

"Well, something kind of weird happened the night of the Moon Dance," I said, grabbing my arm. I looked off to the placid ocean. "I came back, and Coffin said that Jack, my friend from the Earth Territories, came in, gave him a fish, took one of my books, and left. He also left a weird letter."

"What?" Miles asked. "Are you sure it wasn't just one of Coffin's stories?"

"Could one of Coffin stories make one of my books disappear and a letter from Jack appear?"

"Right," Miles said, pursing his lips. "So it was really Jack? Like earth person Jack?"

"Yeah, at least that's what the letter said," I said. Miles frowned.

"Jack... I always thought he was a little weird," Miles said.

"Miles."

"Sorry. But he is weird. Whatever. What did the letter say?"

"Well, he said that he was researching the Setters, and one of the books he needed had a copy... here," I explained. "He went to the library, heard I had it, snuck into my room, found the book, left the letter, and disappeared."

"Jack... researches stuff?" Miles asked. "I thought he had to take care of his family."

"I know, that's why it's weird that he came all the way to Wateria for... research," I said. "Another weird thing, none of the guards stopped him. If an earth person had come here, we would have known about it even if the guards had decided to let him through."

"Maybe he snuck past them?" Miles offered, thinking for a moment. "Yeah... he couldn't have. I don't think he's good enough at earth magic to burrow into the palace either."

"Yeah," I said, biting my lip. When we had met Jack, he'd lived in a relatively poor part of the Earth Territories. His dad died when he was young, leaving him to take care of his mom and several siblings. He just wasn't really the kind of person who had time to sneak into another country to do research. Or learn much earth magic either.

"What book did he take?" Miles asked.

"I almost forgot about that," I said, grabbing my head. "This was the weirdest part. I had a bunch of books, one of them being *Prominent Setters and Their Achievements*."

"And?"

"And he didn't take that one," I said. "He took the *Lives of the Balancers*, which isn't true and isn't about the Setters."

"Why does he even care about the Setters?" Miles asked.

"Oh, because according to him, he recently learned that Mark was the last one," I said, shrugging at the ridiculousness of it all. I had to admit, telling someone about it did help. Even if it was just a small part of everything I was worrying about.

"That's just... all around weird," Miles said, rubbing his temples. "Why does Jack care so much about the Setters that he would leave the family he's taking care of to sneak into a heavily guarded city to find *one* book that isn't even about what he's researching?"

"I don't know, and that's what's been stressing me out," I said. "There's only one reason he'd do that."

"What would that be? He's going insane?" Miles asked. I shook my head.

"There must have been something really important in that book he stole," I said. "If he was willing to do all of that, it must have been important, right?"

"I thought you said the book wasn't true," Miles said.

"Well, Erin said that it's based on a legend, but it's written as if it's fact, by an author that claims she's from a city that is also a legend," I said. "So... it can't be true."

"Well legends have to come from somewhere, right? Maybe he's just using the legend to get clues on the real thing," Miles said. "But then again, clues based on a legend aren't really worth all that he did to get it."

"I know!" I said, exhaling a sigh of relief. Miles grimaced.

"Well now you've made *me* stressed about it," he said, crossing his arms. "But I get it, telling other people about what you're dealing with helps get rid of stress and stuff."

"Thank you," I said. "But... please don't tell Dad."

"Oh, of course not," Miles said.

"Thanks," I said, pushing my hands out. I pulled another stream of seawater out of the ocean. "Let's do some more training."

.<>.

The announcement came a few weeks later, at dinner. They didn't want to just pop in, unannounced, thinking that descending from the sky into a recovering city with no warning would probably cause panic. They wanted to meet with Dad, Sophie, and Drew, although we weren't told for what. It was rare that they ever met with world leaders, so by the time they arrived four days later, there was a certain feeling of occasion in the air.

Maddie, yelling out instructions, organized us to stand behind some of the older lords and nobles in the central courtyard. Dad and his siblings stood detached from the group, in the middle of the open space of the courtyard, ready to accept them. One of the lords in front of me was bragging about a time he had apparently met one of them, which I doubted. They tended to keep to themselves, and meeting one of them in person was rare. Meeting their elites was even rarer.

Suddenly, the sound of a trumpets blasted through the mid-morning air. We all craned our necks up, seeing a small flurry of dark dots detach themselves from the clouds. The strange vehicles spiraled down, their pale wooden frames and stretched linen wings coming into focus. The three airships slowed a few hundred feet above us, floating into a triangular formation. We could hear the roar of the winds keeping them in place.

Suddenly, hatches opened on the bottoms of the airships along the bottoms of their hulls. Two robed men came out of each of the ships, dropping into the air. They began to spin and windmill their arms, the air under their command. They slowly turned down towards the courtyard, the six of them descending in a synchronized circle. The water people cheered, for most of us it being our first time seeing anything like this. The men slowed down, their winds buffeting against our crowd. They softly touched down in front of Dad, Sophie and Drew, the water people clapping.

The air people had arrived.

"Master Kiahta," Uncle Drew said, bowing to the one at the head of the circle. "It is an honor to be graced with the presence of the air people."

"It is an honor to be welcomed into the home of the water people," Kiahta said, bowing back to him. I could only see him from behind and from far away. All I could really see was a pale green robe and a few wispy white hairs around his head. The other men looked to be of similar age, all wearing different pale colored robes. I'd only met an air person once before, while searching for Mom near their territory (not that they would have really noticed, most of their villages were in the sky or on the tallest mountains). I really had no idea what to make of them, other than stereotypes I'd grown up with. People mostly just thought of air people as being stuck-up, as they made it a point to never take a side in a conflict. That usually meant they did nothing, giving the impression they thought they were better than us.

That's what made it so weird for them to be here, in the capital of the Water Kingdom. Even visiting us would be seen as favoring us and anger the fire people.

"Come, let us take you into the palace so we can discuss matters," Dad said, leading the air people towards an open door on the other side of the courtyard from us. They broke their circle and followed Dad in a perfect line. The crowd began to break up, the water people talking about seeing six air people at the same time. I started to walk back into the palace as we dispersed, Miles walking after me. I glanced back as Kiefer limped away with his thickly wrapped leg, Jamie helping him. Jamie glanced at me for a moment, gave me a glare, and turned back to Kiefer.

"Samz," Miles said. "Do you want to train or go try if we can see the air people?"

"I..." I glanced back at Kiefer and Jamie. "... neither."

"Oh... okay," Miles said, frowning. "Are you alright or—

"I'm fine," I said, turning and walking back into the palace.

.<>.

I marched across one of the bridges of the palace, gardens and courtyards spreading out below me. The three airships still circled ahead, the spiral of wind keeping them aloft periodically blowing through the spires of the palace. I pulled my coat closer around me as one of the gusts blew through. I paused in the middle of the bridge, terraces falling away into the city. I could even see the garden where the rosebush had bloomed. It was a just a red speck in the middle of the brown garden.

It was kind of dumb that I'd let that stupid rosebush completely destabilize me. It was a random occurrence. I didn't know why it happened, but did it really matter? It was a rosebush. What was the worst it could do? Make Dad think I was some anomaly? Prick someone's finger with a thorn? It wasn't going to kill me, it wasn't going to hurt me. It was just a rosebush. I didn't know if it was some subset of water magic, but I'd already learned that I was terrible at research. And what was there to research when I'd already done it? It was just a rosebush. I looked down at the garden.

Just a rosebush.

My eyes bulged.

Dad and the air people were now walking through the garden, surrounding the rosebush. I couldn't hear what they were saying, or see what they were doing, but they were all fixated on the rosebush. They looked concerned, Dad explaining something while motioning to the rosebush. My rosebush.

That was when I realized.

The air people hadn't just come by to talk to Dad. Dad had called them here. Because of the rosebush. The rosebush blooming hadn't been some weird water magic thing. It had been something big, exactly as big as I'd feared based on Dad's reaction. What else could merit a visit from *the air people?*

My heart started to pound. I couldn't breathe. I'd done something terribly wrong.

The air people were here, because of *me.*

THE CITY IN THE SKY

"Samson," I heard my Dad say. The overcast, morning light filtered in between the gaps of my blanket. I'd been silent during dinner the night before, not even talking to the air people. I was trying to skip breakfast, where Dad should have been when he found me.

"What?" I asked, pulling the blanket away from my head. The top half of Dad's face was in shadow, where he stood in the doorway. He was frowning, the dark morning light carving deep crevasses in his skin.

"Why aren't you down at breakfast, with everyone else?" he asked, on hand on the doorway. I turned over to face Miles' bed.

"I'm not hungry, and I'm tired," I mumbled. "Can I just have some time to sleep?"

"Are you feeling alright?" Dad asked. I groaned softly.

"If you actually noticed me you wouldn't have to ask," I whispered into my pillow.

"What?" Dad asked, not having heard what I'd said. I pulled the blanket over my head. He was the last person I wanted to talk to. If he actually had time for me, maybe I wouldn't have been so stressed. If he had actually told me what was happening, I would have been okay. But he'd seen what had happened to the rosebush and never explained his reaction to me. He let Jamie and Kiefer have a private trainer and let them hate me.

"Nothing," I mumbled. Dad took in a deep, shaky breath.

"Samson, I know that the past few days have been a bit confusing," he said. "But I promise—

"The past few *days*?" I hissed, pulling the blanket tighter around me. "I've felt like this for *weeks*."

"Samson..." Dad said. "I had no idea, I—

"Of course you didn't," I said, feeling the barb stab Dad. "You never do. There's always something else that's more important than me."

"I—

"For a while it was Mom, and now it's the war and all you ever do is just send Maddie to go deal with your family problems," I said. Dad huffed.

"It's not like I have a choice," he said, his voice wavering. "I didn't decide to lose your mother or to fight an endless war."

"I know," I said, sighing. "But still. It took you weeks to realize how... not okay I am. You've actually made it worse."

"I've—

"You never tell me anything, or explain anything," I said, pulling the blanket away. Dad stared back, his mouth slightly agape. His mouth suddenly closed, his face turning to stone.

"Well, if you're not going to go to breakfast, then I'll just tell you what I was going to announce there," Dad said, crossing his arms. "At noon, we're leaving with the air people. They've already begun preparations for the spell that will take us there. If you aren't on the airship by noon it will be hours before we would be able to find you again. Please pack your things and be ready to go by then."

"What?" I hissed, sitting up. "Why are we going with the air people?"

"I'll..." Dad grimaced. "I'll explain once we get there. Promise me you'll be there at noon. If we all aren't ready by then we won't be able to go with them at all."

"Fine," I said, swinging my legs onto the floor. Dad huffed and breezed out of the room.

I didn't want to go with the air people. I didn't want to listen to Dad. I didn't want to deal with any of the weird things that were happening to me. I just wanted to get away from it all.

And I could.

I stood up, Coffin yawning awake next to me. I patted his head as I walked over to put my shoes on.

"Coffin?" I asked, grabbing a medium-sized, black backpack from my closet. "Do you wanna go on a little adventure?"

"Sure..." he said sleepily, rolling onto his feet. "Where are we goings?"

"I'm not sure," I said, grabbing an extra robe and other clothes to put in the bag. I grabbed the remaining books from Erin's pile I hadn't read. "That's the exciting part."

"Okay," he said gnawing on the edge of my bed. "When are we going?"

"Right now," I said, pulling the cords of the backpack around my shoulders. I looked in a small mirror at the back of the closet, noticing the dark bags under my eyes. I pushed my hair off of my forehead.

"Let's go."

.<>.

Getting past the guards was easy. Miles and I often left with backpacks for training, so it wasn't that weird that I was leaving with one. They simply saluted me as I walked out one of the side gates. A few citizens noticed me as I walked to the outskirts of the city, one or two of them saying a few words of admiration to me. I smiled at them, the feeling of running away making me happier than I'd been in a long time. I made my way to one of the ridges, and followed one of its dusty roads right out into the countryside behind the mountains. Coffin followed me the whole time, bumping into my knees or tasting the air with his snout.

We followed the road around the mountain until we could see the green and yellow hills and empty pastures rolling off to the clouded horizon. Roads snaked in between the hills, several of them converging into small towns. A

153

river swept through several of them, slicing back and forth until it cut between the two mountains and flowed into the capital.

"Wowee," Coffin breathed, a cold breeze skittering across the valley. "Where are we gonna go next?"

"Hm," I thought looking out across the valley. It had been about an hour since I'd left, two hours until we were supposed to leave on the airships. Dad had probably noticed I was gone, and if he hadn't probably was going to soon. We would do best to stay away from the towns. To my right, a few streets snaked off into a forest, its trees just starting to show the first buds of spring.

"Let's go towards that forest," I said. I'd hiked there a couple times when we'd visited Uncle Drew. It was pretty secluded and rarely visited by civilians. Coffin and I could explore there long enough for the airships to leave.

"Sounds fun!" Coffin barked, throwing his head to the sky. He started to scamper down the road, dust kicking up behind him. I laughed, running after him. We passed by farms, cows grazing on the grass that was just waking up from winter. Coffin and I tried to walk along the low stone walls separating the fields from the road. He told me a 'true story' about the time he and his brother fought a 'narwhal octopus' in the middle of the Great Desert, and another story where he heroically saved a human baby in the middle of the Cold Wilds north of the Fire Empire. I told him real stories about some of the trips Dad had taken us on in the search for mom. I told him about the countless earth people villages we'd been to, including the one where I'd met Jack. I told him about our brief trip to the Coral Colonies, or the time we accidentally crossed the border into the sand

154

people's territory. I wasn't sure how long it had been when we reached the forest, but we were suddenly in the middle of it.

The path dissolved into nothing, dark trees scraping the sky with their skeletal fingers. A few of them were tipped with red buds, others still dormant. A few dead, brown bushes huddled close to the yellow grass, the scattered pine trees being the only green in the whole forest. Dark trunks stretched off as far as I could see, the two peaks of the Waterian mountains barely poking above the barren canopy.

"Let's take a break," I said, sitting down against a hollow maple tree. Most of its branches had broken off in the last winter, laying scattered around its base. It smelled dark and musty, mold not having completely destroyed it yet. The bark was dry and flaky as I leaned back against it, pulling an apple out of my bag.

"This is fun," Coffin said, curling up at my feet. "I like this adventure. We shoulds do this more often."

"We should," I said, taking a bite of the old, chalky apple. Another breeze shook the branches of the forest, bringing the earthy scents of melting ground. I looked up to the sky, and noticed something was churning the flat overcast above the capital. I squinted, and saw as a hole silently blew the clouds apart, three tiny shapes whisked through it and into the blue sky on the other side.

"The airships left," I said, feeling something lift off of my shoulders. I didn't have to go with Dad and the others. I leaned back against the tree in relief. I'd escaped.

"The what?" Coffin asked, poking his head up from where he'd been eating the grass. Some of it was still stuck to his snout.

"Airships were supposed to take us away, but they didn't," I said, smiling softly. "We made it out. We're gonna be okay."

"What weres the airships gonna do to us?" Coffin asked, cocking his head.

"Take us to somewhere I don't want to go, just because Dad said so," I explained. "They didn't care if we didn't want to go with them or not. They weren't even going to tell us why they were taking us. They were just going to... do it."

"That's... bads," Coffin said, laying his snout against the ground. The hole in the overcast began to close, high wisps of clouds closing over the blue.

"So, we're just gonna stay here for a little while," I said, leaning into the tree. "They'll realize because we weren't on the airship, we didn't want to go. They'll understand how serious we are."

"I... kind of gets it," Coffin said. I sighed, smiling softly and closing my eyes. I was safe and free. Nothing could hurt me.

"That's fine," I said. "We're here, and we're safe."

The tree suddenly stiffened. The grass around my legs suddenly began to grow. The palm of my hand began to pulse again.

"Master..." Coffin said, as I opened my eyes. This time, I watched in wonder as the yellow grass around me bloomed to green. I opened my palm, the symbol burning bright, completed. Standing up and facing the tree, the soft and dead bark suddenly hardened back into life, vitality flowing back into it in an expanding wave. The life reached the branches, extending them where they had been broken and opening into tufts of leaves where they were complete. In my hand, the half-eaten apple bulged, the red skin closing over the part I had bitten off until it was whole again. Around my feet, the grass continued to grow outwards, flowers starting poke up from the ground.

The symbol on my hand had two dots, one near the bottom of my middle finger and one at the end of my palm. In between them was a curved line. The glow went out of it, the maple tree now fully restored and Coffin and I surrounded by a patch of revived grass and flowers.

"What just happends?" Coffin asked, sniffing the nearest flower. "What... water can do that?"

"I... I'm not sure," I said, looking at the symbol. It was green, not blue. Then again, sometimes along the coast water could be green. Maybe it was a mark people with my ability had. Water people who could revive plants. It was weird, but it wasn't bad. It wouldn't be that helpful in battle, but that didn't really matter. It was an unusual ability, but it was mine, apparently.

"You're not sure?" Coffin asked, cocking his head. I shrugged.

"Well, evidently it can," I said, grabbing my backpack. "C'mon, let's keep going."

"Can we bring back more trees?" Coffin asked, following me as I walked out of the circle of grass. I paused, the grass slowly starting to grow back the longer I left my feet there.

"I'm not really sure how to do it on command," I said, patting his head. I started to walk again, leaving my patch of revived grass behind. "Maybe we can try a little bit."

"Yay!" Coffin said. "I don'ts like it in the winter when all the trees die and stuff so I really likeds it when you brought the tree back."

"Thanks," I said, chuckling. I took the repaired apple, which was now heavier and a deep red. I took a bite out of it, now crisp and fresh instead of old and chalky. "I guess my power even makes apples taste better."

"Eugh, appleses are *always gross*," Coffin said, sticking out his tongue. I chuckled, descending back into the forest.

The trees became thicker, growing closer together. Coffin and I now had to work our way around some of the trunks, my bag occasionally getting caught on branches and brambles. The sun started to break through, the winds from the airships having whipped the flat overcast into growing lumps of cloud. After a while, we came to a small clearing were a road cut through the forest.

"We should take another break," I said, sighing as we emerged from the brambles. Coffin slumped down onto the road. I turned my back on the other side of the road, trying to catch a glimpse of the Waterian mountains. For just one second.

158

The other side of the forest suddenly exploded with fire. Coffin and I yelped, turning as the trunks and dry branches were instantly consumed with flames. Seven fire people came through the fire, keeping it from touching their skin by outstretching their palms. Coffin growled as we shrunk back against our side of the road. I held one hand out and one back, in one of the defensive positions Miles and I had studied. Not that I'd brought any water. There were a few tiny puddles along the edge of the road, but not nearly enough to fight off seven fire people. They all wore the same armor as the one who had attacked us in the Battle of Wateria. They emerged from the fire and out onto the road, one of them stepping in front of the rest and flipping up his visor. He had a strong, square jaw and a robust mustache. His thick eyebrows were narrowed, looking at my forward palm. It was the one with the symbol on it.

"It's an honor to meet you, Balancer," the man said, who I presumed to be the leader. He stepped forward, grinning widely as his arms were clasped behind his back. The other fire people each ignited a flame in each of their palms. "I'll be honest, when Emperor Conner told us our assignment, I thought it was insane. He told us what you are. You're supposed to be a myth, but here you are, proudly showing me that symbol on your hand."

"Wh-what?" I asked, trying to sound tough but fear getting in the way. *Seven* fire people. I could barely fight off *one* with an adequate source of water. I certainly wasn't powerful enough to produce my own water.

"That symbol, on your hand," the leader said. "I know what you are."

"That symbol just means that, um, I'm a water person who can sometimes revive plants," I said, stepping back against the trees, their branches touching my back. The leader chuckled.

"Don't play dumb with us, we know you can do a lot more than just *revive* plants," he said. He frowned for a moment. "Or... has no one *told* you?"

"You have to leave," I said, trying to use the cold anger Maddie had tried to teach me. It wasn't working. "You need to get out of here, now."

"Or what?" the man scoffed. "Look, I have direct orders from Emperor Conner to bring you back to the Empire. He needs you, and he needs you alive. So, I suggest that you comply with us and keep this civil."

"If you kidnap a prince, you'll have the whole Water Kingdom after you," I warned. I raised my hand, lifting some of the water from the puddle next to me into the air.

"Oh no. Not the whole Water Kingdom!" the leader said, giving me a mocking pout as he rolled his eyes. I thrust my hand forward, the tiny stream immediately burned away by the leader.

"My, my," he said. "Your friend told us you were bad at magic, but it's really a lot more pathetic in person."

"Friend?" A hollow feeling opened up in my chest. What friend? What was he talking about?

"Oops, did I say something?" the leader asked, chuckling. He held a hand out, red fire sprouting from his fingertips.

"What... friend?" I asked, shaking. The leader chuckled.

"I'm sure you'd love to know, but he's requested we keep his identity a secret," he said, grinning down at me. "Now, let's be on our way,"

A gust of wind launched him several feet into the air.

The other six were scooped off of their feet by another gust and thrown back into the smoldering forest behind. I looked up, and saw a tiny airship suspended in the sky. A small figure was tumbling outside the craft, blowing the leader in a circle midair. The figure was wearing a practical tunic as he danced through the air, carrying a spiraling rope behind him. The airship was also rapidly descending, the fins on its sides flapping wildly.

They were air people! Air people had come to rescue me!

The air person, who looked to be an older boy, threw his hands out, wind throwing the leader of the troop into the forest below. The boy sharpened into a dive, wind billowing around him as he careened towards the earth. He turned up at the last second, the winds of his descent blasting Coffin and I off of our feet. As we stumbled, the boy ran over to us, swirling his hands through the air. A warm breeze balanced both of us.

"Who... are you?" I asked, my heart pounding so hard I thought it was going to rip itself out of my chest. The boy had dark skin and a thick mop of black hair. He had sharp, hawkish features and thin, willowy limbs. He held out a hand.

"A friend of your father's," he said. "We need to get you out of here."

"What?" I hissed. Another person trying to take me somewhere without telling me why. The boy sighed.

"Would you rather I leave you with the fire people?" he asked, glancing around as the fire people across the road began to stand up and notice us. "We need to go!"

"Fine!" I said, taking his hand. Coffin morphed into a mouse and jumped into my pocket. The boy bent his knees and jumped.

Unlike a normal human, he jumped several feet in the air, a geyser of wind pushing us upward. The rope guided us up to the airship which was slowing from its descent. Below us, the fire people began to regroup, their palms igniting.

"Auntie!" the boy yelled up to the still far away hatch. "A little help!?"

A woman with wild, windswept hair poked her face into the hatch, a broom tightly clutched in her hands. Her eyes narrowed at the fire people.

"Alright!" she croaked, sticking her broom out of the hatch. "I'll give those smoky cowards a piece of my mind."

Just as the fire people launched a volley of fireballs, the woman deftly swept her broom through the air. I felt the shockwave of force travel right by our heads, her gust of wind blowing aside the fireballs and throwing the fire people to the ground. The boy shot another gust of wind towards the ground, propelling us into the tiny airship. We landed just inside the inner belly, the boy's aunt still using her broom to blast gusts of wind down to the fire people.

"My dear! We need to pull up!" a man at the front of the airship said. In front of him stood an array of wheels and levers, ropes connecting them to various parts of the ship.

"Obviously! Do you think I'm *blind* Marty? Do you?" the woman yelled, beginning to churn the air with her broom. Below, I watched as the dust rose in a vortex pushing us up into the air. The air ship began veering towards the clouds, which I could see through the slice of sky behind the wheels and levers.

"Simon! Prepare the spell!" the man said, turning his head for a moment. He wore thick glasses, his hair red and wild. He looked like a frightened, exotic bird. The boy walked around the wheels and held his hands out to the sky.

"*Iaru aya!*" the boy shouted. Great, hurricane-force winds gripped the ship, shaking it as a hole opened up in the clouds above. I blinked, and the winds thrust us through the hole and into the endless blue of the sky. I screamed as the pressure tore through my ears, Coffin unmorphing in pain at my feet. A few moments later, the pain subsided, leaving me feeling sick on the floor of the air ship. We were now hurtling over the ocean, which was just a blue blur dotted by clouds. I had no idea how fast we were going, or who these people even were.

"Who are you?" I asked. "Simon said you were a friend of my father's."

"We are," the woman said. "And he's not going to be very happy with you when we get to Aetheopolis."

"Aetheopolis?" I asked.

"You know," Simon said. "The capital of the air people. The city in the sky."

OUR DESTINY

"So... how do you know my dad?" I finally asked after a few awkward minutes. "And who are you?"

"I met your father when we were teenagers," the man said, while frantically throwing levers and pulling ropes. "I'm Professor Martin Kilting, that's my lovely wife Matilda, and that young man over there is our nephew, Simon."

"Lovely wife. Ha," Mrs. Kilting snorted, earning her a glare from Martin. If Martin looked like a frantic parrot, Mrs. Kilting was a grumpy owl.

"How did you meet him?" I asked. It's not like normal water people became friends with air people every day. And if the air person somehow stayed long enough to become friends with the water person, the water person would usually talk about it. Dad had never mentioned having an air person friend.

"Well, I was testing out a new idea for a smaller, lighter airship and kind of... crash-landed near a lake where your dad had gone off to for solo training," the professor said. "We spent the week he was supposed to be practicing water magic fixing my airship. I've popped in every now and then, mostly to show him my latest innovations."

"Not all of them," Mrs. Kilting said, wagging a finger. She leaned over, away from the professor. "If it weren't for me, he'd be going to see your dad every time he changed a fin on one of his godforsaken cloud-skiers."

165

"Matilda, it's one of my godforsaken cloud-skiers that saved this boy's life," Martin said, holding up a triumphant finger.

"Yeah, yeah, yeah we get it, you've built the fastest airship in the history of the Inner World," she said, crossing her arms.

"And because it's the fastest, we were charged with rescuing the prince," Martin shot back. He turned to me. "We'll be in Aetheopolis in just under an hour."

I turned quietly towards the open sky. Dad would be there, and he wouldn't be happy with me. I didn't know how I felt about it either. I still felt like I had done the right thing for myself by running away. It wasn't like I was planning to be attacked by fire people and rescued by air people! But Dad wouldn't care. All he cared about was leaving me in the dark about what was going on and leaving it to Maddie to fix everything.

I never wanted to be the center of attention. I never wanted to cause trouble. And yet, Dad's actions made me do things that forced the attention on me. I crossed my arms, and pulled my knees in. Coffin rested his chin on my foot.

Why does this airship have to be the fastest in the Inner World? I internally groaned.

.<>.

The city in the sky stood before us.

An hour after being rescued, we'd arrived at the giant floating city. It wasn't balanced on top of a tall mountain, or held up by airships, it was simply a huge chunk of land with a city grown through it, hung in the sky by the power of air magic. Limestone houses sloped from the reefs of wooden airship docks around the edge to an elaborate palace in the raised center of the city. Patches of trees and flowers dotted the city, vines hung down from the underbelly like chains. I could see the minuscule forms of air people floating about the city, either by their own winds or small sky craft.

"There it is, Aetheopolis," Martin said. "Get ready for some stares. It's rare we get visitors."

The cloud skier began to dip, and a gust of wind suddenly shook the craft.

"Don't worry," Martin said, pulling a lever that snapped two of the lateral fins taut. I suddenly felt my lungs relax, my breaths becoming deeper and fuller. "We just entered the pocket of habitable air around the city. It's there just in case the city floats too high."

"It's pretty useless, in my opinion," Mrs. Kilting said. "We're air people, we can handle a little pressure change every once in a while."

"And he's a water person, so the only pressure changes he'd be able to withstand would be underwater," Martin said, the craft descending further. The air was beginning to turn warmer and more humid. Outside the front of the cloud skier, I could see the peaks of the pale buildings rise. I could make out the faint forms of the willowy, ethereal air people. Simon opened the hatch I'd been brought through and another circular one behind it. I peeked down, seeing a dock built on top of a large house, one thick wooden pole lined up with the circular hole. Simon leaned his front half out of the hatch and began to meticulously whirl his hands through the air. The cloud skier bobbed from side to side, trying to line up in the pole. He shouted a few instructions to Martin as the craft slowed. A few seconds later the pole began to poke through the hole, Simon and Martin masterfully guiding it down to the dock.

Martin opened a door on the side of the cloud skier, leading us out onto the dock. The house below us jauntily made its way to the street, several haphazardly added rooms and porches sticking out from an odd number of levels. Wooden stairs led around the room below the dock and into the house. At this level, the air felt normal, slightly warmer than in Wateria.

"Welcome to castle Kilting," Martin said, spreading his arms out as he led us down the staircase. Mrs. Kilting rolled her eyes.

"Marty darling, if you call our house that one more time I will blast you off the edge of the city with my broom," she said, sighing. Martin scoffed as he opened the door, which led to a tight spiral staircase. Doors stood at various levels. We started descending, Coffin looking around as if he were trying to figure out the best place to pee. We reached the bottom, Martin opening a door to a living room at the base of the house.

The room was dimly lit. In the center was a large, low table, made of nearly white wood, was littered with forms, and weird half-finished metal contraptions. They had an empty fireplace behind the table and two couches. A worn rug sat in between the couches, opposite to a door that led out to the street.

I suddenly noticed Dad, sitting on the couch we had emerged behind. He turned when he heard us open the door.

"Aidan, look who we found!" Martin said cheerily, stepping to the side and throwing his hands out as if to present me. Dad stood up, his face devoid of expression. He walked over, looking down on me.

"Dad, I—

"Go upstairs, and find a room," he said, his voice low. I hung my head, and turned away. Simon led me back to the staircase, Coffin following us. Mr. and Mrs. Kitling awkwardly watched me leave. I grabbed the door and shut it behind me. Somehow Dad not yelling at me had been worse.

Simon stopped about three-quarters of the way up, opening the first of three doors set into the curve of the staircase. Inside was a small, thin room with a dresser on one side and a rickety bed on the other. A square window was set into the wall opposite me, a shriveled, dead potted plant on the windowsill.

"Thanks," I said, stepping into the room.

"If you need anything, just ask," Simon said, sheepishly closing the door behind me. I looked at the withered plant on the windowsill.

Strangely, I didn't feel worried. I didn't feel secure either. There were so many things going on, and so many things I was supposed to be worried about, that I just... wasn't worried about any of them.

I just felt numb.

.<>.

A few minutes later, after I'd unpacked the two robes in my bag, someone knocked at my door. I jumped, my heart skipping for a second. Was it Dad? Was he going to yell at me now?

"Come in," I said, glancing over my shoulder at the door. Kiefer limped in, Jamie helping him. I rolled my eyes.

"I don't want to talk to either of you right now," I said, turning my back to them. Coffin jumped up from where he sat at on my bed and growled.

"Samz please, we're not here to talk to you about running away," Jamie said. "We want to... make amends."

"Yeah? Well I don't," I said, pushing my empty bag aside. I turned to them, my arms crossed. "You two have made it very clear that you don't want to be associated with me."

"Look, ever since I hurt my leg, I've been thinking about what you told me," Kiefer said, looking down. "You were right about getting a private trainer. I'm sorry it took an injury like this to figure that out."

I tightened my mouth. Jamie sighed.

"You were right," she said. "All we know are spells. You know actual magic."

I turned toward the wall, tightening my grip on my arms.

"We just wanted a shortcut, and we paid for it," Kiefer admitted. I rolled my eyes.

"Great. You had a change of heart," I snapped. Jamie and Kiefer's eyes bulged.

"That's it? You don't—

"I don't care if you think I'm right," I said, throwing my hand out. "I don't care that you regret getting a private trainer, or that you think I'm a better water mage than you."

"Samz, we *apologized*," Kiefer said.

"Not for what I'm mad about," I said, shaking my head. "I'm not mad about you two finding a trainer, I'm mad about how you acted like I didn't exist."

"We were mad at you for judging us about getting a private trainer," Jamie said. "You can't judge us like that and expect us not to care."

"You can't ignore me for weeks just because you don't like my opinion," I shot back.

"We didn't ignore you," Kiefer said.

"You did, and you never made an effort to fix things," I said.

"We didn't try to fix things, because the only way you would be satisfied is if we'd stopped working with Master Sevett," Jamie said.

"I thought you just said that you now know that was wrong," I pointed out. Jamie threw her hands up and turned to the door.

"Whatever," she said. "It's impossible trying to reason with you."

"Well, you *are* being pretty stubborn," Kiefer said, shrugging. Jamie stormed out of the room.

"Have fun getting up the stairs on your own," she muttered. Kiefer turned to me, grinning about what he'd said to Jamie. I glared at him.

"You heard her," I said, pointing to the door. "Go have fun."

"Ugh, both of you are the worst," he said, limping out the door. I walked forward and slammed it. I knelt down on the floor, resting my head against the wood.

"Master?" Coffin chirped, jumping off the bed. "Why are you sads?"

"A lot of reasons," I said, patting his head as he walked up to me.

"Should we run away agains?" Coffin asked. "That maded you happy."

"I know," I said. "But we can't."

"So... what now?"

"I don't know."

.<>.

Several hours later, Dad opened the door to my room. I glanced up from my bed, his frame taking up most of the small doorway.

"Samson," he said. I pulled my knees in and looked away. "I know you're angry with me. But I need you to put that aside just for a short while."

"Why?" I asked angrily.

"I know you're confused, and maybe scared because of some of the things that have been happening lately," he said. "But I promise, tonight we all are going to get the answers to many of our questions. We're going to go to the air priest palace in a few minutes."

"I don't want to go," I muttered. Dad stiffened.

"I'm sorry, but the invitation is not a choice," he said. "I apologize for being firm, but our attendance at the palace is mandatory."

"Why?" I asked, turning to him. "If you're so sorry about being vague, why not clear this one thing up for me?"

"I..." Dad grimaced. "I can't."

My chest felt heavy as I broke eye contact.

"Of course," I said. "I'm not going."

"Samson please," Dad begged. "The only reason I'm being vague is just so I don't say anything that turns out to be false and worry you even more. Tonight, the air people are going to confirm... something that will allow me to explain everything that's been going on."

"What if they can't confirm it?"

"I..." Dad broke for a second. "We'll see."

I couldn't go. So many weird things had happened lately and I didn't need another. Dad had been so untruthful the last few weeks that I wasn't sure I could trust him.

At the same time, it *could* clear up everything. The chance was small, but it was there. At this point, anything to make things make more sense was worth it. Even if it meant putting aside my anger towards Dad for a bit.

"Fine," I said, gritting my teeth. "I'll go."

"Good," Dad said, lifting his chin. "We leave for the palace in ten minutes."

.<>.

We left the bubble of light coming from the Kilting's home, my stomach swirling with all kinds of emotions. My entire body tingled with anxious excitement. I wasn't exactly swinging between anxiety and excitement so much as I was feeling them both at the same time. Dad led us in a small crowd up the slope of the city, the dark blue sky above dotted with stars and a nearly full moon. The cluster of towers at the top of the slope blazed with light, smaller lights spreading out from the base and through the city.

After a few minutes we reached the base of the palace, a group of ten robed air people standing in front of us. Six of them had been the men who had visited Wateria,

174

four new air women joining them. Kiahta stood in the center, his arms behind his back.

"Welcome, Almas," Kiahta said. "Come with us."

The air people fell into line behind Kiahta, our family following them into the palace. We entered the base of the tallest tower, walking through a hallway that led to the circular center. The hollow tube of the tower extended to the sky, doors poked into its sides. The tower had no stairs. We were directed into the center of the tower, the ten air people spread out along the edge.

"Ready?" Kiahta said. "Now!"

The air people threw their hands up and pushed them down in synchrony. A geyser of air suddenly took all of us off of our feet and into the air. We screamed as the air people flew us in a roaring gust of wind up through the hole at the top of the tower, the city spreading out below us. Their circle flew back, their winds pulling us to the floor.

Two semi-circular slabs of stone pushed their way into the hole, closing the void below us. The Bond was expertly painted into the new section of the floor. Kiahta stepped forward.

"For two thousand years, the Setters kept the balance of the world," Kiahta said. "For that time, the air people, as the stewards of the element of neutrality, have been tasked with training them. Over the centuries, we have gained several crystals containing magic once owned by mages from around the world, so we could better teach new Setters how to use their powers."

Another air person stepped forward. He was tall, skinny, and wore a red robe. He pulled a thin, rolled up piece of paper from his pocket.

"Twelve years ago, Mark knew something was coming. The emperor of the fire people was becoming unstable, and conflict between the water and the fire people was inevitable," he said. "However, he was not to be the Setter to end the war of water and fire. He knew his time was nearly up, so he gave us very specific instructions on how to avoid the destruction of the Inner and Upper Worlds."

Dad walked over to Kiahta and the other air person, now facing us. The second air person continued.

"It was Mark, the final Setter, who told us that we were to give our seven elemental crystals to each of the children of Emperor Aiden," he said, opening the paper. Seven of the air people reached into their pockets, and each pulled out a glowing shard of crystal.

"We will send the crystals into the air, and allow them to select their hosts," said the only other air person who didn't have a crystal. The air people raised their hands, and began to wave them through the air. They let the seven crystals float through the air. They swirled around, like fallen stars, whirling in between everyone in our family.

These crystals each contained the power of a whole other *element*. They'd allow seven of us to become a Setter. A white one latched onto Erin's forehead. She looked up, gasping as the light flowed into her skin. The crystal died, dropping to the ground. An orange crystal attached itself to Anthony's chest, the light entering him as well. Suddenly, all the other crystals began to attach to my siblings. In a moment, they all died, their magic gone. Seven of them looked at their hands and arms like they were brand new, in awe of their sudden new powers.

I hadn't gotten one.

"All of those who received powers, come over here with us," Kiahta instructed. All of my siblings except for Jamie and Kiefer walked over. Dad looked at us, shaking. Kiahta stepped out of the group.

"Mark knew that it would take more than a team of seven Setters to end the war," the second air person said. "The source of his power told him that his magic would not be reborn into another Setter."

"You see, something was returning, something not seen for two thousand years," Kiahta explained. "Something that would require beings far greater than a Setter."

My heart started to beat faster and faster. Kiahta pulled a small wooden bowl out of his pocket. He walked forward, and took Kiefer's left hand, and placed it on the bowl. He did the same with Jamie's, then mine. We held it, standing it a triangle, as Kiahta stepped back. For a few moments, nothing happened.

Fire exploded from the bowl, leaping up into a burning column. It curled into a circle above us, lines of fire burning from the edge to the center. A moment later, the fire had formed the image of the Bond. All the other shapes evaporated away, except for life, lightning and plants. The ring descended, spinning closer towards us.

The fire siphoned down into each of our hands, some unknown force flipping them palm up, the bowl clattering to the ground. My symbol burned with red fire. On Jamie's hand, a circle with three radiating lines burned. On Kiefer's, two lines with a lightning bolt between them. We stepped back, some energy force ripping from my heart, down my arm, and out of my hand.

At once, new elements sprung from our hands.

A flurry of vines, flowers and seeds exploded from my palm in a wave of green light. Moss grew around my feet, spreading across the tower. Lightning bolts crackled out of Kiefer's hand and into the sky, striking stray clouds. Purple silhouettes of animals sprung from Jamie's hand and danced around the tower. The three elements suddenly converged above us, forming a huge column of white light. Raw energy and power awakened every part of my body as the column pierced the sky above and the bowl below.

The column cooled, our signs turning normal. Kiahta stepped forward.

"It appears that Mark was right. You three have been gifted with the power of lightning, life, and plants," he said. Suddenly, he took a knee and bowed his head towards us. Everyone else sunk to their knees, and bowed.

"Two thousand years ago, your predecessors saved the worlds from total annihilation," Kiahta said. "We now know it is you three who must save them again."

Jamie, Kiefer and I stood before their bowed heads.

"It is an honor to welcome the Balancers back to the Inner World."

178

.<>.

I am a Balancer.

What did that even mean? Why was I being welcomed *back*? Who were my "predecessors"? How had I conjured those plants? How had that wooden bowl caused all of that?

I was so struck by confusion that I barely noticed I'd been ushered away from the tower and brought back to the Kilting's until I was at the foot of Dad's bed. Jamie, Kiefer and I stood before him.

"I want to apologize, for the last twelve years," Dad said, sitting on the edge of his bed. He hung his head. "Mark told us a week before you were born that you could be the Balancers."

"Could be?" Jamie asked.

"There was a prophecy," Dad said. "But prophecies are not predictions, they are instructions, and the universe doesn't always follow those instructions. The prophecy said that you would be the Balancers, but there was always a chance you would have just been normal children."

"But we *are* the Balancers," Kiefer said. "So this prophecy or whatever was true. So why didn't you tell anyone?"

"I believed it at first, but lost faith the longer your mother was gone. When you turned five, Marin and I had planned to announce to the kingdom that you were the Balancers, but I just... couldn't do it without her," Dad said. "Prophecies, if followed correctly, will lead to the best

179

possible future. I thought that if my wife was lost, this couldn't possibly be the right future and you couldn't be the Balancers."

"But—

"I know, Jamie," Dad said, looking away. "It was incredibly irresponsible of me. That doesn't change the fact that I decided that I would raise you as normal children. For a while I truly believed that you were just normal children. I believed that the Balancers had been born to someone else, or perhaps a new Setter had been born somewhere."

"Dad..." I said.

"Then Erin told me about what Kiefer did during the battle. I saw what Samson did to the rosebush, and I heard from a guard what Jamie did to Kiefer's leg," Dad explained. "I realized then that Mark was right. You are the Balancers."

"But what does—

"Not now," Dad said, shaking his head as he interrupted Kiefer. "For now, we all need to rest."

"But—

"Not now, Kiefer," Dad said, looking away. "I need some time by myself."

We stepped back, and walked back to our rooms. I opened the door, Coffin jumping up.

"What happened Master? What's goings on? Where did you go?" he asked, running over to me. I walked past him, and up to the withered plant.

I had power over this plant. The magic of its element had been born within me, and I'd never known.

"Someday," I said, slipping into bed.

Mark was the last of all of the Setters, Jack had said.

Mark knew it would take more than a team of seven Setters to end the war, Kiahta had said.

I thought you said Mark was wrong about them, Uncle Drew had said.

Hello, Balancer...Don't play dumb with us, we know you can do a lot more than just revive plants, the fire person had said.

If there was a Setter who was supposed to stop the war, we would know about them by now. But we don't, so obviously whatever magic gives birth to Setters doesn't think this war needs one to stop it, Erin had said.

I looked up at the ceiling, then the plant.

How was I supposed to learn plant magic? How was I supposed to stop the war?

How am I going to save the world?

END OF PART TWO OF

VOLUME ONE

OF THE WATER AND FIRE SERIES

.<>.

PART THREE

.<>.

THE MANOR

PROPHECIES OF BEFORE AND NOW

I am a Balancer, I thought, as I shoveled eggs into my mouth the next morning. The phrase had been bouncing around my head and repeating itself all morning. At first, it had felt cool, mysterious, and powerful. Now it was getting kind of annoying. Being a Balancer had nothing to do with eating eggs.

"Samz, slow down," Maddie said, sitting down next to me. "You don't want to start your first day as Balancer by choking on eggs."

"Hardly edible eggs," Mrs. Kilting interjected, slamming another pot down on the table. "This is why I never let Marty cook."

"Actually, it's not really his first day as Balancer," Erin said, sitting down across from us. "He's had those powers all along, since birth, if he's anything like the first Balancers mentioned in *Lives of the Balancers.* You know, it's really fascinating to find a book though to be inaccurate that's later proved to actually be a true account of events. Anyway, while it may not be his first day as a Balancer those crystals only gave us the power of a second element last night so it *is, however,* our first day as Setters."

"Right," Maddie said, crossing her arms, absorbing Erin's ramblings. "Maybe for you. I don't think I'm going to use my new element too much."

"Maddie, darkness is one of the most useful elements," Erin said. "You can heal blindness, see in the dark, break illusions, and some darkness people can even see emotions and—

"I mean, in actual battle," Maddie said. "Healing blindness and shooting shadows won't stop fire people as well as a blast of water will."

Maddie and Erin dissolved into squabbling, while I choked down Professor Martin's admittedly terrible eggs. For the morning after I found out I was supposed to save the world, it was pretty normal.

At breakfast, once everyone else arrived, we mostly talked about the older seven's new powers. Maddie had gotten darkness, and didn't plan on using it much. Erin had received the element of light and planned on using it with her water magic as much as possible. Ezra was still too brooding to be excited about his new storm powers. Anthony and Emily spent the whole time arguing about whether Anthony's lava or Emily's coral would be more effective in battle.

Luke didn't have much to say about his ice powers. Living so far north, some of our blood did come from ice people, so although we were water people, we could freeze it if we wanted to. Having ice magic was just like having more advanced water magic for Luke, so he was fine with it. Miles talked a little bit about now being able to control sand, although he was pretty tight-lipped about it. Even though the Mesipar Sea War with the sand people was long over, most water people still had reservations about anyone who could do sand magic.

During the whole discussion, Jamie, Kiefer and I sat quietly at the end of the table, not contributing much. Up until this point, we'd been arguing for weeks. Now, we suddenly had to work together to save the world. It wasn't really the best conversation topic for breakfast.

Finally, after breakfast, we got ready to head back to the air palace. Dad told us that mages from all over the world have been called upon to teach all of us our new magic.

Everyone, except for the Balancers.

.<>.

When we arrived, our siblings were quickly ushered away by air people who introduced them to their new teachers. Us three Balancers were left with Duddurn, Splee, and Kiahta.

"Good morning Balancers," Kiahta said, bowing to us. "I'm sure you have many questions, and this morning we hope to answer as many of them as we can."

They led us through the main tower, to a door in the back. It opened up into a beautiful garden.

Trees, bushes, and ivy grew around white stone arches stretching to the tall wall that bordered it. The white stone walled off small sections of the garden dotted with circular pools and beds of flowers. They led us into the garden, until we reached a circular stone table with a linen sheet stretched above it to shade it. Small, circular stools of stone surrounded the table, which was carved and painted to resemble the Bond. We sat down across from the three priests.

"Long ago, all humans, magical and normal, lived together in the Upper World," Kiahta began. "However, three thousand years ago, our ancestors discovered the existence of the Inner World. They forged a bond between the two worlds and made the Inner World their home."

"The legends and stories are unclear exactly how we got here," Splee continued. "Some say only three of the pioneers had magic, others say all of them did, and countless other explanations. But the fact remains that our presence here meant that our world was responsible for the elemental balance in the Upper World."

"The Bond, the magical force that holds our worlds together and grants us our magic, is affected by the types of power we draw from it," Duddurn explained. "Too much negative energy, and both worlds could be destroyed by the imbalances in the Bond."

"Um, I'm sorry, I'm a little... confused," Kiefer interrupted, coughing.

"What is it, Balancer of Lightning? We would love to clarify anything that confuses you," Kiahta said, smiling softly.

"Oh um, I'm just kind of confused about, well... everything," he said, sheepishly grinning. Jamie shook her head, disappointed.

"Kiefer, they mean that when people do bad things with magic, like starting wars," Jamie explained, "the energy causes the thing holding our worlds together to become unstable. If it becomes too unstable, both worlds are destroyed."

"Okay, kind of getting it now, um," Kiefer glanced back at the priests. "Continue. Sirs."

"This imperative that our worlds be balanced is why we had the Setters," Kiahta explained, stepping forward. "Setters were granted power over extra elements, so they could solve conflicts, to prevent the Bond from becoming unstable."

"But what very few know, is that the origin of the Setters can be found in the story of the Balancers," Duddurn said.

"Two thousand years ago, during the Great Catacomb War, every nation except for the fire people were consumed by great and bloody conflict," Splee said. "After years of silence, the fire people suddenly called out to the other nations in distress."

A cold breeze blew through the garden. Kiahta looked down, gulping.

"For years we have searched for records of how... *they*... came into existence, but the chaos caused by their creation has made that search impossible," Kiahta said. He reached into his pocket and pulled out a stack of circular stone disks. He placed them in a circle in the middle of the Bond. Each had a different, strange symbol.

"Five terrible forces, birthed from some unknown darkness, ravaged the old fire kingdom," Kiahta said. "They went by many names."

"We call them the Untamable Mights," Duddurn said.

Kiahta held his hands out and raised them, each of the disks spinning into the air. One detached itself from the group and began to float with its face pointed towards us. A broken throne was carved into its face.

"The first was called Domination," Kiahta said, letting the first disk drop. The next showed a staff with a large gem on it.

"The second was known as the Thief."

A quill.

"Third, the Liar."

A sword etched with runes.

"Fourth, Hatred."

Finally, the last disk turned to us. This one simply showed a pair of eyes.

"Their master was the great Untamable Might of Power," Kiahta said. "All the other Mights answered to him. He was stronger than any force the Inner World had encountered before."

"It was Power himself that led his Mights from the ruined fire kingdom to conquer the rest of the world," Duddurn said. "Under his leadership, the world quickly began to fall under their reign of darkness."

"However, soon after the creation of the Mights, three strange humans emerged from similarly mysterious origins," Splee said, pushing air into a hole in the side of the table. The cracks hissed as the symbols of life, lightning and plants pushed up a few inches.

"In the one thousand years that the Inner World had been inhabited, no one had ever controlled life, lightning or plants, until the original Balancers arose. However, instead of getting their magic from birth, they got it from a mysterious force they called the Sol," Kiahta explained. "The eldest possessed the gift of lightning, the second possessed the gift of life, and the youngest, the gift of plants."

"Together, they were able to contain each of the Mights into objects where they could never escape," Splee said. "Their intervention ended the Catacomb War and saved the world from the Untamable Mights."

"Wait, me again, sorry, but what do you mean by... contain them?" Kiefer asked. "Why didn't they just destroy them?"

"Well," Kiahta said, glancing at the other priests. "We're not... quite sure. At that time, the Inner World was in such chaos that accurate histories are hard to come by."

"So..." Kiefer said. "Aren't there at least some ideas?"

"Well, containing them prevented them from taking over the world again," Splee said. "They didn't need to be destroyed if there was an easier way to stop their reign."

Kiefer nodded silently, pursing his lips.

"Got it," he said weakly. Duddurn stood up to continue.

"After the last Balancer died, the Sol took the magic of all three of them, and gave it to the very first Setter," Duddurn explained. "For two thousand years, the Sol passed power down from Setter to Setter, to Mark, and finally, to you three."

"Thirteen years ago, Emperor Conner of the fire people... discovered something," Kiahta said, lowering his voice. "According to Mark, who was Conner's friend at the time, he had discovered one of the objects containing an Untamable Might."

"Wait," Kiefer said. "If Conner has an Untamable Might, how has he not... you know..."

"Let us finish," Splee said. "Mark knew that if Conner had found one of the Mights, he would soon find the other four. He knew that because Untamable Mights could only be defeated by the magic of a Balancer, he realized that he would have to die so new Balancers could be reborn."

"Before the first Balancers died, five prophecies were made about the second coming of the Balancers," Kiahta explained. "Four of them were stolen by the Mights, only the first one saved by the air people."

"So you guys have the prophecy? About us? When do we get to see it? What does it say about us?" Kiefer asked excitedly.

"In good time, we will show the prophecy to you," Duddurn assured Kiefer.

"But I thought prophecies weren't real," I said, remembering what Erin had told me. Kiahta wagged a finger.

"They certainly are real," Kiahta said. "One led Mark to your mother, leading him to strongly believe that she was to give birth to the Balancers."

"Strongly believe?" Jamie asked.

"Prophecies are not accurate predictions," Splee explained. "They simply give instructions that will lead those affected to the best possible future. The prophecy said that the queen of the water people would give birth to the Balancers, and even though that's what happened, it didn't necessarily have to."

"We weren't even sure if you truly were the Balancers until last night," Kiahta admitted. He looked away. "However, Emperor Conner knew some of the prophecy."

"He..." Splee paused. "All he knew was that the Balancers would most likely be born in the Water Kingdom."

"You see, because it was Balancers that trapped the Mights, Conner knew that it would take Balancers to free the Mights," Kiahta explained. He looked at us, sadness in his eyes. "They could only be freed by the ones who contained them."

"To try to find the Balancers, and free the Untamable Mights, Emperor Conner attacked the water people," Kiahta said. My stomach dropped.

"I thought the war was because of how we treated the sand people after the Mesipar—

"It was a lie your father and his siblings told you and the Water Kingdom," Kiahta said. He looked directly at us.

"It was never about trade, or war crimes or anything else your father told you," Kiahta said.

"The war is because of you."

TRAINING, AGAIN

"The legends say... very little about the element of plants," Kiahta said. A day had passed since he had gathered Jamie, Kiefer and I to tell us about the Mights. After telling us that the past twelve years of war had been because our existence, they gave us the rest of the day off to deal with that. Instead of thinking about it, I shoved it far enough back in my mind so it wouldn't come out for a while. For the time being, it was working.

Since air people are great at reading people, they had Jamie, Kiefer and I wake up extra early the next morning to start training, because we all definitely did not stay awake all night having an existential crisis. And on top of it all, Kiahta's opening lecture on plants... was not going well.

"The only human to ever control plants lived two thousand years ago, so I will be training you based on magical theory written by the storm person scholar Chi Izina," Kiahta explained. I sat across from him, a small, circular pond between us. A thin book lay closed at his feet, written in fancy Pataoban script. He had been poring over when I'd walked in.

Kiahta stood with his hands behind his back in front of a curving tree, leaves fluttering down. At this point, they were more interesting than him. Kiahta held his hand out and caught a leaf in a tiny vortex of wind. He pinched the leaf and held it up to the sun.

"Plants get their energy from each of the four core elements," Kiahta said. "The air, the earth, water, and the light from the fires of the sun all allow plants to grow."

He glanced down at me as if to get some sort of response from me. I briefly considered being cheeky and looking behind me but decided against it. It was too much of a Kiefer thing to do. Kiahta coughed and looked back up towards the sun.

"You must be a substitute for all of the energy to create plants," he said. "You must be the sun, the earth, the water, and the air."

Was that supposed to mean something? What did Chi Izina know about plant magic? Even Dad's explanation of water had been easier to understand. I could kind of get earth, air, and water helping plants, but the sun representing fire was a bit of a stretch. Fire burned plants. And I thought that the sun represented the element of light, not fire. And even then, light usually represented illusions and purity, not helping plants grow. Kiahta glanced down at me and dropped the leaf.

"Perhaps, we could try some magic, instead of just magical theory," Kiahta said. "Have you ever been able to do plant magic?"

"I've been able to revive dead plants, a few times," I said, shrugging. "Roses two times. A tree once."

Kiahta paused. He opened his mouth and faltered.

"Well, I... Chi Izina only mentioned revival in passing," Kiahta said, nodding. "Perhaps we can start with growing grass?"

195

That wasn't at all what I'd told him. Besides two nights ago, I'd only ever revived plants. Whatever plant magic I'd done that night was because of the ceremony. He wasn't listening!

"Now, hold your hand against the grass," Kiahta instructed. I placed my hand in the grass, the cold blades wet on my hand. "Be the fire of the sun, be the nourishment of the earth, and the water, be the air."

That didn't make sense! He wasn't telling me what to do, he was just spitting elemental nonsense at me that didn't even make sense (I was still stuck on how the sun represented fire instead of light). He was an air mage. Chi Izina was a storm mage. Neither were a plant mage.

"Concentrate, concentrate, concentrate," Kiahta urged. I tried to, but instead of thinking about plants all I could think about was how unfair it was. I hadn't asked to have plant magic, but I had to learn it, no one was going to teach me, and the one person who was teaching me wasn't listening to me.

I pushed my hand further into the grass, trying to make it move or grow or do anything. Kiahta said some comments that I didn't listen to. The sun was hot on my neck and in no way, shape or form was helping me grow any plants. Maybe the sunburn was how the sun apparently represented fire and not light? Even if I asked, Kiahta wouldn't have given me a real answer.

This is going to be a long day.

.<>.

196

"Now, as a Balancer, it's important to be able to fight those of another element," Kiahta explained, motioning to the circular pond next to me. "Every Setter, at some point in their lives, has had to fight. As a Balancer, you'll need to fight even more. So far, all you've learned is how to spar against another water person and the occasional fire person."

"It's not exactly as if I've had a lot of options," I said, crossing my arms. Kiahta sighed.

It had been three days since we'd started training. The second day I'd made a patch of grass grow a few inches, and the third day Kiahta said he thought one of the flowers I was trying to control might have budged. It hadn't. He'd given me a translated copy of Chi Izina's book to read, but most of it just talked about hypothetical comparisons to other elements. I'd also successfully compartmentalized the whole "I'm-the-reason-people-are-dying" thing; there would be time later to work through that.

"Samson, one of the reasons Setters often turn to the air people, is that our magic can be helpful in teaching others how to fight against different types of magic," Kiahta explained. He extended his hands, walking in a tight circle. A rock near the pond was suddenly lifted into the air by a tight collar of wind. "See?"

"Kind... of...?" Lifting a rock with air was completely different from what an actual earth person could do. Besides, the earth people were neutral in the war, so I'd never actually need to fight one.

"Today, you and I are going to practice fighting against someone with a different element than our own,"

Kiahta said, assuming an air person fighting stance. His feet and arms were wide, his heels in the air like he was trying to be as off of the ground as possible.

"Hold on, hold on, hold on, I'm not going to fight you," I said, shaking my head. Kiahta chuckled.

"You can use as much water as you want. For now, I won't expect you to use plants, unless you want to," he smiled, a breeze starting to stir his robes. "Let's start with air. Ready?"

"Wait, I'm not—

Kiahta leaped up several feet into the air, his wind scattering leaves from the trees. He suspended himself on a swirling cushion of air above the tree, grinning. I groaned and pulled a stream of water out of the pond into a loop around me.

"I don't see how this—

Kiahta spun in mid-air and whipped one arm out and back in. A moment later, a wind gust pushed me back, then thrust me forward. My water splashed into the dirt. I glared up at Kiahta. I stepped forward and thrust a hand up, the water from the pond blasting towards Kiahta from below. He threw his hands down, a gust of wind blowing apart my blast and sending him calmly spiraling to the ground. I changed directions, weaving my jet of water horizontally and aimed it at his shoulders. Kiahta jumped into the sky again, my water just scraping his toes. I groaned. Fighting an air person was like trying to punch a butterfly.

"Think Samson," Kiahta said as he floated on his column of air. "Watch how I fight. Think about my element. What do you think my weakness is?"

I rolled my eyes, and ran over to the pond. I stepped right into it, feeling a shiver of power run from my legs up to my spine. I tried to blast him two more times, but both times he dodged nimbly. Still floating, he spun three times in a circle, a blast of wind sending me stumbling back into the pond, soaking me up to my legs. He floated down to the ground, putting his hands behind his back and his feet flat on the ground.

"Get up, let's try that again," he said, winds already starting to swirl around him. I groaned, shakily rising to my feet.

"Ready?" he said, raising his arms and standing on his toes.

"I guess," I said through my teeth.

"Let's go."

.<>.

Kiahta and I sparred all day. He never gave me any hints as to what his weakness was. Sometimes he would even use winds to lift rocks into the air to send at me, so I could practice fighting off an earth person, even though that would never happen. By the end of the day, I was covered in bruises and was sorer than I'd ever been. Back at the Kilting's house, Jamie tried to heal some of my bruises with her life magic. We were in the living room, sitting on the same couch.

"I'm pretty new at this, so stop me if anything is hurting," she said, closing her eyes and holding one of her palms out. She concentrated, and her palm slowly began to glow with purple light. Her hand shaking, she pressed the palm into the largest bruise on my forearm. The pain instantly eased, the warmth of her hand spreading all the way up my arm.

"Is it working?" she asked, opening one eye.

"It is," I said wearily. I was happy that she was doing well with life magic and she could use it to heal me, but it made me feel a little disappointed. I still hadn't made that much progress with plants, and I was *still* not great at water.

"Ooh, cool," Kiefer said, poking his head into the room. He then saw me, bruises and scrapes covering my arms and legs. "Eugh, what happened to you? You look like crap."

"Kiahta had the brilliant idea to teach me how to fight other elements today," I said, shrugging. "Which as far as I could tell only involved blowing me into a tree and launching rocks at me."

"It's important for us to learn how to fight other elements, be grateful that Kiahta is expanding your training and not just concentrating on old history lessons," Jamie said, releasing her hand. The bruise was still there, but it was smaller and paler than it had been before and it didn't hurt. She moved onto a slice of cuts on my shoulder that had come from being blasted into the tree.

"I thought you liked history," Kiefer said, slumping into the couch on the other side of me.

"Normally I do, but all Splee talks about previous Setters and all the ways they settled conflicts and what lessons we can learn from them and he never actually teaches me much life magic," she said, releasing my shoulder as the cuts faded away.

"At least you don't have to read Chi Izina," I said.

"At least you get to read about your element," Jamie said. "Splee is making me read a book about a light Setter. It would be bad enough on its own but it's written in the light people language Zoben, with the Andlurran translations written in the margins and Splee has terrible handwriting."

"So Kiefer, how's your priest been annoying you?" I asked, turning to him. He shrugged.

"Duddurn's fine he just doesn't actually know anything about lightning magic," he said, holding his hand up. He snapped, and a small crackle of electricity popped out of his hand. "Cause he's like, an air mage or whatever and I'm the only lightning mage to exist in two thousand years. It's not too bad. I get to shock stuff. Sometimes I 'accidentally' shock Duddurn. I guess I have bad aim."

"They're doing their best with what they have," Jamie said. "We have to appreciate what they're doing for us. Especially letting the whole family stay here."

"What?" Kiefer asked. Jamie looked at us as if this was something we were supposed to know.

"What do you mean 'what'?" she asked. "The air people are currently neutral in the war. They're housing and training us, royal members of the Water Kingdom."

"Well if we're the Balancers, we're technically supposed to save the *whole* world, so does it really count?" I asked.

"Maybe not for us. But Dad, a water emperor, is here," she said, finishing a bruise on my leg. One of the doors opened suddenly, Simon walking through.

"Hello," he said, sitting down across from us. "Having a secret Balancer conference?"

Jamie said 'no' and Kiefer said 'yes' at the same time.

"What happened to you?" Simon asked, pointing to me.

"Ugh," I said, crossing my arms. "Kiahta made me spar with him the whole day so I could figure out what his weakness is."

"Well, he's old, right?" Kiefer said. "I'd say that's a weakness. Go for the weak knees."

"He might be old but that doesn't stop him from jumping around on air," I said. Simon chuckled.

"Well, like all air people, he's only good if he's far away from you and as far off the ground as he can get," Simon said, shrugging.

"Huh?" I asked. Simon leaned forward, glancing sideways for a second as if he were letting me in on some forbidden secret.

"Next time you spar with him, get him as close to you as possible, and as close to the ground as you can,"

Simon said. "Especially if he's on the ground, he'll be more vulnerable. The closer he is, the weaker his blasts will be."

"Really? Thanks," I said, smiling. "I'll try that."

"And if any of you want to spar with someone who doesn't have joint pain, I've always wanted to try fighting someone of a different element," he said, standing up. "If you ever need anything, I'll be here."

"Thanks Simon," Jamie said.

"How are they doing at teaching you magic?" Simon asked. We looked at each other. "Not great?"

"Kiahta just repeats unhelpful magic theory," I said.

"Well, that's to be expected," Simon said, shrugging. "That's how people learn air magic."

"That's awful," Kieter said, crossing his arms. Jamie jabbed him with her elbow.

"No, it's just different," she hissed.

"It is," Simon said. "Each element is different. Air magic requires a lot of magical theory and meditation. Water magic requires making a personal connection to the element. Even within each element, there's no one right way to learn."

"I guess," I said, sitting back on the couch.

"Don't get discouraged," Simon said. He glanced over at the door, and put a hand to his mouth. "One second. AUNTIE!"

Mrs. Kilting threw the door open, broom in hand.

"What is it Simon? I have a pot of stew going," she said.

"It's quick," Simon said. "Can you tell them about how you learned magic?"

"What's there to tell?" she scoffed. "I went to air magic classes with those priests for years, and could hardly blow a scroll off a desk. One day I was doing chores, sweeping my family's house, and got so fed up with how far behind I was, I used my broom and BAM! I could do air magic."

"See? And now she's great at it," Simon said.

"Eh, I'm alright. As long as I have a broom or a fan, I can do it. Take it away and I'm basically useless," she said, shrugging. "The air priests weren't exactly happy with how I did magic, so I stopped learning from them. That's when I found Marty, who never even *used* his powers, and didn't care that I couldn't use mine without help. And now, I'm stuck with him for life."

"Thanks Auntie!" Simon said. "You can go back to your stew!"

"Okay," she said, walking through the door and blowing the door shut with her broom.

"So, I don't know if that helped at all, but I guess just... don't lose hope yet," Simon said. "My aunt is living proof that you don't have to learn how the priests want you to. You can find your own way."

.<>.

The next morning, when I got to the garden, no one was there. I waited on a bench by the wall. Above the bench, there was an overhang that left a bed of flowers in deep shadow. They were wilted, and almost dead.

Kiahta wants me to do plant magic, I thought, *but the only plant magic I'm good at is reviving dead ones.*

It couldn't hurt to practice. And if I couldn't do anything, it wasn't as if Kiahta was there to chastise me.

I knelt down next to the wilted flowers and touched one of my fingers to a bleached petal. Kiahta and Chi Izina's way of being all four core elements had never worked. It was looking at plant magic as something purely theoretical and technical, which I realized was not how I had been originally taught magic. Dad and Maddie had taught me water magic by helping me find emotions and situations that strengthened my magic, and that had worked for me. Mrs. Kilting had been taught by air priests, rejected their practices and found her own way. Maybe I could too.

The three times I'd revived plants before had been moments of respite in the middle of chaos. Moments of calm and protection. I inhaled, and exhaled, letting the feeling of being protected, invulnerable, and safe wash over me. I let it flow down my hands, and into the flowers.

Slowly, color began to bloom back into the petals. Breathing steadily, I spread my arms apart, a wave of rejuvenation following my palms. The bent stems righted themselves and filled in with a deep green. The petals burned purple and reached for the sun. I began to stand up, making repeated motions of pulling the plants up with my

205

hands. The stalks rose higher and higher, out of the shadow of the overpass. They finally reached the sun and rested.

I looked down the overhang and saw more bushes that had been left to wilt in the shadows. Feeling optimistic for the first time in days, I continued down the edge of the wall, reviving the dead plants and growing them until they touched the sunlight. Once I finished with them, I healed any other plants that were wilting or dead. I brought color and life back into my section of the garden. Even the surrounding grass seemed greener as if it too had been healed in the backwash of my powers.

Finally, after I had revived the last wilted plant, I turned to the plants that were healthy. If I could command the plants that were too weak to grow, I could do so much more with the plants that already were healthy.

I knelt down in the grass and spread my arms. The blades tickled my hands, as I let my feelings of safety and clarity spread into the grass. Slowly at first, but quickening by the second, the blades began to shiver and grow where they touched my skin. My heart soaring, I pulled the grass back, the blades thickening and elongating.

Almost giggling, I ran over to a sunflower that stood with its petals facing the sun. I grabbed its stalk and evened out my breathing. It began to grow, the stem moving and tingling with power against my palms. I stepped back and began to grow it without contact from my hands. The sunflower stretched even closer to the sun, its leaves curling larger and larger.

I can do plant magic. I'm a plant mage.

I went through the garden, growing each of the flowerbeds to at least twice their size. I healed any of the yellow grass until the entire section was green. The smell of pollen and leaves was thick in the warm morning air.

I finally approached the tree in the center. I placed my hands on it, and could instantly feel the power that concentration of my element it held. It wasn't like the throbbing, pulsing feeling I got from being submerged in water. It was strong and silently growing, stoic and powerful and *there*. I felt the sun, I felt my breath.

I began to feel the power of the tree, and slowly began to shape it. It responded to me, the trunk curving up higher to the sky. The grass and the flowers lent me their strength as I lifted the tree to the sky. Leaves fell in a rain around me. New branches twisted from the old, buds rapidly grew from red to full leaves.

I stepped back, marveling at my work. I took a few deep breaths, and sat across the pond, facing my newly grown tree. A few moments later, Kiahta rushed into the garden.

"I am so sorry I got tangled up in a—

He stopped cold. That morning, the garden had been small and nearly dead. Now it was vibrant, colorful, and much bigger and much more alive. He looked at me, his mouth slightly agape.

"Don't worry about it," I said. "Shall we begin?"

THE LAST ELEMENT

"So, what are we learning today?" I asked. I had woken up in a strangely optimistic mood. The past several days of learning plant magic had been so much better than the first few, I didn't dread walking into that garden every morning anymore. "Fruits again? Grass? Are we finally going to start trees or something?"

"Alright, alright," Kiahta said, shaking his head. "We actually are going to take a break from plant magic today."

"What?" I asked, my shoulders sagging. I was finally getting the hang of it, and he wanted to take a break?

"Don't worry, we'll get back to plant magic in no time," he said. "Since you were doing so well with it, I thought it would be worth it to take a moment to teach you more about the other half of your duties as a Balancer."

"What would... that be?" I asked. Kiahta waved me closer and turned to lead me deeper into the garden.

"Well, we're going to start with a little history lesson," he said, leading me towards a wall at the edge of the garden. He reached a moss-caked door in the wall and held his hand up to a metal-rimmed hole in the center. He pushed a gust of wind into the door, air hissing out through the cracks. It swung inward a tiny bit, Kiahta pushing it the rest of the way in. He pulled a candle from the pocket of his robe and lit it, illuminating a staircase that descending down into darkness.

"What... kind of history lesson?" I asked. Kiahta was silent as he led me down the staircase, the mossy door shutting behind us. The stairs descended deep, far into the depths of Aetheopolis.

"Just a moment, you don't need to be impatient," he said. After a few minutes, we reached the bottom of the stairs. Across from us, the candle illuminated a floor to ceiling carving in the yellow stone.

It showed sharply drawn clouds with people standing atop them, their forms filled in with white paint so faded it took me a moment to notice.

"What is this?" I asked, placing a hand on the carving. The people atop the clouds had crazed, jaggedly carved looked on their faces. Smaller people huddled on the ground below, running from the air people. The carvings continued to the left and right, fading off into the shadows outside the candle's light. The hallway seemed to curve off in either direction.

"To be a Balancer, you must not only learn the magic of your element," Kiahta said, ruefully bowing his head towards the grotesque illustration. "Your job is to preserve the balance of the world. To do that, you must understand the very concept of balance itself.

"I meant," I said, noticing one of the carved air people seeming to pull something long and wispy out of the mouths of one of the people on the ground, "what are these carvings?"

"This is the past of the air people," Kiahta said, motioning to one of the people jumping from the clouds and terrorizing those below. "You know us now as the nation of

209

neutrality, but a few hundred years ago this was not the case."

We began to walk to the left, seeing more illustrations of destruction. Air people gleefully tore villages apart with tornadoes, others seemed to have strings from their fingers attached to other people, as if they were puppets.

"There was a time when we were the country of war and terror," Kiahta explained. "Our ancestors believed that since we had been given power over the air, wind, and sky, it was our right to do with it as we pleased. In those days, everyone lived in fear of the air people."

He paused at a large carving. An air person floated above a choking man clutching his throat. The air person was drawn to be pulling thin, wispy lines out of the man's throat.

"We committed many great sins," he said, placing a hand on the carving of the choking man. "We'd destroy those who defied us in cruel and unusual ways. There were once spells that..."

He looked up at the carving, shaking his head.

"There was a spell that could suck all of the air out of a person's lungs," he said. My eyes widened. The carving was of an air person suffocating another person, pulling the air right out of his lungs. The thin wispy lines were their stolen breath. "Another allowed air people to control the movements of others, by harnessing the oxygen in their blood."

"Control their movements?" I breathed, my chest feeling hollow. Kiahta turned back to me.

"The water people once knew a similar spell, one that could control a person's movements by controlling the water in another's body," he said, his voice hovering dangerously above a whisper. "It was far more effective than the air magic spell."

"Was?"

"It's not important," Kiahta said, waving the thought away. He continued down the hall. "What is important is what happened *after* our centuries of aggression."

"What happened?" I asked.

"We changed," he said, continuing down the hall. The carvings suddenly changed. The air people began to bow before figures dusted with pink pigment. The pink figures touched the foreheads of the bowing air people. "Our violent ways were not sustainable. We stopped attacking innocent people, and we erased many of those terrible spells."

"Erased them? But you can't destroy spells," I said, shaking my head.

"That is true, as far as we know," Kiahta said. "One cannot destroy a spell, but one can *forget* a spell."

"How did you make everyone forget?" I asked. Kiahta motioned to the pink figures. I noticed faded carvings behind them that looked almost like palm trees.

"The coral people, often overlooked by the other nations, possessed the key to ending our era of war," he explained. "Once we resolved to end that chapter of our history and move on, we called on the coral people to help facilitate that change."

"The *coral* people?" I asked. I didn't really know a whole lot about them. They weren't important to the war, or really any nation except the Storm Empire. I'd always thought that their element was weak and kind of useless.

"Coral is the element of harmony and memory," Kiahta said. "Many overlook the critical role that the Coral Colonies play in the Inner World."

"What do they do?"

"There are many among the coral people who possess the ability to manipulate memories," he explained, touching a hand to the pink people. The pink people were coral people, and they were touching the minds of the air people. "As a society, we agreed to bring in coral people to erase those spells from our memories."

"And they really did it?" I asked. Kiahta sighed.

"They were thorough, but not complete, that would have been impossible," Kiahta said. "Almost every nation, at least once in their history, has called upon the coral people to erase dark spells from their kingdom. But people and records slip through the cracks..."

"Slip through the cracks...?"

He paused, grimacing. "Never mind, it's not important to this lesson."

"Okay…" I said, as Kiahta moved past the coral people and onto more carvings. These ones still showed air people fighting, but always among people pigmented different colors. In the center was an intricate carving of Aetheopolis, with radiating lines like sunlight spreading from it.

"We became a nation that would be neutral in all conflicts," he said. "In a war, we would try to get each side to compromise. If we couldn't, we would either try to stay out of it, or help each equally. For twelve years we have stayed out of the War of Water and Fire."

"I see… so is that balance? What you're trying to teach me?" I asked. Kiahta shrugged and brought me farther. The wall suddenly turned blank, the carvings ending.

"There's one more part to this lesson," he said, the wall now starting to fill with carvings. These ones showed air people huddled in tents clinging to the sides of mountains, air people peacefully descending from clouds with hands kindly outstretched. It was the polar opposite of the first carvings I'd seen. Their forms were soft, curved, and serene.

"This was how the air people began, before neutrality, and before violence. We originally believed that the air people were to be the people of peace," Kiahta explained. "We never provoked any other country, but we also never struck back against anyone who attacked us. Our obsession with peace had made us weak. Other countries attacked us just because we were an easy target."

"But what does this have to do with—

"Come," he said, walking further. I saw the air people being struck down by multi-colored figures in the carvings. They still tried to extend their hands of peace, but they were swatted away.

"Eventually, our people became fed up with being pushed around by the other nations," Kiahta explained. Certain air people began to clench their fists, angrily carved winds slicing around them. "In response to our vulnerable peacefulness, we became angry."

Suddenly, we were standing just where we had been at the beginning, back to the carvings of the violent era of the air people.

"First, we were too peaceful. Then, we were too violent. And now, the air people have found balance in our policy of neutrality," Kiahta explained. "We leaned too far one way, and in response, we leaned too far to the other. And now we lie in the middle."

"So... that's balance?"

"Yes, Samson," Kiahta explained. "Often history will balance itself, as it did with the air people. Sometimes it will swing back and forth several times before achieving balance. Some might even balance themselves for a time, and then fall back into the cycle of swinging back and forth between extremes."

He placed a hand on the wall.

"However, sometimes we need help in balancing our world," Kiahta said, turning to me. "And that is why you are here. You and your siblings are to stop the scales from tipping too far in any one direction."

"I know, we need to end the war," I said. "Since we're on the side of the water people, we can help them win and—

"No," Kiahta said, shaking his head quickly. His voice was rushed and hollow. "You are a Balancer. You may be born of the water people, but you are not on their side."

"What?" I hissed. Kiahta sighed, something breaking inside him.

"I'm sorry," he said, looking away. "Perhaps this was too much to explain to you at once. This early. I'm sorry."

"But—

"Let's go back to the garden and work on your plant magic," he said, walking up the stairs. I paused, looking back at the carvings of the air people pulling the air from people's lungs.

"I want to understand but—

"Samson please, I'm sorry," Kiahta said, turning away from me and hunching his shoulders. He glanced at me nervously. Fear flashed in his eyes for a moment. "It was too early. Just... forget about this lesson. For now."

He turned back and began to march up the stairs. I paused, looking back at the carvings of the violent air people. Although I was so confused about the lesson being 'too early' or that I should 'forget' about it, something else had bothered me.

"Kiahta, when you were talking about the spells, do you know if anyone still knows them?" I asked. He paused on the stairs.

"There have been dark outbreaks in the past, when people discovered abnormally powerful spells that had previously been erased," he said. "But we are living in a time of peace. If there are any spells like those out there, they are safe, hidden, or forgotten."

"Okay..." I said, not entirely convinced as I went up the staircase.

.<>.

I sullenly went through the motions of learning plant magic for the rest of the day. We mostly reviewed forms and abilities I'd already learned, Kiahta not wanting to push me after what he'd told me. Finally, the end of the day came.

"That's enough for today," Kiahta said. I lowered the vine I'd been practicing with then reached for my bag. I turned to leave, but Kiahta put a hand on my shoulder.

"Samson," he said. I turned around. He sighed, looking down.

"What?" I asked.

"I'm sorry I showed you the carvings and told you those things about balance," Kiahta said. "I see now how those things have upset you."

"No, it's okay," I lied. "I need to learn about balance at some point, right?"

216

"I suppose," he said, releasing my shoulder. "Let's just... not talk about it for a while."

"Okay," I said, turning to go. I paused. He said I couldn't fight for the water people. Did he mean that I would have to fight for the fire people? Both? Neither?

"Wait," I said, turning around. "Before I go I just... can you tell me about fire?"

"Fire?" Kiahta said, looking up. He put his hands behind his back and squinted. "What do you want to know about fire?"

"Just... I've been told a lot of different things about what it's supposed to be for, and it's confusing," I said. "You're an air person, so you have a neutral view of it, right?"

He was silent, his face stone.

"Look, I understand water, because I'm a water person, so it would be balanced if I learned about fire too, right?" I asked. He paused for a moment.

"No," he said. "If you weren't ready to hear about balance you certainly aren't ready to hear about fire."

I groaned, my fingers briefly clenching.

"I... I *am* ready," I insisted. I was tired of people not telling me things. First Dad, now Kiahta. I was done being left in the dark with scraps of answers.

"No," Kiahta said. "You're not ready."

"You... can't decide when I'm ready or not," I said, anger boiling in my throat. "I know I'm ready, just tell me. If it hurts me, then it will be my fault."

Kiahta turned away from me, looking at the ground. His shoulders and neck were tense. Suddenly, he relaxed.

"Fine," Kiahta said, looking toward the sunset. His voice was deep, nearly a whisper. "Since you are so foolishly insistent, I will tell you about fire."

I sat down on the grass, Kiahta's fist briefly clenching.

"You know well that water was the first element," he said. "Fire is the last element."

He looked over his shoulder to me, his face outlined in red by the sun.

"After all the other elements had come into existence, fire was born out of the greed of man," he said, his voice shaking. "Unlike all of the other elements, fire is the only one that was solely born out of humanity. Humans created fire because we were impatient and our need for results outweighed our need for safety."

He turned around to face me, the sun burning behind him.

"Fire has one goal," he spat, his words now openly venomous. "To consume."

I shivered. I had asked, hoping his explanation of fire wouldn't be like Ezra's. It was worse this time because Kiahta wasn't a moody teenager who had just seen battle.

He was an old, wise man who had studied all of the elements for his entire life. He knew what he was talking about. He was right.

"Without the control of a human, the other elements will simply dissipate and eventually become inert. Even great storms will evaporate and lava will harden into stone," he said, anger igniting in his eyes. "But fire will continue to burn until it has consumed and destroyed everything."

I grabbed the grass behind me, tearing the ends off.

"It is the duty of the fire people to be in control of the element gifted to them," Kiahta said. "Lack of control is the greatest weakness and the greatest strength a fire person has."

The wind shifted direction, angrily whipping through the garden.

"A fire person without control can destroy all of his enemies," Kiahta said. "But he will also destroy himself."

Kiahta held both of his hands out, the wind gusting around him.

"Water is the first element, and fire is the last," Kiahta said. "The conflict between your nations, two opposite elements, puts the greatest strain on the Bond. The war must end."

Kiahta composed himself, putting his hands behind his back. The wind died down, his robes and hair resting.

"You, Jamison, and Kiefer must end the Mights, so they do not destroy your people," Kiahta said, "and so the fire people do not destroy themselves."

Kiahta folded his hands, the lecture over.

"Oh..." I said, standing up. Kiahta released his hands. I shouldered my bag, my arms shaking. "Thank you."

"It is always my honor to guide you," he said, bowing. "I will see you tomorrow."

"Yeah," I said, turning away from him. Trembling, I left the garden.

THE ONE WHO KNOWS

We spent the next two weeks just working on plant magic and fighting. He never brought up the carvings or talking about fire again. Neither Jamie or Kiefer had been brought down to see the carvings, not after what happened when Kiahta took me. For two weeks we focused solely on the magic aspect of being the Balancer of Plants.

Two weeks after showing me the carvings, Coffin had come along for the day to watch me do plant magic. After I finished reviving a whole row of dead corn stalks, Kiahta pulled me aside.

"Samson, I know that I have been reluctant to discuss the more... abstract side of your role as Balancer of Plants for a while," he said. "However, the other priests and I have decided that it is time to show you and your fellow Balancers the prophecy."

"Really?" I asked.

"Yes, young one," Kiahta said, smiling. "Let's go now, your brother and sister are waiting."

"Master?" Coffin asked as he waddled along. "Whassa prophecy?"

He led me over to the same pavilion where he'd originally explained our roles. Jamie and Kiefer were already there with their priests. I sat down next to them, the priests organizing themselves across from us.

They lifted their hands and pressed them into holes on the side of the table. Air hissed between the cracks of the elements. The center four, water, earth, fire, and air, rose up. The priests swiped their hands forward, three gusts of wind lifting the four blocks right out of the Bond, and sending them spinning to land on the edges of the table. They raised their hands, a geyser of air pulling a stone tablet up from within the table. The tablet floated over towards us, the ancient stone sprinkling dust onto the table. Nearly faded words were carved into its face.

"This is the only prophecy that was not taken by the Mights, the one that led Mark to identify your mother as the mother of the Balancers," Kiahta explained.

Jamie, Kiefer and I leaned in. Jamie started reading it aloud.

"If the throne is found by a king of fire

The Balancers will return

Seek the mother, a queen of water

Or the Inner World shall burn

Beware the one who hears the heart

Beware the thorny rose

Beware the power of the spell

Beware the one who knows

Go to the sky, go to the caves

Reveal to them the light

They will make the fire surrender

In the home of betrayal's night," she read.

I read it again. The first part seemed pretty straightforward, and it was all things that had happened. The second one was weirder, though. *Beware the one who hears the heart?* What did that mean? *Beware the thorny rose.* I'd healed a rosebush, and it had freaked me out for a few weeks. That part made sense. *Beware the power of the spell?* Maybe that had to do with Kiefer using the spell that hurt him. *Beware the one who knows?* Knows what?

"Hey, we've already done some of this!" Kiefer said, jabbing a finger towards the first sentence of the third stanza. "*Go to the sky,* um, we did that."

"Then what *caves* are we supposed to go to?" Jamie wondered. "And what does it mean by *thorny rose?*"

"You're confused about *that* part? What about '*In the home of betrayal's night?*'," Kiefer asked.

"We understand you have many questions about the prophecy," Splee said. "There are already many interpretations of the prophecy that might ease some of your questions."

"To answer your question, Jamison, many believe the thorny rose is a metaphor to refer to jealousy, for it could tear you three apart," Kiahta said.

"And since you have come to Aetheopolis, the sky, it would make sense for you, at some point," Splee began, making a sour face. "It would perhaps benefit you to also go to Ar Shaa, the capital of the earth people."

"I'm not sure what, if anything, you could find there, but if the prophecy recommends it, then I suppose it must be the best course of action," Kiahta said, grimacing. I guessed, earth being the opposite of air, the priests would be opposed to sending us to the earth people, even if a prophecy said we should.

"Okay, what about the *home of betrayal's night?*" Kiefer asked.

"Again, some things we are not sure about," Kiahta said, picking the Tablet up and tucking it under his arm. "For today, we just wanted to show it to you."

"What?" Kiefer whined. "But—

"Kiefer, be patient, please," Kiahta said. "This prophecy is incredibly important. Just the first few lines that Emperor Conner knew prompted him to start a war against the water people. In the wrong hands, the knowledge it possesses could be catastrophic."

"We understand," Jamie piped up before Kiefer could say anything. "Thank you."

"As always, it is an honor to guide you three," Splee said, bowing to us.

"Master? You never tolds me what a prophefy is," Coffin asked later that night. I was in my room at the Kiltings, reading *Prominent Setters and Their Achievements*. Even though I now knew why Kiefer could control lightning, the books Erin had picked out for me were still interesting. I was reading a chapter on Thera, a Setter who'd controlled lava, light, and water. In her lifetime she resolved four conflicts before they could descend into war.

"It's kind of like... there's a problem, and a prophecy describes the best way to fix it," I explained, petting him as he curled up next to me.

"Oh," Coffin said, yawning. *"Bewares da thorny nose. Beware the heart who rose.* How is dats helpful?"

"I'm not sure," I said, chuckling. I closed my book, placing it on the side table. "Maybe we should sleep on it."

"Yes!" Coffin yipped. "Sleep is good!"

I grabbed Coffin's morphing collar and tightened it around his neck. The past few nights he'd been morphing in his sleep, so he'd started wearing his collar to bed. I blew my candle out, the thin ribbon of smoke curling to the ceiling. I leaned back in my bed, Coffin springing off of my legs and landing in his collection of blankets by the foot. I pulled the sheets in and fell asleep.

.<>.

"Get him, now!" a voice hissed. My eyes darted open for a moment before a pair of hands clamped themselves

over my eyes and mouth. Another pair pushed my shoulders into my bed, my flailing feet not catching on anything.

"Get the sedative!" another voice hissed. I heard the sound of someone fumbling with a glass vial, their footsteps creaking across the ground as they walked towards me. I tried to scream as the thin neck of a vial was pressed between my lips, a burning liquid dripping down into my throat. Someone plugged my nose, forcing me to swallow the burning liquid. My skin suddenly started to turn numb everywhere the liquid had touched, my arms and legs drooping.

"Quickly, we need to get him out of here," the first voice hissed.

"No," another voice said sharply. "We have another option."

"What?" the first voiced asked. Starting from my stomach, a warm, buzzing numbness began to seep into my muscles and bones.

"The wolf has also seen it, I can see it in his memories too," the second voice said. "He will be easier to contain, and there is a lesser chance of them coming after us than if we take the Balancer."

"But I thought the Emperor—

"Trust me, taking the wolf now is going to help in the long run. The Balancer knows but so does the wolf," the second voice interrupted. Why were they talking about Coffin? I suddenly panicked, remembering how I had put his morphing collar on right before bed. He couldn't fight back!

"Are you certain?" the first voice asked. He sounded quieter, the numbness nearly up to my neck. I felt the room begin to spin.

"Yes, we need to go, now," the second voice said. I was suddenly released, but I couldn't open my eyelids. I squirmed, only my fingers and toes still moving. I heard a yelp as something grabbed Coffin, then nothing.

The smell of smoke filled my room as it spun one final time, before spinning away into darkness.

.<>.

I'm not really sure when I woke up. I could feel the sunlight and see it faintly through my closed eyelids when the sedative had worn off enough for me to be conscious. At that point, I could hear people rushing around me, their voices all weird and distorted. I remember deliriously finding their voices hilarious. More time passed, and I started to make out words. They were worried about me. They were pretty sure it was a sedative that was keeping me from waking up. A few people were wondering where Coffin was. I opened my eyes before I could open my mouth, and even then, it was a while before I could speak.

Around dinnertime, I finally felt alert enough to hold a conversation. I'd been left alone for a while in my bedroom until Kiahta came in.

"Samson," he said, bowing as he entered the room. "How are you feeling?"

"I still can't really feel my legs, or most of my arms," I said, trying and failing to shrug. "Has anyone seen Coffin?"

227

"We were very worried when we heard you weren't waking up," he said, ignoring my question about Coffin. "Might I ask what happened last night?"

"I can, but has anyone seen Coffin?" I asked again, trying to sound insistent but the sedative still slurring my words.

"Please, if this was some sort of foul play by upset air people, we need to know so we can punish the guilty party," Kiahta insisted. "Do you know who gave you the sedative?"

"I..." I tried to remember from last night, but my memories were also muddled. "They pinned me down."

"Who?" Kiahta asked.

"I don't know," I said, again trying to shrug. "They gave me the sedative, and then were going to take me, but I think they ended up taking Coffin instead."

"Who is... Coffin?" Kiahta asked. I tried to roll my eyes.

"My morphing wolf," I said. "The one who sometimes comes to training? They took him."

"Who are *they*?" he asked, leaning forward. He was still ignoring Coffin.

"I... they mentioned the 'Emperor,' so I think they at least work for Emperor Conner," I said. "But then after they left, I smelled smoke."

"The fire magic teleportation spell turns the user into a plume of smoke," Kiahta said. "These weren't some air people mercenaries; these were *actual* fire people."

"And they took Coffin," I insisted. "That's what I'm trying to tell you. They took Coffin."

"Do you know why they would take it?" Kiahta asked, finally somewhat acknowledging Coffin.

"They said... I can't really remember... something about him having seen... it," I said.

"It?"

"I don't know," I said. "They said that I 'knew' and so did Coffin, but Coffin was easier to control so they took him."

"Do you know what they were referring to?" Kiahta asked.

"No, but there must be some sort of information we both have," I said.

"And now that information is in the hands of the fire people," Kiahta said, grimacing. "I'm sorry, I should never have shown you the prophecy or the carvings or anything besides plant magic. I promise we'll scale back your training for now."

He stood up, tidying the hem of his robe.

"The sedative should have worn off by tomorrow, so I think we could begin working on trees," he said.

"Wait, but what about Coffin?" I asked, my chest twitching.

"I'm afraid there's nothing I can do," Kiahta said. "I'm an air person. I cannot chase after the property of a water person just because it was stolen by a fire person. Even if that property knows something about the war that could help the other side, I am powerless to intervene."

He was just going to leave Coffin? He was in captivity of the fire people! And he was going to ignore it just because he had to be neutral? He was going to let Coffin, who he kept calling my 'property,' be captured just because of some outdated moral code.

"You..." I grimaced, trying not to yell. I kept my voice low, but powerful. I called up the cold anger Maddie had taught me.

"You might be an air person, so you can't act," I said, "but I am a water person. And I choose to go save Coffin."

"But Samson, you must be trained in your duties as a Balancer," he said. "You must remain in Aetheopolis."

"You don't have power over me," I said. "You cannot force me to stay here, and you cannot keep your morals while forcing me to give up mine."

"No," Kiahta said. "I'm going to go talk to your father and see what he has to say about this."

He disappeared into the doorway, leaving me alone for a few minutes. Suddenly, Dad burst through the door.

230

"Samz," he said, looking down at me. "Kiahta told me what you said."

"I... I'm sorry I got mad at him—

"We need to respect that he is an air person and must follow the values of his element," he said sternly. He suddenly knelt down beside my bed and placed his hand on mine.

"However."

He looked up at me, grinning.

"He needs to respect that we are water people, and we must follow the values of our element," he said. "Coffin is a part of you. I promise, your family will help you get him back. Because unlike air people, we can *choose*."

"Dad," I said, a tear forming in my eye. He smiled, chuckling.

"Do you mind that I kind of stole that line about morals and being a water person?" he asked.

"It's fine," I said, smiling.

"When Kiahta told me you said that, I was so proud of you," he said. "You're growing into a fine young water person."

"Thanks, Dad," I said, as he hugged me. "Coffin knows something, something big enough for fire people to want to capture him."

"We'll find out what it is, I'm sure of it," Dad said. "Kiahta told me that whatever it is, you know it too."

"I know," I said. "But still, even if we have the information, so does Coffin. We need to get to him before the fire people get it out of him."

"From what I've seen from that wolf, it won't be easy for them," Dad said. "We're going to save him. I promise."

I'm going to save Coffin, I thought, *no matter what.*

THE CITY IN THE GROUND

The letter came nearly a day after we told Kiahta we were leaving Aetheopolis. We were at breakfast, Professor Martin and Mrs. Kilting squabbling while Simon brought the mail in.

"Hey, this one's for you," he said, pulling one out of the stack, just as Mrs. Kilting wacked Martin on the head with her broom, the gust of wind clattering through our plates and blowing out the candle in the middle of the table. I took the letter, a name scrawled on the front.

"It's another letter from Jack," I said. Jamie and Kiefer suddenly leaned in from either side of me, their eyes wide.

"Another?" Kiefer asked, his mouth still full of eggs.

"When did you get the first one?" Jamie asked. "Why did he send you a letter? How did he send you one, all the way from the Earth Territories?"

"How did he know to send it *here?*" Kiefer said, snatching the letter. The address of the Kilting's was written across the front, my name underneath. I grabbed it back.

"I mean, he knew I was in Wateria, so I guess he's just good at finding people," I said.

"He was in *Wateria?* Jamie asked.

"I thought I told you guys," I lied. I hadn't told anyone about Jack giving me the letter, because the story involved admitting that he had somehow gotten past the guards and into my room, without anyone noticing. Yet another weird thing that still didn't make sense.

"I think I would remember you getting a letter from an earth person," Kiefer said. "And no offense, I never would have thought that he could afford to send a letter."

"That *is* a little offensive," Jamie said, giving him a judgmental look as she took another bite of her eggs.

"How do you know it's offensive? You're not Jack!" Kiefer said, rolling his eyes.

"Well, usually assumptions based on class structures, especially from someone like you who benefits from his class, are offensive," Jamie said.

"How about I just read the letter," I said, scooting my chair in between them. I opened the envelope and pulled out the note.

"*Dear Samson,*

I hope this letter finds you well, if at all. Aetheopolis is not the easiest place to reach by letter if you can imagine. Anyway, I was just in Wateria to give that book back to you, but when I got there, I found out that you'd left to go to the air people's capital (does it suck? It does, doesn't it? Air people are the worst). I kept the book with me, just so I can bring it to you once you go back to Wateria. Or, if you can, you could even come to Ar Shaa. My family just moved there, and I can give you your book back and we can talk about the project it helped me with.

From,

Jack," I read. Jamie and Kiefer sat back in their chairs.

"So Jack, an earth person living in poverty, sent a definitely very expensive letter to the capital of the air people... to return a book and ask to hang out?" Jamie said. "...what?"

"Well, he kind of... I wouldn't really say *broke* into as much as *sneaked* into Wateria to borrow the—

"Hold on, hold on, hold on," Kiefer said, leaning forward, grabbing the table.

"Jack *broke* into Wateria to borrow a book from you?" Jamie said

"Awesome," Kiefer said. Jamie smacked his shoulder.

"No, not *awesome*. Weird and... unnecessary," Jamie said. "What *project* was he working on? Why did he need to break into Wateria to take a book?"

"He said that he was doing research because he found out that Mark was the last Setter," I said. "Which I guess makes sense now. Mark was the last Setter because his death allowed us to be the second Balancers."

"What was the book even about?" Jamie asked.

"The Balancers," I said. It was weird how something that had stressed me out a few weeks ago now made perfect sense.

"Do you... no, that's impossible," Kiefer said, waving his thought away.

"No, what is it?" I asked. Kiefer shrugged.

"Could he have known that we were the Balancers?" Kiefer pointed out. "Think about it. Why would he have taken the book about the Balancers if he didn't know they were back?"

"He might have just known that the Balancers and Setters were related," Jamie said.

"I think Kiefer might have a point," I said. "He might not have known that *we* were the Balancers, but he was definitely doing an investigation to see if there *were* Balancers."

"And," Kiefer said, jumping in before Jamie could say anything. "If he has all the research about the Setters and the Balancers, maybe we could learn more about ourselves from him."

Jamie thought for a moment.

"Ar Shaa," she said, taking the letter. "That's the capital of the Earth Territories. It's underground."

"And...?" Kiefer and I both asked.

"That line of the prophecy," Jamie said. "*Go to the caves.*"

"But I thought we were looking for Coffin," Kiefer said, glancing at me. They both looked at me, waiting for an answer.

I wanted to find Coffin, that was true. However, we had no idea where he was, and sitting in Aetheopolis wasn't going to make us any closer to finding him. Just getting out of the city would take us one step closer. Also, we were all tired of the way the priests were teaching us how to be Balancers. If Jack had information about us and our predecessors, it could help us. And of course, the line from

236

the prophecy said to *"go to the caves."* If it was in the prophecy, that meant going there would help lead to the best future.

"We should go to Ar Shaa," I said. "Then look for Coffin. I mean, we're not going to be there for that long, right?"

.<>.

Once everything came into place, getting to Ar Shaa actually didn't take that long. It was getting out of Aetheopolis that cost us almost two weeks of time. While the priests weren't exactly happy that Jamie, Kiefer and I were leaving, they were more than eager to get the rest of my family out. They didn't seem to understand that all of us should leave, and not leave the Balancers behind to train. I barely saw Kiahta and the other air priests myself, most of the arguing done by Dad, Mrs. Kilting, Martin, and even Maddie a few times. Each day I became more worried about Coffin and less sure that going to Ar Shaa was worth it.

Finally though, after struggling to get out of the grasp of the air mages, we found ourselves loading our stuff onto one of Martin's airships. This one was much larger than the cloud-skier I had come in on, the prow much more prominent and the wings wider. This one was parked near the edge of the city, alongside a fleet of other airships in various stages of completion. The air priests had allowed Professor Martin to use the yard to experiment as long as he made enough airships for their purposes as well.

"I think that's the last one," Kiefer said, passing me the last bag from the stack. I wiped the sweat off the back of my neck. The day was hot and sweltering, Aetheopolis having drifted closer to the equator since we'd arrived. Our assembly line dissolved as we climbed in through the back hatch, into the spacious interior of the airship. On the opposite end of the airship, Martin was up on a raised chair, an array of wheels and levers spread out before him.

"Simon! Close the hatch!" he shouted. Kiefer and I stepped in, Simon pulling his hands down. A gust of wind pulled the back hatch into place. Simon and Mrs. Kilting walked around our pile of bags to the front of the airship, positioning themselves on either side of Martin.

"Everyone! Buckle yourselves onto the airship!" Martin yelled out, pulling a few wheels taut. Two benches lined the interior of the airship, periodically marked by buckles attached to straps. I sat down between Jamie and Kiefer.

"Ready?" Martin called out to his wife and nephew.

"Ready," Simon said.

"Whatever," Mrs. Kilting said, readying her broom.

"On three," Martin said, throwing two wheels into a spin. "One... two... three..."

Simon and Mrs. Kilting both shouted a spell at the same time, Simon throwing his hands out while Mrs. Kilting slashed her broom forward. A torrent of wind launched the airship forward, the bottom scraping towards the edge as it tried to lift off.

"Lift up! Lift up!" Martin shouted. Straining, Mrs. Kilting used her broom to stir the currents below the airship, while Simon continued to push it forward. Suddenly, the airship dipped over the edge, the nose facing the dark ground thousands of feet below. My stomach dropped, Kiefer grabbing my shirt. We hung there for just a moment, Mrs. Kitling and Simon quickly pulling us upright and off of the ledge. Martin furiously pulled a few more levers, until the airship settled down and we began to softly descend.

"Alright, about four hours until we reach Ar Shaa," Martin said. We looked back through the small opening along the back hatch.

Slowly, the city in the sky disappeared into the blue.

.<>.

Several hours later, the Kiltings brought the airship down into the middle of a rocky desert. We unpacked all of our bags from the airship, gathering on the burning ground. We had flown closer to the equator, and the sun shone much harder than it had in the Water Kingdom. After we got all of our stuff off, we said goodbye to the Kiltings. They flew off, leaving us in the middle of the desert.

"So... where's the city?" Miles asked, after the Kiltings had disappeared from sight.

"Below our feet, actually," Dad said, stomping on the ground with one foot. "Like we are at our most powerful when fully submerged in water, the air people are more powerful the higher their altitude, earth people are at their most powerful underground. They built their capital underground so, in case of an attack, their magic would be at its strongest to defend it."

"Okay," Miles said, pursing his lips. "So... how do we get there?"

"Any minute now," Dad said, looking at the ground. "There are certain earth people that are extra sensitive to vibrations in the ground. In our correspondence, they told me that they would have a few on standby to notify a welcoming committee when we arrived."

"So how long will—

Two huge slabs of rock broke apart and lifted out of the ground, cutting Miles off. A trio of earth people emerged from the hole.

Unlike the willowy and ethereal air people, the earth people were stocky and tough. One, wearing a crown of bristling crystals, stepped forward, the two guards on either side of him assuming wide, low earth magic attack stances.

"Chieftain," Dad said, bowing to him. "It is an honor to meet with you."

"Indeed," the Chieftain said. "I hear that you have business here in Ar Shaa, after your visit to Aetheopolis?"

"Yes, I do," Dad said, straightening up. The Chieftain cocked an eyebrow.

"Hmm," he said. "If there's one thing I know about water people, they always have an ulterior motive. You must understand my suspicion, as you have just come directly from the capital of the air people."

"I promise you Chieftain, we are not agents of the air people," Dad said. "You must know that one of the main values of water people is independence."

"Hrmm," the Chieftain said, scratching his chin. "Fine. Come in."

"Thank you," Dad said, bowing. Kiefer and I glanced at each other, as the earth people led us down into the city of Ar Shaa.

We descended for several minutes before we emerged into the underground city, instantly illuminated by an array of glowing crystals. Crystals of every color illuminated the three-dimensional city. The cavern stretched farther than any of us could see, stalactites dripping with earth people dwelling obscuring its true boundaries. Streets lay stacked upon each other, suspended walkways connecting countless levels of the city. The bustling sound of the thousands of earth people all around us echoed loudly through the cavern.

"Now, these men will take you to Jack's house, while I discuss matters with the Chieftain," Dad said, motioning us to a few guards that had arrived. Silently, they led us through the streets while Dad and the Chieftain began to walk down the main thoroughfare to the palace at the center of Ar Shaa.

The guards led us through the streets that stretched into midair and curled around great columns of stone. Bats soared above, while strange, white-eyed fish swam in the waterways. The earth people barely seemed to notice us, most of them continuing to go about their business. Even after spending over a month in Aetheopolis we still had gotten stares from air people.

Finally, we reached the edge of the cavern, where a huge wall of stone stretched up towards the surface. A small street, only a few feet wide, clung to the edge of the cavern, small dwellings punched into the wall along its length. The guards led us single-file down the tiny street until we reached a simple wooden door carved into the side of the cavern. Maddie approached and knocked it.

The door swung inward, revealing a young man with curly brown hair and a bony frame. He looked down at us with his strikingly dark eyes, a smile breaking across his usually weary face.

"What are you guys doing here?" Jack smiled. "It's been forever!"

He let us into his tiny home, our family alone taking up most of the main room. A fire crackled merrily in the fireplace, a few children playing around it. The walls and ground were made up of the same stone as the cavern.

"Mom! The Almas are here!" Jack called, leaning his head through a doorway to the right. The rest of us came in and started to mingle with the family members spread about the room. Jack approached me.

"It's been such a long time," he said. "I have your book."

"Oh, thanks," I said. "I was going to ask about that."

"Could I... pull you aside? To talk about it?" he asked, cocking his head towards the door. "I have all of my stuff in one of the tunnels surrounding the city. I can explain it better if I have all of my research."

"Okay," I said, glancing back at my family. It felt a little weird leaving them here, but I had to find out why Jack had gone all the way to Wateria to borrow a book.

"Great," Jack said. "Let's go."

.<>.

Jack led me lower and lower into the city until we reached a tunnel at the end of a road. We took a few turns through the tunnel until we reached a certain point where Jack stopped.

"Where's your research?" I asked.

"Mostly in my head," he said. "I just wanted to bring you here, so we wouldn't get interrupted. I love my siblings and all, but they can—

"I get it," I said.

"Right."

"So, what was the project you were working on?" I asked, sitting down on a shelf of stone. Jack paused. "You said you wanted to talk to me about it? And you came all the way to Wateria to get a book from me, so..."

"Right," Jack said, turning back. "Well, you remember what I said in the letter. Mark was the last Setter."

"I remember," I said, shrugging. "I guess the part that I don't get is how you found that out in the first place."

I also didn't get why he had to come all the way to Wateria and leave his impoverished family for a book, but that question was a bit too loaded to start out the conversation with.

"This is going to need a little bit of background," Jack said, sitting down across from me. "It's kind of a long story, are you sure you want to hear it?"

"Yes," I said, sitting up straight. Jack smiled.

"Good," he said. "The first Balancers came into power because of a war. The Arken War."

"I thought it was the Catacomb War?" I asked. Jack shrugged.

"It has many names, one of them being the Catacomb War, as your people call it," Jack said.

"Yeah, I read a book about that. Or at least, I tried to," I admitted. The version Erin had picked out for me was written in such an old style of Andlurran it was almost impossible to understand and completely impossible to stay captivated by. I gave up about a quarter of the way through before the Balancers were even mentioned.

"Well, the war began because of a simple land dispute," Jack said. "The fire people, peaceful at that time, owned an island in the Great Ocean. However, the storm people, who at the time lived on the same continent as the fire people, also claimed ownership of the island. The dispute led to a costly battle between the fire people and the storm people."

I vaguely remembered this part. It was the first part of the actual battles of the war, the first few chapters of the book having tediously discussed the context of Inner World politics that contributed to the Catacomb War.

"There were so many dead, that the fire people created a deep tunnel on the island with enough space to properly honor each of the fallen," Jack explained. "They called these the Catacombs of Nar Shaa.

"The Catacombs became an incredibly popular place to bury the dead, its tunnels rapidly expanding. People even began to use the tunnels as links between cities, increasing the demand for more Catacombs to be built," Jack said. This was the part when I'd finally put the book down. It had gone through almost every instance of some random fire town requesting to be connected to the Catacombs and how they went about building it and so on. "However, some of the tunnels began to stray too close to the territory of the lava people. Unnerved by the proximity of the fire people, they attacked the Catacombs and took the network for themselves. As they expanded the Catacombs south into their territory, they renamed it Alune Shaa.

"Years later, the Coral Union began to spread across the Great Ocean. As their strength and confidence grew, they sought to find a way to exercise power over the fire and lava people they were encountering. After finding out about the existence of the Catacombs, they bided their time until they were strong enough to take them from the lava people. The now Catacombs of Lanrun Shaa began to stretch across the Great Ocean, from the eastern lands of the fire and lava people to the western reefs near the capital of the Coral Union.

"However, the coral people knew that both the fire people and the lava people had lost the Catacombs. Not wanting to make the same mistake, they decided to build a city that all the tunnels of Lanrun Shaa would flow into.

"Unfortunately for the coral people, the darkness people had begun to set their eyes on taking the Catacombs," he continued. It was hard keeping track of all of the countries trying to get to the Catacombs, but Jack has gotten so into telling the story I didn't want to interrupt him.

"They made a deal with the lava people, to help them take the Catacombs back. Together, the darkness and the lava people overtook the Catacombs, the tunnels now stretching all the way to where the Water Kingdom now is," Jack said. "However, just before they had driven the last of the coral people out, the darkness people broke their promise with the lava people. Taking the Catacombs for themselves, the darkness people successfully built the city of Ultone Shaa, connected to the Catacombs," Jack said. "Are you following this?"

"I..." I paused for a moment. "A bunch of countries wanted tunnels to bury people in? But most people just use them to get around most of the world at this point? I think...? And now there's a city that the darkness people built. Is that right?"

"Close enough," Jack said, shrugging. "Just to review, we have the fire people, the storm people, the coral people, the lava people, and the darkness people connected to the Catacombs."

"So... I'm *guessing* that meant...war? Probably?" I guessed.

"Exactly," Jack said. "The previous owners of the Catacombs, except for the fire people, teamed up. The darkness people chose a few allies to fight. And a third side of bystanders rose up to try to stop them from fighting, that coalition being led by the earth people."

"So who won? And what does this have to do with the Balancers?" I asked.

"Well, halfway through the war, the Untamable Mights came into being, destroying most of the Fire Kingdom," Jack explained. "After they came to life, most of the war became concentrated on stopping them."

Jack looked at my hand and the symbol.

"The Balancers rose out of the ashes of the Fire Kingdom, and they trapped the Untamable Mights. The war ended in the City of Ultone Shaa, where they captured Power," Jack said. He suddenly stood up and looked down the tunnel.

He turned back to me, his eyes cold.

"But they shouldn't have."

"What?" I hissed, my heart jumping. What did he *mean* the first Balancers shouldn't have captured the Mights? He turned back to me, his face devoid of emotion. The shadows suddenly seemed longer than they had a moment before.

"The first Balancers made a mistake," Jack said, his fist clenching momentarily. "This project that I've been working on... you can help me fix their mistake."

"Jack, what are you talking about? Fix what?" I asked, shrinking back into the cold stone of the tunnel. He held his hand out.

"The Mights are far more powerful than the Balancers. Their abilities can change the world much more than your elements can," he said, his voice suddenly hopeful. "They are trapped... but you, the Balancer of Plants, can free them."

"Free the Mights? Jack, they're evil I can't..." I trailed off. Besides the fact that he had just told me to free the Mights, he'd also called me Balancer.

I had never mentioned being a Balancer to him.

Before I could puzzle over how he knew I was a Balancer, he continued talking.

"Is that what the air priests told you? What do they know?" he scoffed, his hand dropping. "They fear power and think any form of it is inherently bad. The Mights are powerful but they can be used for good."

"Jack, I can't," I said, shaking my head. "Why... who... how did you... Why did you leave your family to... learn all of this?"

Jack grinned.

"The water people would never help me with something like this," he said, still smiling. "So, there was only one other place I could turn to."

"You..." I felt like the cave was shrinking, the walls suffocating me.

248

"You're working for the fire people."

Jack grinned, a cocky, toothy, terrible grin.

"Of course," he said. "They listen to me, I help them, and they pay me handsomely."

"Jack, you can't trust the fire people," I said, standing up.

"I've trusted them for years and all they've done is help me," he said. "They appreciate my talents. I'm an asset to them."

"I thought you never learned earth magic," I said. Jack rolled his eyes.

"I did, but that's not the magic they need me for," he said. "*Beware the one who hears the heart, beware the thorny rose.* We have both of those right here."

"You know the prophecy?" I hissed. Jack crossed his arms. He knew the prophecy *and* he knew I was a Balancer? "But... it was just us in that garden. Who told it to you?"

"*Beware the power of the spell,* still not sure about that one, although I do agree it probably refers to that accident Kiefer got into. It could have killed him and you would have lost the Balancer of Lightning," he said. "*Beware the one who knows,* well, I've had a lovely time getting to know *him* over the past two weeks."

"Jack what are you..."

Two weeks. Coffin had been taken two weeks ago.

And Coffin had seen the prophecy.

"Coffin is the one who knows?" I asked.

"Correct, thorny rose," he said.

"And you?"

"Yes?"

"You're the one who hears the heart?" I said. "What does that mean?"

"It means I can sneak past Waterian guards because they never remember seeing me. It means I can tell fire people exactly where you're hiding in the woods outside Wateria," Jack said. "It means I can pluck the memory of a prophecy from the mind of a morphing wolf."

I stepped backward. What was happening?

"The Setters are not the only beings to pass their abilities down through the ages," he said. "There is another power."

"You... you knew I was a Balancer without me telling you," I said. "I haven't mentioned it this entire conversation."

"Yes, I do realize I perhaps blew my cover a bit," Jack said. "But I knew you'd figure it out eventually."

"You can read and... manipulate minds," I said, stepping back. "But I thought you were an earth person. I thought only coral people could—

"Coral people can erase small memories, nothing compared to what I am capable of," Jack said. "They cannot read and change thoughts, they cannot have complete control over another."

"But that's impossible, there's no such thing as—

"It's not impossible," Jack said, flexing his fingers. "In fact, it should help everything make sense, as you so desperately want it to."

My heart dropped. There was no other way he could have known that. He was a mind reader.

"There's no time for that now," Jack said, pulling something from his bag. It was one of Dad's crowns, the simple golden ring he often wore around his head.

"I must be going soon, so I'll leave you with this," Jack said. "So you don't try to follow me, I'm going to activate a little curse. The Untamable Might of Domination cursed the Catacombs to become unstable every time a leader's symbol of power was destroyed."

He threw the crown onto the ground with one hand, and with the other, he tore a chunk of rock out of the wall. He thrust it down, the stone breaking Dad's crown in half. Rumbles suddenly began to echo down the tunnel.

"Now, since you have refused my offer, my orders are this," Jack said, gathering his bag. "Come to the Basin of Betrayal in three days, or your morphing wolf is killed."

"Jack," I croaked. Cracks began to form along the ceiling, dust and rock chips raining down.

"I'm sorry," he said, shrugging. "Your family visited me and yet, you never gave my family any money. You had the power to help us and you let us struggle. Where did you think I was going to turn?"

"I thought we were friends," I said, my eyes stinging with tears. Jack laughed, his voice cold and hollow.

"And I never thought you were so naïve," he said. "Well, until next time!"

The tunnel suddenly broke into a thousand pieces, the torches snuffing out as I plunged into darkness.

THE CATACOMBS OF NALUR SHAA

My eyes opened to darkness. I was freezing, cold shards of stone covering me up to my waist. I held a hand up, checking to see how close the ceiling was. My hand waved through the void. Slowly, I pulled my legs out of the pile of rocks, most of them sliding away, down some unseen slope. My back trembling, I stood up, waving my hand through the air so I didn't bump into anything. Finally, I was standing.

"Hello?!" I shouted. My voice echoed sharply, reverberating down some unseen tunnel. No one responded. "Hello?! Is anyone there? Hello?!"

I don't know how long I shouted. Being in complete darkness completely threw off my sense of time. I was cold, starving, bruised, and completely alone.

"No one's here," I muttered to myself, my chest caving in. I dropped onto the broken stones, trying to take in deep breaths. I was alone. No one knew where I was. I didn't know where I was. I could have been in the same tunnel Jack and I had been in, or miles underground.

Jack had mind powers? How was that even possible? The only explanation was that he was half coral person, but even then, any memory manipulation magic he got would have been diluted by earth magic. And as Jack said, not even a full-blooded coral person could read minds. Whatever magic Jack had had come from... somewhere else.

I never would have been in that tunnel if I'd never met Jack. I never would have met Jack if Mom hadn't just disappeared. Jack would never have attacked me if I wasn't a Balancer.

Why am I a Balancer?

I'd never been given a choice. No one ever asked me if I wanted to learn plant magic and stop the Untamable Mights. Why did *I* have to do it? What had I done to deserve that responsibility?

I sat down, a few rocks scattering down the tunnel.

"I don't want to be a Balancer," I said. All my life, all I ever wanted was to be unnoticed. All nine of my other siblings had caused Dad enough stress that in everything I tried to do I tried to attract the least attention. To be simple and normal. To not cause trouble. The only reason Maddie ever got mad at me was that I never told her if I was hurting.

Now, there was no hiding. The sole fact of my existence pushed me into the spotlight wherever I went. Whether it was air priests that always found it 'an honor to guide me' or earth people who kidnapped my friends just to manipulate me, people would have whole agendas about me just because of my status. It would never matter what my personality, history or abilities were, from now on, being a Balancer was going to affect how everyone treated me.

It was happening already. Dad had moved our whole family out of Aetheopolis just because Jamie, Kiefer and I thought that there might be some answers to the prophecy in Ar Shaa. Family members who had known me my entire life already were treating me differently because my identity had become the Balancer of Plants.

It's like I'm being erased, I thought. *It's never going to be like before.*

But...

Before finding out the truth about my identity, I was always confused. Those months in Wateria had been so bad I ran away from home and almost got captured by fire people. Now that I knew, things would be better.

Or they could be worse.

Now that I knew things, I knew that there were people all over the world that would want me for their own purposes. I knew that the Fire Emperor had started a war because of me. Now that I knew who I was, I would always know about the danger always surrounding me.

"Ugh," I said, standing up. Worrying about being a Balancer wasn't going to change the fact that I was stuck alone, in pitch darkness with no ideas of how to escape. The cave didn't care about me being a Balancer.

I slowly started to walk forward, my feet sinking down into the pebbles and shards of stone. Every now and then, the whole pile trembled as cascades of stone dribbled down the tunnel. I kept one of my hands waving above my head, making sure that I wouldn't hit my head on a ceiling. Slowly, my eyes adjusted to the darkness enough to barely make out my own body parts.

I stepped on the wrong stone. My leg dove into the rocks, the pile pulling me down a sudden sharp decline in the tunnel. I screamed, trying to grab onto anything, but it was all just falling rocks. The ground disappeared, throwing me into a cascade of earth.

A moment later I landed on my side, sharply crying out. I clutched my ribs as they roared with pain. Warm blood seeped from my shoulder and into my robe. More rocks fell around me, small shards starting to bury my legs and lower torso. I pushed against the tide, trying to pull myself out of the rocks, but my bad shoulder gave out, leaving me half tangled in stone.

The rocks finally settled, and I was able to pull myself out of them once again. I dusted myself off, checking the rest of my body for injury. My right leg had also been hurt by the fall. Grimacing, I started to limp forward. Now I was on solid stone, no more piles of pebbles to navigate.

The darkness took away all sense of time. I could have been wandering for an hour, half a day, or even ten minutes. It was too slow for me to really notice, but light suddenly began to glow ahead. The tunnel became less jagged and random, clean lines cut into the stone. Finally, I came around a neatly cut corner and found the source of the light.

In front of me, an empty archway stood. Rusted metals with gold accents still shining brightly wove around the archway. Within, an unearthly golden-yellow glow shone from glowing crystals growing along the cracks. The same crystals had been cut and refined to display words along the top edge of the arch:

The Catacombs of Nalur Shaa

.<>.

Limping, covering in stone dust, and grabbing my right side, I hobbled into the Catacombs. Along the walls, ancient drawers marked with archaic names periodically disrupted the sharply cut rock of the tunnel. In the first hallway they were all the same, but as time went by and I explored more branches of the Catacombs, I found some were more ornate, and I even saw a few with a whole antechamber before a locked door where the body was held. The Catacombs were silent, even more so than the cave.

Eventually, I turned into a new section of the hallway and stopped cold. The tunnel had been torn apart by battle. Cooled flows of lava melted through several drawers, interspersed with columns of ancient, white, petrified coral. Broken pieces of armor lay shattered by spears of coral or melted into the cooled lava. I carefully sidestepped through the wreckage, only finding more the farther I went through this new part of the Catacombs. The coral and the lava people had left the biggest mark on the Catacombs. Burn marks would have faded, darkness was intangible, and storms would have dissipated. But lava cooled into rock, and coral left shards of white stone.

Going through the Catacombs felt surreal, like I was partially in a dream. It might have been from the unearthly glow of the yellow crystals. It could have been from the perfectly preserved battle. It could have even been from the fact that something that had been told to me as almost a legend was actually real. Whatever it was, it numbed the pain in my ribs and my legs and lulled my mind into a thoughtless blur.

.<>.

Some unknown time had passed, but I had left the site of the coral versus lava battle, and gone into a relatively unscathed hallway. An intersection opened into a high ceiling chamber, a large chandelier of branching crystals growing down. I was looking up at the chandelier of crystals that I tripped on something small and wooden, nearly decking myself. I steadied myself and looked down at what I had tripped over.

It was a small wooden box, with the emblem of the fire people burned onto the top. I picked up the box, a few small objects rolling around inside. It was new; fire people had been here recently. Inside was a bruised apple and a few strips of half-eaten dry meat. The food was relatively fresh! Forgetting about the fact that fire people had gone through this part of the tunnel recently, I ate the entire apple and all of the meat. The meat was harder to get down, as I hadn't had anything to drink in a while. I'd tried a few times to produce water from nothing, but I didn't have my water staff and wasn't skilled enough to do it on my own. I kept the seeds of the apple in my pocket, so I would have some plants with me in case of a fight.

After my hunger subsided a tiny bit, I looked closer at the box and the intersection. There was nothing remarkable about the box, but after a few minutes of inspection, I found that the fire people had created burn marks on the sides of the walls inside the tunnels. They must have been marking the hallways they went through so they couldn't get lost. I could follow the fire people!

No, I can't follow the fire people, I remembered. I was injured, still hungry, dehydrated and I could fight with the only element I had with me, a few apple seeds. There was absolutely no way I could fight them off if I actually found them. Following their trail, I could either go in their direction or the exact opposite.

However, maybe there would be others looking for the fire people, following their trail. This part of the Catacombs was close to the Earth Territories, so there were probably earth people in charge of making sure it wasn't invaded. They would probably notice fire people sneaking around, and go after them.

I found a comfortable nook and rested my head on a stone. I decided to wait there for someone chasing the fire people to find me. Even if there was no one coming to look for the fire people, I needed to rest. My exhaustion immediately caught up with the rest of my body, and within minutes I was asleep.

.<>.

My vision was covered by a film of deep blue.

I saw an older man with a beard, his fingers laced together and placed on a large desk in front of him. Behind him, two large windows showed a sprawling town made out of gray stone. A woman sat across from the man, a stack of papers in her hand. She quickly flicked through them, reading off quotes.

"Here it says that we cannot get more fertilizer until we send fifty men to go fight or soldiers from our province capture twenty-five water people," the woman read, holding up and official document and placing it on the desk. "We have three troops that are close to the front lines that might be able to capture at least a few water people."

"Perhaps if we ask for less fertilizer, they'll lower the amount of water people our men need to capture and we can at least get something for our people," the man said, wearily wiping his forehead. "We can't afford to send any more men to go fight, not now."

"I'll prepare a request for half as much fertilizer," the woman said, scribbling a note on a sheet of paper beside her.

"Have they responded to the request for livestock from the Lianes islands?"

She flicked through the pages and pulled out another, older one.

"Your request to have more livestock imported from the south was met by a request for more armor produced by our blacksmiths," she read. "And even if we do get them that armor, they can only send us half as much livestock as we requested."

"That can't be right, they know we're out of ore," the man said, looking down at his desk. He turned over a few papers, shaking his head. He gave up, dropping his hands on the desk.

"That's absurd, did they not get the request saying we needed more ore to actually make the armor they want?" the man said, leaning forward. The woman flipped through the pages again, pulling out a few pages clipped together.

"They did," she said, placing it on the desk. "And in response, they said you can have all the ore you need if you bring the age for advanced fire magic training down to eleven."

"Eleven?" the man breathed, his eyes widening. "I cannot do that to the youth of my province. Even if I was okay to lowering the age to eleven, I don't have enough fire masters to teach them because they're all off fighting in the war!"

"Governor, if we can lower the age of advanced fire magic training, then we can get the ore to make the armor to get more livestock," the woman said, keeping her voice as low and as calm as possible. The man took in a deep breath, closing his eyes. "I know it's not ideal, but doing so will get us at least some relief."

"Has the Emperor said anything else about these requests?" he asked, gritting his teeth.

"Well, in all of the responses, they mentioned provinces that have complied with similar regulations," the woman said, holding up the papers that were clipped together. "The Karn Shaa province agreed to lower the age of advanced training, and in the months since the government has provided them with enough resources to bring back their lumber industry."

"Hmm..." the man said, spreading the papers out on his desk. "Julia, please have a staffer draft a letter to the Governor of the Karn Shaa Province, and ask him for advice on how he dealt with lowering the age of advanced training. I want it in Aneta within the week."

"Yes sir," the woman, Julia, said. She stood up and marched out of the room. The man, left alone, began to rub his temples.

"Please," he muttered, before falling silent.

.<>.

"Samz! *Samz!*" Jamie said, shaking my shoulder. I blearily opened my eyes, my vision immediately was overtaken by waves of purple light coming from Jamie's hands.

"Get him some water!" someone, I think Miles, said. My cuts melted away, while my ribs and leg simply dulled away into a low ache. My vision began to sharpen, and I saw Miles pull a length of water out of a pouch strapped to his back.

"Ready?" he asked. I opened my mouth, and he gently floated the water into it. My body greedily gulped the water down, my muscles relaxing. I stopped, Jamie and Luke helping me to my feet. In the intersection stood all of my siblings. Dad was nowhere to be seen.

"What are you guys doing here?" I croaked. Maddie stepped to the front.

"Fire people attacked Ar Shaa right after you left with Jack," Maddie explained. "One troop in particular cornered our group, and gave us an... ultimatum about Coffin."

"I know," I said, coughing. "Jack gave me the same one."

"Jack?!" Their expressions exploded into an array of worry and anger.

"Jack... he has mind powers and he's using them to help the fire people," I said. "He stole Coffin because he has a memory of seeing the prophecy, plus a lot of other Balancer and water people things that can help the Fire Emperor."

"Mind powers? Those aren't a thing," Luke said.

"Some coral people have them," Emily said. Even though she had gotten coral magic, she hadn't received any powers of memory manipulatation.

"Jack can do way more than what coral people can do," I said. "He can read minds, change memories and, even though I've never seen him do it, he said he can... control people."

"Well, I have read a few legends about people with powers like that," Erin said. "I guess, like the Balancers it is plausible that—

"Erin, not now," Ezra said. "Jack doesn't have mind powers."

"I'm sorry, but Samz is right," Miles said. "Why else would Jack steal Coffin?"

"To lure us into a trap?" Emily said.

"There are better ways to go about laying a trap than stealing a morphing wolf," Anthony said. "I mean if *I* were a fire person—

"Anthony!" Ezra growled. "You can't say that."

"No, I just meant—

"You're so—

"Just—

They melted into chaotic argument, Maddie trying to keep order. I stepped back until I was standing in the archway of one of the hallways. I tried to take in deep, slow breaths but their arguments were setting me on edge. Kiefer and Jamie noticed me and detached themselves from the group.

"Are you okay?" Jamie asked. I shrugged.

"Not really," I said. "I don't like it when they argue. Especially about me."

"That's it?" Kiefer said. "You did almost just get lost in a huge underground maze."

"Well, it's not really the maze," I said, looking away. "I just... recently I was thinking..."

I couldn't tell them. I couldn't let them know how much I was struggling with being a Balancer. Maybe it was my exhaustion, or maybe I was just feeling honest, because I did croak out an answer.

"... none of this would be happening if I wasn't a Balancer," I said, exhaling. Jamie and Kiefer sighed.

"Samz," Kiefer said, grabbing my shoulders. "I am SO glad one of us finally said it."

"Wait, what?"

"I know," Kiefer said. "I don't like the responsibility either. It's not fair. I didn't get to choose."

"You're right," Jamie said. "I didn't do anything to deserve all of this upheaval in my life. I didn't ask for another element that no one actually knows how to teach me."

"Yeah... you two are both right," I said. "But... you're also wrong."

"What?" they both asked. I looked up.

"I think the priests made a mistake by teaching us separately," I realized. "They made us feel like we were alone and they all told us different things. We might be three different people, but we're all Balancers."

They both smiled.

"We're the only people that can stop Emperor Conner from bringing back the Untamable Mights," I said. "The only way we can do something that big is by starting to do things as a team."

"Yeah!" Kiefer said, beaming.

"I know we didn't ask to save the world, but we have to," I said, putting a hand on each of their shoulders. "But we can't do it if we keep thinking of ourselves as apart. From now on, we do this together. Deal?"

"Deal."

.<>.

After the others calmed down, Maddie finally filled us in on the rest of the story. Unlike Jack, the fire people had told them where the 'Basin of Betrayal' was.

"It's a small island in the Lesser Ocean, between the Fire Empire and the Water Kingdom," Maddie said, pulling out a map. It showed most of the world, with a few black lines scrawled across it. "It's accessible through the

Catacombs. That's how the fire people got so many troops to Wateria without us noticing."

"But we're only around here," I said, pointing to the area surrounding Ar Shaa. We would have to walk under hundreds of miles of Catacombs just to get to the border of the Water Kingdom.

"Before we left, we met with some of the officials Dad was talking with. The earth people created moving tunnels to traverse the Catacombs faster," Maddie explained, pointing to a star she had drawn on one of the black lines. She had drawn several others along sections of the lines. "Using them, we can get to the Basin of Betrayal in a day or two."

"Is there any way for us to get there not using the Catacombs?" I asked.

"There is," Erin said. "That's the route Dad is taking."

"Then why are we going through here?" I asked.

"Dad is taking a portion of the water army and a few squadrons of earth people to attack the island," Ezra said. "We're there to scout out the territory and see if we can get Coffin out on our own."

"If Dad and the earth people can secure the island, it would be incredibly helpful in the war," Maddie explained. "If everything goes well, we should get there right before they arrive. If something goes wrong with our mission, they can help us, and if they need help securing the island we can help too."

"Wait, but if the earth people are helping, does that mean—

"Oh, right," Ezra said. "The earth people agreed to be our allies in the war. Getting their capital attacked by fire people was a pretty good motivator. Forgot to mention that."

"Okay," I said, smiling. This plan was going to work. We had the earth people on our side. We were going to save Coffin. "Let's go."

.<>.

The moving tunnels consisted of chains of stone compartments slightly smaller than the surrounding tunnel. Ancient earth magic enchantments caused them to move incredibly fast, pausing occasionally when they intersected with new tunnels. Inside benches were carved into the rock. The two days of travel were incredibly boring. We spent most of the time planning what we would do once we got to the Basin of Betrayal. Finally, two days later, we arrived at a dead end.

The moving tunnel rumbled to a stop, the open section showing a decrepit, barely intact tunnel. We took our remaining supplies and got off of the tunnel, just as it started to slide back to Ar Shaa. The new tunnel slowly sloped up, haphazardly carved. Most of the glowing crystals, red in this section of the Catacombs, were shattered and lying in the cracks. Maddie led the way.

Finally, we could see light at the top of the tunnel. We crouched down, Maddie glancing down at us.

"Everyone," she whispered. "We don't know what kind of situation we'll be going into. We know they are prepared for us. Follow my lead, and fight with everything you have."

"Stick to the strategy, but be prepared to improvise," Erin advised, uncorking her pouch of water. "Communicate out there."

"Remember what the fire people did to us," Ezra said. "This is our time to strike back."

"Alright," Maddie said, standing up. "Let's go."

We moved forward, opening our water pouches. Jamie held her water in loops bunched around her arm, Kiefer held his in two hoops around his fists, while I held mine in a swirling shield. Maddie waved us forward, our family exiting the tunnel.

"There you are!" Dad's voice suddenly said. He sounded scared and relieved at the same time. My eyes adjusting to sunlight after being underground for three days, it took me a few moments to make out what was in front of me.

It was a camp, bustling with earth and water people. Tents perched themselves precariously on the edge of a cliff, protected by earthen walls drawn up by the earth people. Dad stood at the mouth of the tunnel, in full battle armor.

"Dad?" Maddie breathed, putting her water back into her pouch. I put my water away.

"We've been here for a day," he said.

"How's the battle going?" Ezra asked. Dad sighed.

"Samz, Kiefer, and Jamie? Can you come with me?" he asked. We looked at each other, Dad leading us to the rock wall that protected the tents. Leading us along the edge, we came to a staircase leading up to the top of the wall. He paused, keeping his head below the top.

"Don't let your head go over for too long," he said.

"Dad, what is it?" Jamie asked.

"This is the basin where Mark died," Dad explained.

"Okay... what does that have to do with what's happening now?" Kiefer asked.

"Mark used to be friends with Emperor Conner before he began to dabble in the Mights," Dad explained. "He came here to try to warn Conner before he gave his magic to you."

"Oh, so that's why it's called the Basin of Betrayal," Jamie realized. "But again, what does that have to do with what's happening now?"

"Well," Dad said, briefly glancing over the wall. "There's no easy way to put this."

"What is it?" I asked. Dad grimaced.

"We haven't been able to take the Basin because..." he paused. "There's a manor in the center of the Basin. It's... protected. I'm not really sure how to—

"Protected by what?" Kiefer asked. Dad closed his eyes.

"The Untamable Might of Domination."

My chest froze. Jamie and Kiefer's eyes went wide. I walked up a step and looked over the wall, my heart pounding.

A dome of red light surrounded an opulent manor in the center of the Basin. The dome appeared to be powered by a beacon of red light piercing through the center of the manor itself. I saw the tiny forms of fire people walk back and forth across the boundary of the dome.

"Domination increased the strength of all of the soldiers," Dad explained. "I'm sorry to ask so much of you, but if we're ever going to take the Basin and find Coffin, you three need to destroy Domination."

"*If the throne is found by a king of fire,*" Jamie muttered. "*They will make the fire surrender.*"

"*In the home of betrayal's night,*" I recited. Jamie, Kiefer and I looked at each other, our faces illuminated by the glow of the red dome.

"The prophecy says we can make the fire surrender," Kiefer said. "So that's what we're gonna do."

"Alright," Dad said, a tear forming in his eye. "I'll gather a force that will get you into the manor."

He stepped down the staircase. Jamie, Kiefer and I looked down into the Basin of Betrayal.

This is where Mark died to give us his power.

This is our first chance to use it.

Suddenly, a cloud of mist burst to life in front of us. We gasped as it collapsed and coalesced into Shinux.

She was larger than the last time we'd seen her, now big enough to carry all three of us. Kiefer beaming, he held a hand out as she nuzzled him.

"Dad said she would return when we needed her most," Kiefer said, Shinux extending a wing. Jamie and I brushed her feathers. I felt soothing waves of water magic run up my arm and swirl around my heart.

"Get Dad," Kiefer said. "Shinux will get the three of us into the Manor."

"And we'll get Coffin back," I said. Jamie grinned, looking down into the Basin.

"And we'll destroy an Untamable Might."

THE THORNY ROSE

"Are you sure you're ready? We can camp here for as long as—

"Dad, please," Jamie said. We were all atop Shinux, water staffs strapped to our backs. Kiefer sat at the front, then Jamie, then me. The camp bustled around us, earth and water people shouting to each other. "Shinux will magnify our water magic enough to get us into the Manor."

"I'm sorry, but I'm not going to let you three go into a situation you're not prepared for," Dad said. "Trust me, we've tried fighting these soldiers under Domination's influence, but it's useless."

"Dad, you haven't had an aquanix on your side until now. Shinux can boost our magic enough to counter those fire people," Kiefer said. "You said yourself that Shinux would come back when I most needed her."

"You don't understand, you've never been in any sort of battle like this," Dad pleaded. "I won't—

"No."

Maddie appeared behind Dad, placing a hand on his shoulder.

"Maddie, what are you talking about?" Dad asked. Maddie stepped forward, folding her hands.

"Dad, they have a job to do," Maddie said. "They just need to get into the Manor and destroy Domination. The only way we can help them is to be there to hold back the fire people in any way we can."

"Maddie you don't understand, I can't just send my children into battle," Dad said, crossing his arms. Maddie straightened herself.

"You think I don't understand? I've had to help raise them their entire lives, it's hard for me too," she said. "But we can't let our own fears stop them from fulfilling their destiny."

Dad sighed, his shoulder falling.

"You're right," he said, looking at the ground. "Help me gather as many men as possible to help get them into the Manor."

"Dad, they're going to be fine," she said, looking at us. "They're going to do great."

"Great, wonderful, we got all the mushy feelings out of the way," Kiefer said, rolling his eyes. "Can we go now?"

"Wait a minute for us to gather our forces," Dad said, Maddie running off to rally the water and earth people. Kiefer held onto the base of Shinux's neck, signalling her to spread her wings. She flapped a few times, momentarily struggling to pull the three of us into the air. She flapped up onto the top of the wall, putting us in full view of the Manor and the red dome of light. We looked back, watching as lines of blue and brown-clad people organized themselves. Dad walked up to the base of the wall, looking to us.

"We're ready when you are," he said. "I love you."

"We love you too," I said. Kiefer rubbing Shinux's neck, glancing back at us.

"Ready?" he asked. Jamie and I nodded. Kiefer let out a battle cry, Shinux launching herself off of the wall. Just as her talons let go, the wall crumbled, earth people tearing it down. The debris rolled down the side of the basin, kicking up a huge cloud of dust. I looked down as earth people pushed shelves of stone carrying troops down into the Basin. Ahead of us, lines of fire people began to rush out of the dome, red light burning in spirals on their armor and skin.

"Stay high up where they can't reach us," Jamie said, Kiefer commanding Shinux to fly higher. Below us, fire people began to form circles.

"What are they doing?" Kiefer mumbled, just as a huge column of fire erupted right next to us from one of the circles of fire people. My skin screamed in pain as Shinux veered away, the column continuing to burn higher. Another column began to burn in front of us.

"Seela!" Jamie screamed, extending her staff. A thick bubble of water encased us, glowing faintly. Shinux *really* was increasing our powers. We flew right through the column of fire, the Seela falling away a moment later. I glanced back, watching as the two columns began to curl and break into smaller tendrils. They looked like two huge octopuses of fire, stabbing the ground with their tentacles.

"We're almost halfway there," Kiefer said. We had nearly reached the dome of red light. "We need to start descending."

Shinux began to dip, the huge door of the Manor coming into view.

"We're about to pass through," Jamie said, closing her eyes. The red light danced in front of us, tendrils and spirals burning in midair. Shinux went straight on, right into the light. We felt nothing; the power of the dome wasn't intended for us.

Inside the dome, all of the soldiers continuously burned with red light. Three lines of soldiers noticed us and began to shoot spears of fire at us. I held out my staff, and began to produce water from the tip. Jamie and I created a large bubble of water for us to work with just as the spears of fire began to reach us. As Kiefer concentrated on controlling Shinux, Jamie and I send volleys of water to counter the fire. Being with Shinux made the water respond instantly to my commands, and I could control much more than I normally would have.

More fire people began to attack us, Jamie and I produced a double-layered Seela. The fire harmlessly bounced off of the shield.

"We're almost there," Kiefer said. "I'm gonna blast the door open with lightning, and then Samz can grow the wood back together."

"Got it?" Jamie asked, turning back to me.

"Well, I think so, I mean, I've worked a lot with flowers and more leafy plants and I haven't really had time to work with wood and I—

"No time! Figure it out!" Kiefer screamed. Shinux was flying lower to the ground, the huge mahogany door standing before us. "We need to drop the Seela so I can blast the door. Jamie, Samz, cover me."

Our Seela melted away, and seemingly every fire person sent fire at us. Jamie and I held our staffs aloft, as lightning began to dance around Kiefer's fingertips. We produced water as fast as we could, the water and fire exploding against each other. Shinux continued to barrel towards the door. Jamie turned to blast the few remaining fire people in our way while I fought off the ones behind us.

Suddenly, Kiefer launched a huge, crackling lightning bolt at the door. It exploded along the middle, the lock breaking and the door opening slightly inward. Shinux ducked into the Manor, the doors still slightly open. I jumped off of her back, landing on a glossed floor. I ran forward to the doors and slammed them shut. Concentrating, I placed my hands along the gap. The two wooden halves began to fuse and meld together. Raising my hands, the change continued to the top until they were just one wall.

"We made it," Jamie said, panting. Now that we were in the silence of the Manor, I could feel how hard my heart was pounding and how weak my knees were. I turned around.

A single hallway stretched into obscurity. The walls were red, periodically interrupted by marble columns. Paintings of moments in Fire Empire history hung on the walls.

"Alright," Kiefer said, stepping off of Shinux. "Let's find Domination, and let's end this battle."

.<>.

It quickly became clear that there was no one else in the Manor. The sounds of the battle outside had been completely silenced. The halls were illuminated by red torches hung in between the pillars.

"Hey, guys?" Kiefer asked. "Do any of us actually know how to destroy Domination?"

"I... I'm not actually sure," Jamie said. "He's inside of a throne, right? Maybe we just need to destroy the throne."

"Sounds easy enough," Kiefer said.

"But if we just have to destroy the throne, then why hasn't anyone else destroyed Domination?" I pointed out. "If only the Balancers can destroy Untamable Mights, we must have to do something more than just destroy the object they're in."

"It probably has something to do with our Balancer elements," Jamie said. "No one has controlled them since the first Balancers, so they must be what we need to destroy it."

"I guess that makes sense," Kiefer said, shrugging. "But first we have to get past the Emperor's son."

"The who?" I asked, stopping cold.

"Oh, right, you were with Jack," Kiefer said. "The fire person we captured told us that the Manor was guarded by the Emperor's oldest son. Had some weird name."

"Kiefer, he was named after the very first fire Emperor, Iekaantared," Jamie said.

"Ick... an... ta... what?"

"Iekaantared."

"She said Ikenterd," Kiefer said. Jamie rolled her eyes.

"No, *Iekaantared*," Jamie said. "Did either of you ever pay attention in history class?"

"Jamie, you know I didn't," Kiefer said. Jamie crossed her arms.

"It doesn't matter what his name is, what matters is that he's the only thing left standing between us and Domination," Jamie said.

Ahead, I finally made out a huge black iron door. We were nearly at the center the Manor, the origin of Domination's dome of light.

"It's in there, isn't it?" Kiefer asked, pointing to the door.

"It must be," Jamie said. "Are you two ready?"

"I hope so," I said, as we arrived at the door. Scenes of war, crowns, and destruction were carved into the black iron. A single golden knocker carved in the shape of a crown hung in the center of the door.

Kiefer reached towards it, Shinux letting out a low coo. Kiefer grabbed the center; Jamie and I grabbed the left and the right.

"Ready?" Kiefer asked. We nodded. We knocked three times, the entire door vibrating. Stepping back, the door began to rise, great rumbling mechanisms hidden in the walls lifting it up into the ceiling. Inside, burning red light glowed.

We saw his sharp boots first, his feet in front of the bottom of an ebony throne. The door rose further, revealing the rest of a large dais and a wall adorned with gold flames. Streams of red light curled off of the throne and into the air.

Finally, we could see the Emperor's son. His pale face was twisted into a sneer. His jet black hair was pulled back behind his head. He wore red armor that glowed under the power of the throne. The throne itself rose high above the young man's head, the back dissolved into jagged spears of polished ebony. Light burned from the spears, coalescing into a pillar that pierced the high ceiling.

Iekaantared looked down at us. Silence.

"Well," he said, his voice hoarse. His face suddenly jerked into a grin, and then he started to laugh. His laugh cackled up and down, his neck thrown back. He was *not* stable.

"Is he okay?" Kiefer mumbled, leaning over to me. Iekaantared composed himself, folding his hands on his lap.

"I apologize, I just find it... amusing," he said. Jamie scowled.

"What? What's so amusing?" she hissed.

"It's just that, my father told me that the Balancers were great magical forces that were the greatest threat to our Empire," he said, holding back a chuckle. "And you're *kids.*"

"And you have a weird name, sounds about even to me," Kiefer said, shrugging. "So... are we fighting, or just talking?"

"*Kiefer,*" Jamie hissed. Kiefer rolled his eyes.

"It's an honest question," he said.

"He kind of has a point," I mumbled. Jamie rolled her eyes. Iekaantared stood up, holding his fists out.

"Now, you can either let me capture you three, no casualties, or you can make the foolish decision to fight me. I have an Untamable Might boosting my power," he said, spirals of red light curling off of his shoulders.

"We have an aquanix, and more elements than you have," Jamie said, gripping her water staff. "You can either let us have that throne, no casualties, or you can make the foolish decision to fight us."

"Ooh, that was good, you turned it around on him," Kiefer said, chuckling.

"Okay the first joke was funny but we should really focus," I said out of the side of my mouth.

"I'm just trying to keep it light an—

"Are you three finished?" Iekaantared hissed.

"Yes," Jamie said, glaring at Kiefer and me before turning back to the prince. "We do not surrender. We need to get to that throne and we will fight you if we have to."

"Fine," he said, he fists igniting. "All though, it won't be much of a fight."

He thrust his fists forward, two huge tongues of fire twisting towards us. We scattered, the fire burning down the hallway. I pulled a length of water from my staff, holding it in a swirling shield in front of me. Kiefer, on the other side of the room, held his water staff aloft and aimed it at the prince.

"*Carwavo!*" he shouted, a cone of water knocking the prince aside before he could react. He landed against the wall near me. I lunged forward, extending my shield into a whip. Before it could reach him, Iekaantared kicked a barrage of fire at me. I contorted my arm, my whip of water barely dodging out of the way. I ducked, the fire burning over my head and setting the pillar behind me on fire.

Jamie charged forward her palms open. Purple light leaped out of it, taking the form of a hawk. Iekaantared opened his mouth and blew a stream of fire at it, but the hawk silhouette dove around it. It slipped under his stream of fire and flew up, scratching his face. The prince stumbled back as Jamie's hawk dissolved.

"She can *do* that?" Kiefer yelled, looking at me. "Did you know she could do that?"

"Kiefer!" I shouted, pushing him out of the way right before a blast from Iekaantared could burn his hair off. We landed on the floor, Jamie rushing forward to cover us.

"Melanga!" she shouted, three cords of water exploding out of the end of her water staff. They latched onto Iekaantared's arm, yanking him towards Jamie. I threw my whip of water out and connected it to his leg. He screamed, weakly punching a slice of fire at Kiefer. Shinux flew in front of the fire and beat it away with her wings. Kiefer dove towards Iekaantared, his fists crackling with electricity. Jamie and I tightened our grips at Kiefer launched a lightning bolt at him.

The lightning connected, its power booming around the room and throwing Iekaantared backward. He landed on the ground, convulsing as his armor smoked.

"Get to the throne, now!" Kiefer shouted. We rushed forward, Jamie jumping over Iekaantared's limp form. The throne of Domination stood before us, crackling with red light.

"So, what now?" I asked.

"Let's each attack it with our Balancer elements," Jamie said, her hands starting to glow purple. Kiefer's hands started to crackle with lightning. I pulled the apple seeds from my pocket and began to germinate them.

"Now!" Kiefer shouted, electrocuting the throne. Jamie opened her palm, whorls of purple light slithering through the throne. Branches exploded from the seeds and latched onto the throne. For a few seconds, we continued to bathe the throne in our elements. The throne just sat there, still producing the red light.

"Stop, stop," I said, letting go of the branches. "It's not working."

"What do we do?" Jamie asked. Behind her Iekaantared was starting to stand up. Shinux flapped over to him and started to peck in his face.

"Maybe we have to get Domination out of it somehow," I suggested. Kiefer rolled his eyes.

"And how would you suggest going about that?" he asked. "Should we knock on the throne and see if he's home?"

He reached forward, holding his hand up to mockingly tap on the back of the throne.

"Kiefer don't—

"Hello, Mr. Domination, are you—

The second his hand touched the throne, his body dissolved into yellow light and was sucked into the heart of throne. Jamie screamed, reaching for the throne.

"Kiefer!" I shouted. I looked all around the room, but he was gone!

"I'm going in after him," Jamie said, reaching forward.

"Jamie—

She grabbed the throne, dissolving into purple light and diving into it.

"No!" I yelled. They were both gone! I looked back, Iekaantared dragging himself to his feet. The red spirals of power were returning, and I knew I couldn't face him alone.

Out of options, I reached forward and touched the back of the throne.

.<>.

I blinked, and was suddenly floating in midair. Milky gray clouds spread out into infinity. I looked down at my body, jumping.

My body was made out of green light! I could only really distinguish the outline of my body; it was too bright to make out details. I looked up, and saw two other forms. One was purple, who I assumed to be Jamie, and the other was yellow, who I assumed to be Kiefer.

"Where are we?" I asked, floating towards them.

"I don't know," Kiefer said. He opened and closed his hand a few times. "I don't think we're dead, but I can't use any magic here."

"Who... is there?" a voice suddenly croaked. It seemed to come from everywhere. The clouds in front of us parted, revealing a dark, chained figure.

"Who are you?" Jamie asked, holding her fists out.

"I am Domination," the figure answered.

Domination's features were black and blurry, the edges of his form flickering as if they weren't really there. A twisted crown of silver adorned his withered head that wavered in and out of existence. Chains wrapped around his arms, hands, legs and neck. They disappeared into the mists. Domination floated forward, holding out a dark, flickering hand.

"*It has been a long time... Balancers,*" he said. His voice was raspy and weak. "*Have you come here to free me?*"

"No, we've come here to destroy you," Jamie said. *It would be great if you could tell us how,* I quietly thought.

"*I wouldn't... if I were you,*" Domination said. His fingers curled into a fist. "*I could help you defeat the fire people. I could make you kings and a queen.*"

"We don't want that," Kiefer said.

"*What about you, Balancer of Plants?*" Domination asked. "*Wouldn't you... like to defeat the fire people?*"

I did. I wanted to defeat the fire people. Kiahta had told me that I had to bring an equal end to the war and that as a Balancer I was not a part of the Water Kingdom. But I was. The fire people had hurt my country and they needed to pay. Domination could help me.

Lost in my thoughts, I had barely noticed that one of the chains now floated in front of my glowing hand. I had to free Domination. I reached out, and grabbed one of the links. It instantly began to dissolve into green light, the magic burning right through the—

Kiefer punched me. My mind reeled as I was sent careening off into the mist. I watched as wisps of black smoke billowed off of me. Looking down, nearly my entire body had darkened to black. The green was slowly starting to inch back. I had to free Domination! I *had* to! He could help us! They were trying to stop me!

"What are you doing?" I hissed. Kiefer and Jamie grabbed me. The light from their bodies burned through the

285

black, restoring my body to green. The change suddenly washed through my head, and I woke up.

"Woah," I said, shaking my head.

"Are you okay?" Jamie asked. "Domination touched you and you started to break his chains and—

"I'm okay," I said. "He tried to control me, but I'm fine."

I didn't want to free Domination. He wasn't going to help us defeat the fire people, he was *working* for the fire people.

"Let's go before he tries to take over someone else's mind," Kiefer said, floating back towards Domination.

"*Foolish decisions,*" Domination rasped. "*The fire people will destroy—*

Kiefer kicked Domination in the stomach. Yellow light spread from his foot, pieces of Domination's stomach breaking off and dissolving into nothing.

"Get him!" Kiefer yelled. I floated forward and grabbed his arm, his skin burning white-hot against my hands. He screeched as I tore his arm off, throwing it into the clouds as I burned away. Jamie dissolved his arm as Kiefer destroyed his chest. His remaining body parts flailed, his form barely keeping focus.

"Go for the head!" I shouted, holding a hand out. We rushed forward, the light of our signs burning through the clouds. Domination screeched, a sound so loud it shook the entire realm. We connected with his head, cracks of light tearing through his face. A ball of light in the center of his skull exploded, white light erasing everything. It passed up our arms, and past our heads.

The light cleared, passing through us. We were back in the throne room, standing in front of the throne. It was cracked in half. The light continued, burning through the pillar of red light until there was nothing left.

Domination was dead.

We grabbed each other, our hearts still pounding. We had defeated our first Untamable Might. In front of us, the ruined throne smoldered.

"What's that?" Kiefer asked, reaching towards the crack. There was something wedged in between the halves of the throne! He pulled out a stone tablet, holding it up for us to see.

It was the next prophecy.

A REUNION AND AN ANNOUNCEMENT

The battle did not last long after we destroyed Domination. Without his influence, the fire people succumbed to the combined efforts of the earth and water people. Many escaped, but we were able to secure a good amount of them to be kept as prisoners. After we reunited with our family, we searched the abandoned camps until we found Coffin.

He had been left in a cage, a thick morphing collar clamped around his neck. When we came into the tent, Coffin jumped up, and started barking. The earth people smashed the lock open, letting Coffin run out of the cage.

"Master!" he yelped, jumping into my arms. His fur was oily and matted. He licked my arms and my clothes, wherever he could reach. "I missed you, I missed you, I missed you so muches!"

"I missed you too," I said, choking on my words. He was back, and he was okay.

"Geez, I was wondering how long it was goings to take for me to rescue you," he said, slipping out of my arms. "I thought they'd gottens you for sure."

"Me?" I asked, pointing to my chest.

"Yeah," Coffin said, cocking his head. "They took me, that guy who gaves me the fish poked my head a bunch

288

of times so I bits him, but the whole times I was just waiting for the best moment to save you."

"Save me?" I said, chuckling.

"You're welcomes," Coffin said. "They weres holding you down and made you drink something that smelled really gross. They knews I was too powerful, so they had to stop me. But nothing could stops me from saving my Master."

"Well, thank you, Coffin, for saving me," I said, patting him on the head. I reached down and unclipped his morphing collar. He shook out his neck, beaming that he was finally free of the collar.

I realized that even if he wasn't showing it now, being captured had probably traumatized him. He could just as easily have thought it was all some sort of game, and he could have been truly fine, but still. It had traumatized me, and I knew I had to do something to ease any of his fears. If he had any. I was pretty sure he still thought he was some sort of undercover spy.

"Coffin," I said, holding up the morphing collar. "I know that having a morphing collar on all of the time isn't fun for you. Sometimes, it can be scary. Sometimes you need to morph, but you can't."

"Yeah, I do *nots* like the morphing collar at *all*," he said, coughing and spitting something onto the ground, which he then sniffed.

"Coffin," I said, trying to get his attention. He glanced up at me.

"What."

It was probably a stupid decision. Coffin still had a lot more growing to do, and he still was far from mature. He could cause a lot more havoc if I didn't go through with it. But, I was committed. I had to do it for Coffin.

"I promise from now on, you'll never have to wear a morphing collar again," I said, throwing the collar to the ground. Coffin's jaw dropped.

"Really?" he squeaked. His fur began to glow, and then suddenly, he was a bird. A moment later, he morphed into a fox. Then a rhino. Then a mouse. Then a fish.

"Yay!" he barked, as he unmorphed. He ran around and through my legs. "Thank you thank you thank you thank you thank you thank you thank you!"

"I love you, Coffin," I said, picking him up and squeezing him tight. He rested his head on my shoulder.

"I loves you too."

.<>.

After Coffin ran off to greet the rest of my family, I looked out across the Basin of Betrayal. Several medical tents had been set up, people waiting in lines outside. We'd won the battle, but there had been casualties. I could hear the moans and whimpers of burn victims, even from across the Basin.

"Samz," Ezra said, coming up behind me. We hugged, Ezra lifting me up into the air. I chuckled as he put me down. "What you did was just... amazing."

"Thank you," I said, beaming. He put a hand on my shoulder, looking over to the nearest medical tent.

"Do you understand now?" Ezra said, still looking at the wounded soldiers.

"Understand...?"

"Fire," Ezra said. "The element of destruction."

I looked around the Basin. The abandoned camps were burning, black ash spewing into the sky. Soldiers were covered in blistering burns. Even the manor had caught on fire, flames shattering the ornate windows and turning the walls to cinders. The cries from the medical tents carried over to us on the smokey breeze.

"I guess I do," I said. Fire had destroyed the basin, and had hurt so many of our people. And this was just one battle. There had been twelve years of this, twelve years of destruction.

"It's okay though," Ezra said, kneeling down. He put his hands on my shoulders and looked me in the eyes. "I know you're going to fix it. You're going to bring an end to the fire people."

"I will," I said, looking back at him. "I promise."

.<>.

A week later, we arrived home. Spring had melted through the thick snow, leaving beds of mountain flowers. Everything inside the castle seemed dustier. A few weeks after we arrived, Dad gathered Jamie, Kiefer and I in his office.

"What is it?" Kiefer asked. He sat in between Jamie and I, Dad across from us behind his desk.

"I wanted to apologize, for the past few months, the past few years, really," he said. "After your mother left, all I wanted was for you three to have the most normal life you could. Part of that involved me denying for years that you were Balancers."

"I still don't understand why you had to do that," Jamie said. "The prophecy clearly said that the queen of water would give birth to the Balancers."

"Prophecies are not predictions, only suggestions to produce the best outcome," Dad reminded her. "I never wanted to burden you, but in doing so, I only made your lives worse. Not telling you that you were the Balancers was my biggest mistake as a father."

Jamie, Kiefer and I looked at each other. There were other mistakes we could have brought up. How he'd always been focused on finding Mom. How he'd left so much of our upbringing to Maddie. But this wasn't the time to bring that up.

"When Mark told us that your mother was to give birth to the Balancers, we planned to announce it to the water people and the world when you were five," he said. "But she never returned, so we never told anyone."

"So... where is this going?" Kiefer asked. Dad paused, sighing.

"People in our kingdom and around the world are wondering what happened at the Basin of Betrayal," Dad said. "Our citizens have been wondering why the fire people

292

attack us because of the Balancers if we don't seem to have any."

"What are you suggesting?" Jamie asked.

"If it is okay with you," he said, "I want to formally announce to the kingdom that you three are the Balancers."

We looked at each other, then at Dad. I glanced down at the green symbol on my hand.

.<>.

A month later, a near summer breeze blew brightly through the city of Wateria. A huge crowd of water people dressed in the colors of the ocean stood before us. We stood on the terraced garden of Drew's Palace, the same one where I had revived that first rose. Now, the whole garden was in bloom. Jamie, Kiefer and I wore robes made of the colors of our Balancer element. We stood opposite the three rulers of the Water Kingdom. Our family and an assortment of water masters stood behind us.

"For twelve years, we have fought against the fire people," Uncle Drew shouted, his voice booming across the capital. "We come before you today to finally put to rest the rumors about the causes of this war."

"This war was never fought about land disagreements or leftover resentments from the Mesipar Sea War," Aunt Sophie said. The crowd began to murmur. I clenched my hand nervously. Dad and his siblings had spent weeks preparing the speech so it didn't cause panic. I hoped it would work.

"There were rumors that the next Setter was born in the Water Kingdom, and that the fire people wanted them for their own ends," Aunt Sophie continued.

"Two thousand years ago, five evil spirits, the Untamable Mights, were born out of the chaos of the Catacomb War," Dad said. "They were defeated by the Balancers, magical beings who could control the elements of life, lightning, and plants. They began the chain of Setters that kept peace in the Inner World."

"Thirteen years ago, Emperor Conner began to reawaken these forces of evil," Uncle Drew said. "The only ones who can free or destroy them, are the Balancers."

"After two thousand years, the Balancers have been reborn into the Water Kingdom," Aunt Sophie said. "Over a month ago, in the Basin of Betrayal, they slayed the Untamable Might of Domination."

"The Emperor of the fire people wishes to take the Balancers from us and use them to free the Mights," Dad said. "But we will not let him. We will stand up to tyranny and darkness."

"Leading us into the coming era of peace will be the new Balancers," Uncle Drew said, gesturing to us.

"Prince Kiefer, the Balancer of Lightning," Uncle Drew said. Kiefer stepped forward. He held his hands out, electricity crackling along his fingers. He took in a deep breath, and punched his fist to the sky, sending a lightning bolt thundering into the sky. The crowd screamed, in awe and fear.

"Princess Jamie, the Balancer of Life," Aunt Sophie said. Jamie stepped forward, her hands glowing purple. She held her arms out, purple silhouettes of birds flying into the audience. My stomach dropped.

I couldn't hide anymore. I couldn't fade into the background. That choice had been taken from me. Maybe I wasn't okay with it yet, but I had to learn how to.

"Prince Samson the Fourth, Balancer of Plants," Dad said. In front of me, along the edge of the terrace, they had filled a long hollow with dirt and placed rose seeds along it. I'd picked out the flower.

Kiefer used his magic for power and force. His will to change things gave him his magic. Jamie used her magic for precision and control. Her dedication and clarity gave her power.

I used my magic for protection. Protection of myself, my family, and the Inner World. I loved my family, I loved my country, and I loved the world I lived in. That was where my power came from.

I was safe. There was a country protecting me. There were only four Untamable Mights left. I was protected by people who loved me, and I could protect the ones I loved. I reached out with my magic and exhaled.

The roses burst from the ground, their buds burning to life. They climbed higher in the sky, their vines and thorns spilling over the side of the terrace. Their red petals grew, basking in the light of the sun.

The crowd cheered, waving their hands in the air. The Water Kingdom was behind us. We were together.

We were ready for the future.

END OF PART THREE OF

VOLUME ONE

OF THE WATER AND FIRE

SERIES

EPILOGUE

She could hear her father's screams from the other end of the hall. She paused, biting her lip. Evidently, her brother had returned from the Basin of Betrayal. She had heard a few rumors about what had happened the week before, but she wasn't quite ready yet to accept what happened. However, the sounds coming from the end of the hall only confirmed those rumors.

Her brother had lost Domination.

"Liliana, what are you doing?" someone hissed. She jerked her head back. Her older sister stood behind her. Her black hair was perfectly cut and simply arranged, framing her serenely bored face.

"Helen, you have got to stop sneaking up behind me," the girl said. "And you have got to stop calling me Liliana. You and Dad are the only people who still call me that."

"Why shouldn't I?" Helen said, shrugging. "Lee isn't even a real nickname you can make from Liliana. Do you want me to call you Lily? Even Anna would make more sense."

"No, I want you to call me Lee," she groaned. When she was younger, her mother had called her Lily. Now the name only made her feel trapped, so she had switched to Lee.

"Whatever," Helen said, stepping around Lee and looking down the hallway. The doors to the throne room were firmly shut. "Looks like the rumors were true."

"I know," Lee said. "I can't believe he really lost one."

"From what I heard, it only took a few minutes for the Balancers to overtake him," Helen said, straightening her shoulders. "Looks like I'm Father's new favorite."

"*Helen*," Lee hissed. "You can't say that."

"Calm down Lee, I'm only joking," Helen said. Lee turned away, walking in the opposite direction of the throne room. Helen's face softened. "Lee, I'm serious. I'm devastated that Iekaantared lost Domination to three kids."

"Sure you are," Lee said, storming away. Iekaantared was the eldest of eight, their father's favorite. Since she had been born, Helen had always been his clear second favorite. This was Helen's perfect opportunity to take his spot. Any sympathy she said she supposedly felt for their brother had to be fake.

"Oh please," Helen said, crossing her arms. "Even you have to realize that Iekaantared's failure will help your standing with Father too."

"For the last time Helen," Lee huffed. She paused. There wasn't anything else to say. Helen knew that their father had never been very impressed by Lee. She knew how Lee tried everything she could to prove herself to their father. She knew that he always thought Lee was too forgiving, too lazy, too weak, too—

She's trying to get under your skin on purpose, Lee realized. *Just get out of here.*

"I'm going for a walk," she said, her voice trembling. Helen sighed.

"Lee calm down, I'm trying to compliment you," Helen said, her hands curling into fists.

"Just leave me alone," Lee hissed. Helen groaned.

"You're such a drama queen," she muttered, as Lee turned the corner.

A few minutes later, Lee had gotten herself out of the palace and into the gardens, only the guards at the gate standing between her and freedom. Above her, the crescent moon illuminated the expansive gardens between the terraces of the palace and the high walls surrounding it. She ran to the west gate, two ax-wielding guards standing under torches.

"Your Majesty," they said, bowing to her. Their masked armor obscured their faces.

"Thank you," she said, smiling. Lee hated being fake, but to get the guards to do what she wanted, sometimes she had to really play the part of the helpless, naïve, youngest princess. "I just wanted to take a quick walk outside of the gates."

"Princess, both of us will have to accompany you," one of the guards said, towering over her. Lee inwardly sighed, but she knew that arguing with the guards about chaperoning her would only end up with a lecture from her mother and ban from leaving the palace for weeks.

"Thank you," she said. The guards pulled a lever, the gate swinging up into the wall. They led her through, saluting to the guards on either side of the outside. There was a cliff by the ocean that she liked to go to, and the guards would usually stand far enough back so she could have some privacy. Ahead of her, the road snaked in between low hills to the nearby capital city. To her right, the ocean sparkled under the light of the moon.

Suddenly, she saw a dark shadow pass across the road. She paused, the guards also taking note of the strange figure. It was a man! He was running up the road towards the palace. The guards crossed their axes in front of Lee, the blades igniting with fire.

"Wait!" Lee shouted as the man shambled into the light of the axes. He had a scraggly, matted beard and torn clothes. He fell to his knees and clasped his hands together.

"Stand back!" one of the guards growled, his left palm igniting. The man cowered. He looked in between the axes, the flames... and looked right at Lee.

"Please, Princess Liliana," he croaked. "I am the governor from the Senali Province in the North. I came all this way to—

"Step away from the princess," the guard warned, punching a warning blast of fire right over the man's head.

"No!" Lee said, sinking to her knees so she was at eye level with the governor.

"Please, we've been sending the Emperor requests for increased rations for months and we've been ignored. Every request for aid is met with demands for resources we don't have. My people are starving and—

"You have five seconds to get away from the Princess before you are arrested," the first guard warned. Tears formed in the governor's eyes.

"Princess, if you could just have mercy on my province, we've been ignored due to the war and—

"Alright, that's it," the second guard said, grabbing the governor's scrawny arm. The other sent a blast of fire into the sky, alerting other guards to the situation. Both guards grabbed the governor and lifted him off the ground. He weakly tried to kick blasts of fire at them, but they landed pitifully on the ground.

"Please, I beg you, send aid to the Northern Senali province, talk your father, anyone who can help!" the governor said. "And we're not the only ones, others are suffering. The Alio, Gensi and Yaur Provinces are—

"Enough," one of the guards said, shaking the man. He turned to Lee. "Princess, go back to the palace."

"I..." Lee trailed off, her heart racing. She looked at the man. She looked at the guard.

"Go back to the palace, that's an order," the second guard said.

"Please help us," the governor said.

Lee ran towards the ocean.

The guards shouted after her, but they couldn't chase her. They had to take care of the governor. Her feet pounded against the ground, the ocean glowing closer every second. Holding a palm out, she ignited a small flame with which she could find her way. Ahead was a grove of cherry trees that had yet to bloom, their branches outlined by the moon. She ran into the grove, her golden flame lighting up the trunks and closed buds. She paused where the ground dropped away into the ocean below, where it crashed into the cliffs.

Her whole life she had been told that the Fire Empire was the most prosperous nation in the Inner World. She'd believed it, but it was only now that she realized she had barely left the Fire Palace. Her parents and teachers had filled her mind with images of bountiful farms, innovations and a caring leadership that guided it all. They had conjured pictures of strife and disorganization across the ocean in the Water Kingdom. They'd read her stories of starvation, corruption and greed that had led the water people to hide the Balancers away from the world. Twelve years ago the Emperors of the water people had rejected her father's request to share the power of the Balancers, and the resulting war had only made things worse for them.

But they had just been stories. She'd never actually seen the Northern Senali Province. She'd never even met a real water person. She wasn't there when the war began. She'd never seen if everything she'd been told was true.

She looked down into the ocean. She'd been told that the water people were weak and cowardly but it had only taken three of their children to take down her brother.

Lee didn't know all of the truths yet, but she did know one thing.

Lee, the youngest princess of the Fire Empire, had been lied to.

ABOUT THE AUTHOR

Sam Bell originally wrote the story of *Volume One* starting in the third grade. He self-published it as his first novel in sixth grade. In his senior year of high school, he rewrote *Volume One* into this version.

In addition to writing, Sam enjoys drawing, painting, acting, and animation.

OTHER WORKS

Water and Fire Volume Two 2015

The Roofrunner 2017

Water and Fire Volume Three 2017

Water and Fire Volume Four 2018

MSGED 2019

AND COMING SOON...

WATER AND FIRE VOLUME FIVE

. <> .

THE FINAL SPELL

Made in the USA
Middletown, DE
21 July 2020